Beneath the Sands

J. Mardis

TOOL BELT
BOOKS

Paperback ISBN: 979-8-9935804-0-1
Hardcover ISBN: 979-8-9935804-1-8
Kindle ISBN: 979-8-9935804-2-5

Author's Note

According to classical legend, King Menes united the Upper and Lower Kingdoms of Egypt to form a dynasty and rule as its first pharaoh.

Little is known about Menes's life. However, recent archaeological discoveries, including a stone carving unearthed in the ancient capital of Memphis, depict him as having fathered twin boys.

One of them succeeded Menes as Egypt's second pharaoh.

The fate of the other is lost to history.

Chapter One

After one cover letter, two preliminary phone calls, four Zoom interviews, forty-seven emails, and countless prayers offered up to higher places, it was all coming down to this for Carrianne Kaucher.

She had to impress one guy.

At stake was no less than her dream job: principal geologist for Blue Diamond Resources, which would install her as the lead of a well-funded mineral exploration team and send her out into the field to find ...

Well, that's just it with geology, isn't it?

Maybe riches.

Maybe nothing.

No one ever knows for sure.

It would be up to her to poke and probe the earth until it gave up its secrets.

That was the thrilling, fascinating, adventurous part of the position that made her want it so badly.

Then there was the practical side: it paid more than anything else she had applied for—no small consideration, given the student loan debt that was about to begin coming down on her like an executioner's axe.

The man who would give the imperial thumbs-up or thumbs-down on whether she would be the recipient of this professional and financial windfall would be none other than Anthony Sebastian, the founder, owner, CEO, and driving force behind Blue Diamond Resources.

In a high-risk industry shaped as much by its expensive misses as its spectacular hits, Blue Diamond had managed to survive all the ups and downs of the market to establish a reputation as one of the best.

Sebastian himself was something of a celebrity among geologists —a rockstar to people who were *really* into rocks. It certainly didn't hurt that he was so handsome: six foot five, with ash-blond hair that had resisted graying even though he was now in his fifties. With his square jaw and dimpled chin, more than a few people said he looked like a blond Tom Brady.

Carrianne had watched his TED Talk, "Seeing Through Stone," at least ten times. It was about how, even in a field that was all about analyzing gigabyte after gigabyte of data—from the wide net of aeromagnetic maps all the way down to ultrafine chemical assays that measured trace elements in the parts-per-billion—you still had to be willing to make what he called a SWAG.

A Scientific Wild-Assed Guess.

Sebastian had turned Blue Diamond Resources into a thriving company—and had made himself fabulously wealthy—thanks to his SWAGs: his consistent ability to find deposits where others had missed them, or to go searching for them in places where no one else had thought to look.

Getting to work for him—and learn from him—was one of the perks of the job.

The other was just getting to work. Period.

It had been four months since she'd earned her master's degree from the Colorado School of Mines. Even though she was eating ramen and living with three roommates, she had just about run through what little savings she had. If she didn't find something soon, she would have no choice but to move back home, a setback—and, yes, a humiliation—that no proud twenty-five-year-old wanted to contemplate.

It never should have gotten this bad. Carrianne had watched classmates with fewer academic honors, less impressive internships, and lower GPAs get hired. Yes, some of those were for jobs that hadn't interested Carrianne. And some were obtained through family connections—something she decidedly did *not* have.

Still, something should have panned out by now.

Her desperation had grown by degrees as the months wore on. Before graduation, she had been picky, passing on many of the companies that came to campus to recruit. In May and June, she had still been applying only to companies that met her high standards.

In July, she had started casting a wider net, throwing her resume around with less care. By August, she had discarded the net altogether.

It was now September. She had applied for entry-level positions at a great many exploration companies, any number of which should have been happy to have her. She had been getting nibbles, though none that had led to an offer.

Was it because she was a woman in a field where men still dominated? Or because, as an introvert, she didn't have the kind of bubbly personality that interviewed well? Or was it because of some other shortcoming she simply couldn't see?

It was impossible to know. In the winner-take-all world of hiring, no one took the time to explain to you why you finished second.

She had also tossed her resume at a few higher-level positions, like the one at Blue Diamond. With those, she kept getting ensnared in that classic new-graduate Catch-22. They all wanted three to five years of field experience. But how was she supposed to get experience if no one would hire her?

Her stress level—and desperation—had only increased as her bank account dwindled.

All those worries would vanish if she could just get Anthony Sebastian to say yes.

With what Blue Diamond was offering, she would even have enough left over to send some money home to her grandmother. Meemaw, as Carrianne called her, had been struggling ever since Paw died of lung cancer last year, which had put an end to his small monthly pension payments.

So, there was a lot riding on this interview.

Like, everything.

Or at least that was how it felt.

That morning, she had taken pains to straighten her naturally wavy blond hair and bobby pin it into a tight, no-nonsense bun that rested low on the back of her skull.

She put on her best (and only) black pantsuit, pairing it with a cream-colored silk blouse that did its best not to attract attention. Then, she squeezed her feet into black pumps with two-inch heels that boosted her height to five foot eight, even though she was the kind of person who much preferred steel-toe hiking boots.

And now here she was, sitting in the reception area of Blue Diamond Resources on the thirty-sixth floor of a sleek high-rise in downtown Denver, trying to ignore the sweat trickling down her back.

After a few minutes that dragged on like ice ages, a woman came out and announced, "Okay. He's ready for you."

He being Anthony Sebastian.

That part scarcely needed to be said.

Carrianne stood and wobbled unsteadily on her heels—she was *really* starting to hate those things—through one door, down a hallway, then through another door and into a corner office that looked like it had been decorated by Indiana Jones.

There were carvings and trinkets and sculptures from every culture and corner of the world. Buddhas competed for space with

African fertility goddesses. An armless Venus de Milo faced a Ganesh, like she wanted to hug the big fella if only she could figure out how. A jeweled funerary mask stared with hollow eyes at a golem, above which a scimitar rested peacefully on pegs.

Then there were the rocks. Quartz. Amethyst. Onyx. Soapstone. Alabaster. A hunk of jade the size of a toaster oven.

And—befitting the company name—set off in its own perfectly lit case, there was a blue diamond that looked to be at least eight carats.

Between the decor and the furnishings—mahogany and leather predominated—it smelled like money.

The man himself was seated behind a glass-top desk that was, in contrast to every other surface in the space, completely devoid of clutter. A stapler, tape dispenser, and small inbox looked like they had been placed there with the aid of a laser measure.

Behind him, floor-to-ceiling windows offered a spectacular view of the Rocky Mountains to the west.

His head was down, and his eyes were fixed to whatever was happening on his laptop screen. For a few long moments, he seemed not to have noticed that she had entered.

Carrianne just stood there, uncertain if she should speak or just cough politely.

Finally, he looked up.

"Ms. Kaucher."

"Yes?" she said, wishing it hadn't sounded like a question.

He pointed to the chairs in front of his desk. "Have a seat."

"Thank you."

She settled in. And then he came out with: "Do you like *things*, Ms. Kaucher?"

Was this a trick interview question? An updated version of "If you were a tree, what kind of tree would you be?" Or was this just his way of starting a conversation?

"Things?" she asked.

"You know. Things. Stuff," he said, gesturing at the bounty that surrounded him.

"I, uh, I'm not really much of a collector, if that's what you're asking."

"Why not?"

"They just slow me down. I pack light."

He stared at her blankly for a moment, then broke into a laugh.

"Are you suggesting I'm a little too encumbered here?" he asked, looking bemused.

"Not at all, sir, I—"

"It's okay. It's okay. I *am* a collector, obviously. And I do like things. I like pretty things, important things, things that have meaning to me, things that tell a story. A lot of people like things. But maybe you're right. Maybe all my things are slowing me down."

"I didn't mean to—"

"No, no, you're onto something, Ms. Kaucher," he said, leaning forward in his chair as he spoke. "Speed. Agility. Isn't that what the modern world is all about? You have to be faster than the next guy— or gal, or whatever they call themselves these days. Sorry. I know that's not—"

"It's fine, Mr. Sebastian. I'm not a snowflake. Words won't make me melt."

He smiled at this. "Call me Anthony, please. You know, I had a feeling about you. And I can already tell my feeling was spot on. You don't like to waste time, do you, Ms. Kaucher?"

"Not when I can avoid it."

"That's perfect ... absolutely perfect. It's exactly what I'm looking for, actually. Too many of my competitors, they do this patient, phased approach to exploration. It's like they're afraid of their own shadows. They hem and haw over the aeromag data for months. Then, they tiptoe through the geologic mapping. Then, maybe—*maybe*—they finally send someone into the field to collect a few samples. Then, they finally decide to gear up for something bigger. It takes them years to get to the point where they're doing core sampling. I know that's the prudent way to go, and it's probably what you have to do if you have timid investors and bosses who are afraid of failure, but I have no patience for it. I call it Wimp Geology.

"At Blue Diamond, we take a different approach—what I call Lightning Geology. We flatten out the phases and perform as many as we can, all at once. It's riskier, of course. But to me, exploration is a go-big-or-go-home proposition. You stake your claim, you get your license, and then you strike out to find your fortune. If you don't believe in yourself and your abilities, you ought to get into another line of work. My investors understand the risks, and they don't want to wait years to get a return. They expect results. How do you feel about that?"

"It suits me fine," she said.

Even though it was the opposite of what she had been taught, it was clearly what he wanted to hear.

He was nodding.

"I knew it would," he said.

Then he leaned back in his chair.

"Do you know how many resumes we received for this position?"

"No, sir."

"Ninety-seven."

He let the number dangle out there for a moment before he continued. "And almost every single one of them is more qualified than you. If I was running one of those Wimp Geology companies, we'd never even look at someone like you. A principal geologist has to do more than just geology. You're expected to be the team leader. You have to be willing to do anything and everything necessary—and I do mean *anything*—to keep the expedition on track. You're going to be in a wild, hostile place, where problems we can't possibly predict will pop up, and you'll have to solve them while wrangling the egos of people twice your age and with twenty times your experience. Every single one of my executives has told me you're too young and green to handle that much responsibility."

Carrianne felt her heart pounding. Why was he telling her this? Why had he even brought her here?

Had this been three months ago, she might have just shrunk in her seat and mumbled some tepid defense of her abilities. But after all the rejection she had faced, she felt like she had nothing left to lose.

"Then, no offense Anthony, why am I here?"

"Well, certainly, your grades and field work are all outstanding. Your recommendations are sparkling. I've known Steve Enders at the Colorado School of Mines for years, and he tells me you're one of the brightest and most promising students he's ever worked with."

And then Anthony fixed her with a steely look and said, "But it's mostly because I know about Greasy Creek."

Carrianne froze. For better or worse, Greasy Creek was where she had grown up. Nestled deep in the folds of Eastern Kentucky, it had a shrinking population, a rising poverty rate, and more overdose deaths than anyone cared to discuss.

She had fought like hell, with varying degrees of success, to get rid of her coal country twang. It wasn't because she was ashamed of Greasy Creek. It was because whenever she opened her mouth and that accent fell out, people made assumptions about her.

It wasn't fair.

But she had eliminated any mention of Greasy Creek from her resume all the same.

"How ... how do you know about Greasy Creek?" she asked.

"Because I do my homework on everyone I hire. I know you were valedictorian *and* captain of the junior ROTC brigade *and* queen of the Pike County Fair—"

"That was a scholarship competition, not a beauty pageant. I just—"

He held up a hand. "And yet you still put on a tiara, held a bouquet of wildflowers, and let the local paper take a picture of you along with your grandparents, who looked so proud their hearts were about to burst out of their chests. The paper reported you sang 'Country Roads' by John Denver for the talent portion. You accompanied yourself on the ukulele. I bet that was a crowd pleaser.

"I'm willing to bet this, too: no one gets out of Greasy Creek unless they're smart, tough, and hungry. And I like people who are smart, tough, and hungry."

She didn't say anything, lest she sound immodest.

"Have you ever heard of Beatty, Nevada?" he asked.

"No, sir."

"That's good. Because I'd know you were lying if you said you had. That's where I'm from: Beatty, Nevada, 'The Gateway to Death Valley.' How's *that* for a tourism slogan? It's basically the Greasy Creek of Nevada. Nobody makes it out of there, either. But here I am. You follow?"

She nodded again.

"Good. I'm glad we understand each other," he said. "Now do you want this job or not?"

Not twenty minutes later, Carrianne found herself face-to-face with an employment contract that included an eye-boggling salary and the most aggressively worded nondisclosure agreement she had ever seen.

In short, she couldn't tell anyone what she was doing, where she was going, or what she saw once she got there.

The penalty for being found in breach of contract was five million dollars.

She looked up from the document.

"This NDA is really something," she said.

"You're right. And I don't apologize for it," Anthony said. "Discretion is everything in this line of work. The business is stuffed rotten with copycats. Everyone watches us carefully because we have a track record of success. If other exploration companies suspect Blue Diamond might be onto something, they'll rush in from every angle, and it will destroy a big part of the advantage we have being first to the party. I don't like to share. And

I *really* don't like to share with people who are just sponging off our hard work."

"I understand," she said. "But I don't have five million dollars."

"Of course you don't. No one in your position does. That's the point. This basically guarantees you'll be ruined if you talk. Do you have a problem with that?"

Carrianne's response was to skip to the last page of the contract and sign her name. Anthony Sebastian nodded with approval as she shoved the contract back across the desk at him.

"I knew I was right about you," he said.

"Okay. Now can you tell me where I'm going?"

"Egypt. The desert. Make sure to pack your sunscreen."

Carrianne scarcely needed the encouragement. She wasn't one of those blondes who tanned easily. She was the kind who came in two shades: pale or burned.

"Believe me, I buy it by the case," she said. "What's in Egypt?"

"Only one way to find out," he said. "Historically, the Eastern Desert has been where all the action is. The Nubian Empire pulled gold out of it for thousands of years and there are several well-funded resource plays going on there right there."

He paused for a moment, then hit her with the punchline. "So, naturally, we've secured several licenses to explore the Western Desert."

"What's in the Western Desert?"

"Honestly? No one knows what might be lurking beneath the sands."

Carrianne just stared at him as he grinned.

"But only because no one has looked in a very long time," he continued. "The technology has improved fifty-fold since a qualified team has gone out that way. And there's been a lot of erosion over the last few decades that has brought some very interesting rock formations to the surface. I'm sure everyone is going to laugh at me when they hear I'm out West, but they've been laughing at me for a long time. I'm willing to bet they're wrong—and I'm willing to put millions of dollars behind my bet. What do you think?"

"I think we won't know until we look," Carrianne replied.

"That's the spirit. Now you better get out of here. Your plane leaves in two days."

Carrianne startled at this. "You already bought me a plane ticket? But how did you know I was going to sign the contract?"

He grinned. "Just another lucky SWAG."

Chapter Two

Two whirlwind days later, Carrianne had either sold or given away nearly everything she owned—beyond the clothes she packed for Egypt and the small box of sentimental items back home in Greasy Creek.

She cut a check to her roommates for the next month's rent that basically emptied her bank account, telling them they needed to find someone else to take her bedroom because she wasn't coming back.

"I'm going overseas" is all she said.

How mysterious.

When she called Meemaw to break the exciting news, she swore her to secrecy, on account of the nondisclosure agreement—though even if Meemaw told everyone she knew, the news still wouldn't cross the Pike County line.

Then, Carrianne gave her grandmother the itinerary, scarcely able to believe the words that were tumbling out of her mouth. "I'm flying to Cairo through Frankfurt on Lufthansa," she said at one point.

How glamorous.

Meemaw asked whether she could afford the ticket, and

Carrianne assured her the company was paying for it. Meemaw's only other question was whether Carrianne planned to get a hot dog in Frankfurt.

Blue Diamond's Human Resources department had done what it felt it needed to orient her to the company, subjecting her to an ancient sexual harassment video, making her sign forms saying she understood company policies, and having her fill out a detailed form attesting that her health was good enough to withstand several weeks in the desert, far from ready access to medical care.

Having dotted every i and crossed every t, she was still somewhat shocked to find herself in the Denver Airport. She was wearing her usual travel outfit: hiking boots, stretchy jeans, and a tank top with a flannel shirt layered over it. She kept nervously checking to make sure she had her passport with her.

Truth was, she was proud of herself for even *having* a passport. When she had first gotten one as a sophomore at Eastern Kentucky University, it had been strictly aspirational. Back then, she had only been out of the state a handful of times. The mere notion that she might someday have a reason to cross an international border was intoxicating.

Now here she was, a world traveler at last. She was riveted to the flight path tracker as they crossed into Canada—her first time in international airspace!—then stared in fascination when she realized they were passing over the tip of Greenland.

Greenland!

How exotic.

Fifteen hours and one German layover later, she was on the ground in Cairo. Customs was a nonevent. After an hour's wait, the agent barely even glanced at the business visa Blue Diamond had helped her secure before waving her through.

From the moment she passed through security, it was chaos. A female foreigner traveling alone might as well have had a bullseye on her chest. A dozen men set upon her with offers to carry her bags, drive her to her hotel, or show her the pyramids. Some had only a few words of English, but they used them like knives, jabbing at her from all angles.

According to the itinerary she had received, Blue Diamond had sent a car. She was relieved when she spotted a man in a dark western-style suit carrying an iPad with "KAUCHER" on its screen.

This was how she was getting to Alexandria, where she would be taken to what was listed as "Blue Diamond National Headquarters." There, she would meet Anthony Sebastian Jr., Anthony's son and Blue Diamond's operations director for Egypt.

What wasn't on her itinerary was what happened fifteen minutes outside the airport, when the driver abruptly exited the divided highway and pulled off to the side of an access road. She was just about to ask what was happening when, from one of the many minarets that pierced the skyline, she heard a loud wailing.

The driver, who had already unrolled a mat from his trunk, knelt and started praying.

Talk about things you'd never see in Greasy Creek.

That thought reminded her that she had promised she'd let Meemaw know when she'd landed safely. Carrianne swapped in her new SIM card—the one that promised more coverage in Egypt than anyone—and fired off a quick text.

It was early evening local time when they arrived in Alexandria. In contrast to Cairo, where it had been in the low 90s, the air was cooler and more comfortable. High 70s maybe. A breeze was blowing in off the Mediterranean, and she rolled her window down to take in the brackish scent.

Even though she had barely slept on the plane, she was wired. To her jetlagged body, it was morning. This was just another all-nighter. She had pulled enough of those in graduate school.

She had assumed that Blue Diamond National Headquarters would be located in one of the tall buildings that hugged the shoreline in Alexandria's densely packed downtown. Instead, they bypassed the city center and pointed westward toward the tall cranes of the port district.

Soon, they were approaching what appeared to be a marina.

"Are you sure this is right?" she asked as the driver pulled up to a twelve-foot-tall gate and said something in Arabic into the intercom there.

"Yes, ma'am," he assured her.

The gate rolled open, and they drove past a security booth and underneath a boom barrier that had been lifted for them. Sailboats and motorboats of varying sizes were tied up to docks laid out in neat rows. They stretched out into a bay that was protected from the full brunt of the Mediterranean by a small spit of land perhaps half a mile away.

The car came to a stop alongside one of the large slips at the edge of the facility. Stretched out in front of her was a cruiser that had to be at least a hundred feet long. Maybe more. It had three decks, topped by a generous flybridge over which an impressive assortment of communications apparatus was perched—several spiky antennae, one rotating marine radar, and two rounded domes that Carrianne guessed were for satellite internet.

This wasn't merely a yacht. It was a superyacht. She had never exactly been in the market for one, but it had to cost at least ten million dollars. Maybe twenty?

She was still just gawking at it as she pushed open the car door and stood up. A man who looked to be in his late twenties or early thirties was walking down the gangplank toward her. He wore an untucked linen shirt with an extra button undone and slacks that billowed just slightly in the light breeze. His evenly tanned face was smiling.

This must have been Anthony Sebastian Jr. He was about five inches shorter than his father, but he had the same jaw and chin.

"Welcome to Egypt!" he gushed.

"Thanks."

"I'm A.J.," he said, approaching her with an outstretched hand.

"Carrianne."

Their palms met. He must have been reading the confusion on her face because he said, "I'm guessing no one told you that our headquarters floats, did they?"

"No," she confessed.

"It was Dad's idea. I don't know how much you've followed the politics around here, but the short version is that after the Arab Spring in twenty-eleven, they tossed out the corrupt dictator who had been in charge since the eighties. Everyone thought the country was on the happy road to democracy. Then, the people voted in the Muslim Brotherhood, which turned out to be just as bad at running things as the corrupt dictator. Then, the government was overthrown in a military coup and replaced by—surprise!—another corrupt dictator.

"Anyhow, the current regime seems entrenched enough, but if things should go wrong in a hurry, Dad worries that whoever comes next might not be as friendly to foreigners—Americans, in particular. You're heading up the third of three exploration teams we have operating here. We might add a fourth, depending on how things go. We like having the means to get our people out fast if we need to. Plus, the power and internet go out *all* the time around here. It's nice having everything we need on board here."

"It's a beautiful boat," Carrianne managed.

"Yeah, she's seaworthy. And she sleeps eighteen, so there's enough room to spread out. I take her out on longer trips on weekends just because it seems like a shame to keep her in the harbor all the time."

He looked wistfully toward the sea. The driver was already carrying Carrianne's suitcase up the gangplank. Carrianne shouldered her rucksack.

"Anyhow, come aboard," he said. "The guys are really excited to meet you."

The first passenger Carrianne saw when she climbed up to the main deck wasn't a guy.

It was a woman with a wide face and bored, glassy eyes. She was lounging on the side of the sundeck with her breasts spilling out from the sides of a bikini top. A sarong that was slit high on one side completed the look, such as it was.

"Carrianne, this is Tatiana, she's a friend of mine," A.J. said. "She's still learning English so don't take it personally if she doesn't ask you about your hobbies and interests. Come on. Your room is down this way."

He led her down some stairs to the lower deck, where they navigated a maze of tight turns. He finally opened the door to a stateroom that had a queen-size bed, a couch that folded out of the wall, and a view of the water from a small porthole. It was, from its handsome woodwork to its polished brass fixtures, about a hundred times more luxurious than any place Carrianne had ever slept.

"Look okay?" he asked.

"Yeah, it'll do," she said, though she was pretty certain he missed her attempt at sarcasm.

"I'm sure you'll want to wash up or whatever. Dinner is in a half-hour if that works for you."

"Perfect. I'm famished."

Once A.J. had departed, Carrianne squeezed into her tiny en suite bathroom and showered off the grit of her long journey. She donned the only dress she had packed—a floral print sundress she had worried about bringing to a Muslim country.

Except now she could see that it was, at least by Tatiana's standards, quite modest.

As she left her stateroom, she realized she should have asked for a map. She took several wrong turns, getting so lost that at one point she inadvertently opened the door to the cargo hold.

A musty scent immediately invaded her nose. She found herself staring at several objects of varying sizes that had been securely wrapped in blue tarps and lashed to the boat's hull. Then, her eyes shifted to a crate that contained flats of vodka, whisky, brandy, and tequila—easily a year's supply of booze, wrapped in clear plastic.

Apparently, A.J. didn't want to be unprepared if a party broke out.

When she finally found her way back topside, she walked up to the main deck, which was a combination galley-dining room-living room that was every bit as grand as her stateroom. The kitchen was larger than the one in her apartment.

The savory aroma of garlic and butter wafted from it. A man in a white chef's coat—with matching hat—was putting the finishing touches on dinner.

"There you are," she heard A.J. say. "All shiny and new."

"It smells incredible in here."

"I borrow the chef from the Four Seasons downtown. Believe me, it's not an everyday occurrence, or else I'd weigh 300 pounds," he said, patting his flat stomach. "On the menu tonight is lamb-something and rice something-else, and *aish baladi,* which is the local flatbread. And, P.S., it's delicious."

A.J. had risen to his feet. He was holding a glass bottle by the neck. Small beads of condensation had formed on its sides. Carrianne couldn't read the label, which was in Arabic.

"Want a beer?" he asked, gesturing toward a refrigerator with the bottle. "Wine? Something harder?"

"No thanks."

"You sure? Officially, there's no booze in the field. That's company policy. This might be your last chance for a while."

A voice came from the couch. "Driving another employee to drink, huh, A.J.?"

Carrianne turned to see a man whose deeply tanned skin was set off by bushy, Santa Claus-white hair and a full mustache that dripped down his face like a frown. He had a husky build that was at least thirty years and thirty pounds on the wrong side of fit.

"Carrianne, meet Jerry Thajer," A.J. said, like it pained him.

"He's your geophysicist. Just try to ignore that he's older than most of the rocks you'll be looking at."

"That just means I've been around long enough to remember the early days with his dad, when we used to play rock-paper-scissors to decide who had to change little A.J.'s diaper," Jerry told Carrianne in a growly voice that betrayed his American Midwest origins. "I always seemed to get the smelly ones. When I say I've been putting up with this kid's crap for a long time, I mean it."

A.J. looked down like the comeback he was hoping for was on the floor.

Jerry continued. "And I may be the oldest, but my last stop in the States was with my doctor, and he gave me a clean bill of health. As I told my wife Patricia before I left, 'Sorry, honey, you're stuck with me for a little while longer.'"

"Nice to meet you," Carrianne said. Then, in an attempt to rescue her host from further embarrassment, she changed the subject.

"So, my itinerary ended with my arrival here," she said. "What's the agenda moving forward?"

"Tomorrow, we fly to Aswan, where we have a warehouse that serves as our staging area," A.J. replied. "Some of the crew is already there. You'll also have to add some locals to help round out the team. We're supposed to give preference to Egyptians in hiring, so if we don't make a show of good faith in employing a few of them, especially for the non-technical roles, we could theoretically lose our exploration license."

"I'll help you with that," Jerry volunteered. "You have to know how to spot the shysters and conmen who are just trying to take advantage. This isn't my first time in a third-world country."

"I don't think they call them third-world countries anymore, Jerry," A.J. said.

"What are we supposed to call them?"

"I believe the term is 'developing economies,'" A.J. said.

Jerry waved this away and turned back to Carrianne. "Whatever. Point is, I got your back."

Carrianne was trying to be mindful of some of the final words of wisdom Anthony Sebastian had given her: that, as principal geologist, she was expected to be the team leader and that—especially as someone who was young, unproven, and, yes, female—she had to be strong and decisive.

At the same time, doesn't a good leader also know how to delegate?

"Thank you. I would definitely appreciate your help," she said. "Why don't you assemble some candidates and then I'll review them? If we have a two-step process, it'll help us both get a longer look at them."

"Sure, sure," Jerry said. "That makes sense."

A.J. smiled with approval.

Carrianne turned toward another man who was seated on the couch—the man whose gaze had been traveling up and down her body for several minutes now, making her wish she had stuck with jeans and hiking boots instead of a dress.

He had short brown hair; small, quick eyes; and a pair of heavily muscled, tattoo-covered arms jutting out from his T-shirt. He looked like he spent most of his spare time doing sit-ups.

"Hi," she said, mostly to get him to stop staring. "I'm Carrianne."

"Oh, sorry. This is Dave Martin, your chief of security," A.J. said. "He's with ETS Solutions. They're a private defense contractor. He's an ex-Navy Seal. He won the Navy Cross, which basically means he would have won the Medal of Honor except he happened to live. He's the best of the best—or at least he'd better be for what we're paying him. You can ask him what the ETS in ETS Solutions stands for if you want."

"Well?" Carrianne asked.

"Embrace The Suck," Dave said, repeating a mantra that became popular among soldiers who had served in Middle East theaters of operation during the 2000s.

A.J. nodded in gleeful approval and generally seemed to be marveling at Dave like a small child looking up at a war hero.

"We'll have three more men meeting us in Aswan," Dave told Carrianne. "They're all veterans, all well-trained in small arms, light weapons, and anti-personnel maneuvers. Don't worry. You're in good hands."

Carrianne felt herself swallowing hard.

"Anyhow, I think dinner is ready," A.J. said. "Let's eat."

Throughout the sumptuous meal, as darkness fell across the Mediterranean, Jerry and A.J. supplied most of the conversation, competing to see who could impress Carrianne with the most outrageous story from past adventures.

Dave said very little.

Tatiana appeared at one point, still in her bikini top even though the sun was long gone. A.J. eyed her lasciviously. Without a word, she grabbed some *aish baladi* and disappeared.

When the meal was over, A.J. and Jerry hinted they were thinking about taking on the ship's brandy collection. Dave announced he was planning to turn in, and Carrianne took that as an excuse to do the same.

"Suit yourself," A.J. said. "We'll see you in the morning. Any last questions?"

"I guess I'm just confused about one thing," Carrianne said, thinking of how to voice the concern that had been rising in her throughout the meal. "Why do we need so many soldiers?"

The mood on board the boat immediately darkened.

"How much did Dad tell you?" A.J. asked.

Nothing, Carrianne thought. *Not a damn thing.*

"He ... he didn't mention anything about ... about needing a security force," Carrianne said.

"It's not like we're sending you into a war zone or anything. It's mostly just a precaution—"

"Don't sugarcoat it," Dave said, cutting him off. "She needs to know what she's getting into."

He shot his employer a look that said, *If you don't tell her I will.*

A.J. sighed heavily. "Alright. The Western Desert is ... well, it's not like the Eastern Desert. Put it that way. The Eastern Desert is more well-traveled. The Western Desert is part of the Sahara ... I would call it no-man's land, but that's actually the problem. There are a few people roaming around out there, and a lot of them are, how to put it ..."

"Bandits," Dave said succinctly.

"Mostly small groups," A.J. clarified. "But they are armed and known to be rather ... opportunistic. Our teams are outfitted with several hundred thousand dollars' worth of equipment. Egypt's economy has been in the dumps these last few years, and it's driven a certain segment of the population toward lawlessness. Desperate times make for desperate people."

Carrianne could feel her heart thumping faster. "Have your other teams been attacked?"

"Don't lie to her," Dave cautioned.

"Yes," A.J. admitted. "But that's why we hire people like Dave and his men. We've run them off every time. They're basically just ragtag groups. The moment you show them you're going to fight back, they scatter. They're only interested in easy pickings. It's really been fine."

An uncomfortable silence settled over them.

"It's only fair to tell you that the U.S. State Department strongly advises against travel to the Western Desert," Dave said.

In a smaller voice, A.J. said, "I'm sorry my dad didn't say anything about this. I guess ... if you want to quit, now would be the time."

And do what? Carrianne thought. *Go back to Greasy Creek?*

She had given up her apartment. She had sold everything. More to the point, she was out of money and had no other prospects.

"No," Carrianne said. "I'll be fine."

"Great," A.J. said, perking back up. "We fly out first thing."

Chapter Three

The Beechcraft twin turboprop had the boxy lines of a kid's homemade go-kart and looked like something that belonged in a World War II surplus sale.

We're flying in that thing? were the words Carrianne had to stifle the moment she laid eyes on it.

Or, even more alarmingly: *That thing flies?*

"What do you think of my private jet?" A.J. asked, beaming.

Carrianne tried to ignore the rust stains dripping from the bolts along the side of the fuselage as she said, "It's ... something alright."

"We picked it up used. Obviously. Its primary purpose is to carry core samples from the field up to the lab we have here in Alexandria for analysis. Believe it or not, when we priced out doing it this way ourselves versus paying a trucking company to do it, it was fairly comparable. Plus, this way is a lot faster. And you know how Dad is with all his Lightning Geology thing. Rather than waiting two weeks or a month just for the samples to arrive and then start testing them, we're testing them in days. That way, if there's an area that looks promising, you're able to go back and drill for more samples right away.

"Plus, it's very *Lawrence of Arabia*, don't you think? There's just something ... romantic about it."

Romantic wasn't the word Carrianne would have picked.

Ramshackle, maybe.

Carrianne put an effort into the smile on her face.

"Don't worry, we have a mechanic check it out regularly," A.J. assured her. "The engines were just overhauled last year. They have plenty of hours left in them."

She watched as Dave Martin wheeled a large crate on a dolly up the ramp in the aft of the plane. His biceps strained at the sleeves of his tight T-shirt.

"What's that?" Carrianne asked.

"Oh, you know, Army stuff," A.J. said.

"This is the reason you're going to be able to sleep at night," Dave volunteered. "You're looking at four M-249 Squad Automatic Weapons and enough 5.56 NATOs to wipe out an entire battalion. When you hear us referring to SAWs, we're not talking about something made by Black and Decker. If we set up one of these bad boys on each corner of camp, we'll be able to mow down anything that comes our way. The hajis won't get close."

"Hajis?" Carrianne asked.

"Sorry. That's what we tend to call our less-friendly neighbors."

"Is it ... polite?" she asked.

"Well, strictly speaking, a haji is someone who has made a pilgrimage to Mecca. So, it could be worse. It's better than towelhead or sand mon—"

"She gets the point," A.J. said, then gestured grandly toward the plane. "We should probably get going. Now boarding all rows and all passengers for your nonstop flight to Aswan."

As Carrianne carried her luggage aboard, the overhauled engines roared to life. Most of the plane's hold was dedicated to cargo, so there were just a few jump seats in a small cabin just behind the cockpit. A.J. insisted that Carrianne take the one nearest the window.

That treated her to an unfettered view of Egypt as the Beechcraft climbed up to a cruising altitude many thousands of feet aloft. The dominant feature was the Nile and its banks, which stood out like a well-cultivated green line winding through the endless—and seemingly empty—yellow-brown of the desert.

What Carrianne knew about their destination she had learned from Google. Aswan was the gateway to the southern Nile, had a population of 380,000, and was a UNESCO World Heritage site. Whatever that meant. Its namesake dam provided enough electricity to power nearly two million homes.

After an hour-and-a-half aloft, they came in for a bumpy landing at Aswan International Airport, which, despite its ambitious name, had only one runway and zero international flights.

They taxied directly from the runway to a large warehouse-like building with two massive doors over which hung the Blue Diamond logo.

"Welcome to our non-floating headquarters," A.J. said over the noise of the propellers. "This is pretty much your home-away-from-home when you're not out in the field."

A few moments after the plane had entered the hangar, the pilot cut the propellers, which slowly spun to a stop. When the main cabin doors were opened, a wall of superheated air forced its way in.

It smelled crispy, like the inside of an oven. Although it was only midmorning, the temperature was well on the way to its expected high in the triple digits. Aswan was located at twenty-three degrees north latitude, roughly the same as the Bahamas. Carrianne could already tell its climate was nowhere near as pleasant.

They gathered their belongings and disembarked via a set of stairs that had been wheeled next to the plane. As Carrianne got her bearings, she watched A.J. greet a burly chunk of a man who was at least six foot two, with a head and neck that were roughly the same width.

A.J. soon waved her over.

"Javier Sauza, this is Carrianne Kaucher. She's your geologist. Carrianne, this is Javier. He's operating your diamond drill rig."

"Which I will refer to as Big Bertha, or Bertha, or sometimes the Beast if she's not behaving," Javier said. "So, if you hear me say 'Bertha needs a kick in the ass' or 'I'm going to slap the Beast around,' don't take it the wrong way.

"Got it," Carrianne said.

Javier addressed both of them. "I got the memo about hiring locals for my team, and I think I've found two guys who aren't total *pendejos*. Do you want to meet them before I bring them on?"

"That would be great," Carrianne said.

"How's their English?" A.J. asked.

"Not as good as my Spanish, but a lot better than my Arabic. One of them worked for ExxonMobil a few years back, so he knows our equipment. Those oil guys go a lot deeper than we'll ever need to go, so that's good. The other guy has a construction background and knows how to work an excavator. Bonus: he once helped lead fishing tours on Lake Nasser, so he can help us catch some of those famous Nile perch I've heard about."

"That'll be a big help in the desert, I'm sure," A.J. said.

"I'll let you know when I can get them in," Javier said to Carrianne.

"Okay, sounds like a plan," A.J. said, then looked at Carrianne. "Let's finish up showing you around."

He pointed toward several pallets loaded with long white cardboard boxes, all of which had printed sheets of data attached to one end. To anyone not in the business, it would have looked like a sequence of meaningless numbers, but Carrianne immediately recognized the standard nomenclature for logging core samples.

"Those are fresh from the Western Desert. Once we get them loaded on the plane, I'll be heading back with them to the lab in Alexandria."

"Got it."

"Great. Moving on, that's the office over there," he said, pointing to a hutch in the corner. "There's a big conference table where everyone sort of spreads out. That tends to be the nerve center while you're here. That's also where you'll find the office manager, whose name escapes me at the moment because we just hired him. There's a printer slash copy machine if you need it. The Wi-Fi router is there, too. I only mention that because sometimes you have to do a hard reset after the power goes out, which only happens about five to ten times a week when the heat is like this. We have a generator for the A/C and some of the other stuff in the living quarters, and reception is good, so you can hotspot if you need internet, but the router itself relies on the grid."

"Got it."

"Back this way are the living quarters. Come on," he said, walking across the large open space of the hangar toward a steel door on the other side.

"What's that?" Carrianne said as they passed a few pallets that contained ... something. The lumpy shapes were draped in white cloth.

"Uh, I don't know. Supplies, maybe?" A.J. said, squinting at it. "I'm not sure. Let's find you a place to live first."

He led her to the steel door, which opened onto an interior hallway.

Cool air beckoned.

"We call these the apartments, but they're really more like dorm rooms," A.J. said. "If you see an empty room, you put your stuff in it and it's yours. Once you head out in the field, you vacate the room, stick your stuff in storage, and leave it empty in case someone on one of the other teams needs it. Make sense?"

"Sure," Carrianne said.

A.J. was peering around doors, most of which were ajar and led to rooms that showed signs of habitation. Some of the rooms were doubles. Others were singles. When he reached a closed door, he knocked, waited a moment, then pushed inside to find an empty space.

It was a single. There was no window, but a vent in the ceiling was bringing in more of that delicious, cool air. A bare mattress on a simple frame sat in one far corner. A wooden desk, like you might find in a hotel room—lamp, outlets, rolling chair—filled the other. There were shelves and a dresser on the wall nearest Carrianne.

"The bathroom and kitchen are down the hall," A.J. explained. "Blankets and sheets are in the utility closet in the bathroom. There's a washer and dryer in there, too. There's no maid service so pick up after yourself. Everything else is pretty well labeled, so it should be self-explanatory. One of the office manager's jobs is to keep the fridge stocked, though you'll be expected to make your own meals. If there's anything you're really hankering for, let him know, and he'll do what he can. Do you need some time to get settled?"

Carrianne wheeled her suitcase into the room, set down her rucksack, and removed the ruggedized laptop Blue Diamond had issued her shortly before her departure. Her mind was already churning with everything she needed to accomplish, not the least of which was to hire the rest of the crew, assemble the equipment, and get provisioned for a long stint in the desert.

They were scheduled to leave in two days. Anthony Sebastian had made it very clear that time was money, that his investors were impatient, and that the only way to find resources was to get out into the desert and start looking.

"No, we have a lot to do," she said. "Let's get to work."

"That's the spirit."

As they returned to the blast furnace that was the hangar, A.J. immediately stopped and swore.

"What?" Carrianne asked.

"We have a problem."

A.J.'s focus had narrowed on an unremarkable man who was standing at the entrance to the hangar with his arms crossed in a defensive posture.

He had a mustache, dark hair, and light brown skin. He wore khaki-colored trousers and a short sleeve button-down shirt whose left breast pocket was stuffed with pens and, of all things, a pocket protector. He topped off the look with a hard hat and yellow reflective jacket, both of which contained a circular emblem.

He was talking with Javier, who had his arms behind his back like he had something to hide. Standing in between them was a woman who appeared to be acting as a translator. She was perhaps slightly older than Carrianne—an American with light brown hair and a round, pleasant face.

"Who's the guy?" Carrianne asked.

"That," A.J. said in a low voice, "is Inspector Mahmoud Yousef from EMRA, the Egyptian Mineral Resources Authority. It's part of the Ministry of Petroleum and Mineral Resources."

"That's who grants us our exploration license, yes?"

"Exactly."

"And who is the translator?"

"That's Ciarra Colyer. She's one of ours. Technically, her title is ESG liaison—environmental, social, and governance. But, yeah, her main function will be to translate for you."

"Okay. What's the story with the inspector?"

"Oh, geez. Where to start? The licenses are actually pretty cheap —like, five thousand bucks a year for the first two years, then ten thousand a year for the next two years and so on. It's chump change compared to our other costs. Except, in Egypt, there's what you think you're going to pay, and then there's the real cost of things."

"What do you mean?"

"Okay, so a lot of this is history from before we were here. But it used to be the Egyptian government's deal was basically: if you're a foreign company and you want to come here and mine, fine, but we're taking *half* of whatever you get. Few foreign companies even tried, because who can make money under those circumstances? It left the Egyptians to exploit their own resources, at least in theory. The only problem was, they didn't really have the capital to invest in exploration, so there wasn't much happening.

"Then, in 2019, they passed a law that knocked the royalty down to five percent. That opened the door for companies like us. It's been a good thing for the country, on the whole—because something is better than nothing, right? The problem is, most of these EMRA inspectors act like the old ways are still in place. They know they don't *officially* get half anymore, so they try to get as much as they can unofficially."

"You mean like a bribe?"

"I mean exactly a bribe" he said, as he pointed a finger "which is completely illegal, of course. In the exploration license contract we sign, there's even an anti-corruption clause. They still walk around with their hands out all day long. The contract gives them the right to inspect our operation at any time, and they use that to play this game with us. They never just say, 'Give me money.'"

He glanced across the warehouse at the inspector, who was scribbling notes on his clipboard while interrogating Javier though the translator. "This is an Arab culture, so they're more polite and less direct about it. They find something quote-unquote wrong with your equipment. They find something wrong with one of your employees. They find something wrong with how you tie your shoes. It doesn't matter. The contract is incredibly vague. For example, it says, 'The Company shall train its employees in accordance with generally accepted health and safety procedures and practices.'"

"What does that mean?"

"Exactly. It means everything and nothing all at once. And EMRA people use it to come in here and make a big fuss. It's all nonsense. But the whole time, they wield this incredible power. What it comes down to is that they can cancel the license because they don't like the way you look at them."

"So—I'm sorry to say it—why don't you just pay him off?"

"I have. Generously. If we find something out there, I'll probably have to pay him off again before we can exploit the resource. But in the meantime, I've made it clear he's squeezed us hard enough and that there's no more juice here."

"Then why is he still here?"

"I don't know," A.J. said. "But we had better find out. Because the reality is that guy right there—that mild-mannered nerd with a pocket protector—can put us out of business and kick us out of the country with one stroke of his pen."

"Do you want to talk to him or should I?" Carrianne asked.

"I've got to get those core samples back to Alexandria," A.J. said. "Besides, he already hates me. Why don't you give it a try?"

Chapter Four

C arrianne touched the back of her head, where several of the bobby pins that held together her once-tight bun had been knocked askew.

There was no time to fix it now. She just put on what she hoped was a pleasant face and approached the trio.

Javier shot her a quick, wary look. The translator, Ciarra, made brief eye contact before returning her attention to Inspector Yousef. He had been keeping up a steady stream of Arabic directed toward Javier, but it ceased the moment Carrianne walked up.

She had taught herself a few Arabic phrases during the plane ride over, so she repeated the standard greeting she had learned.

"*Asalam alaykum*," she said. Peace be with you.

"*Wa-alaykum salam*," the inspector replied. And upon you be peace.

"My name is Carrianne Kaucher," she said. "I am the principal geologist for this expedition."

Ciarra repeated the introduction in Arabic, listened for a moment, then said, "He wants to know where your husband is."

It was all Carrianne could do to not let her eyes bug out of her head.

"What?" she half-spat. "Is that literally what he just said?"

"Yes," Ciarra said.

Are you bleeping kidding me? Carrianne wanted to say back.

But then she remembered Anthony Sebastian's words during their interview. *You have to be willing to do anything and everything necessary—and I do mean anything—to keep the expedition on track.*

In this case, that meant keeping her cool around the man who could make her first-ever field leadership experience an exceedingly brief affair.

"Tell him I don't have a husband," Carrianne said.

Ciarra did as asked, then was met with a long burst of Arabic.

"He says you are very beautiful. He says your beauty will cause a distraction and men won't be able to think straight while you are flaunting yourself in such an open manner. He says that if they know you are single, men will think of you as a ... oh my ... they will think of you as a prostitute. And they will ... I'm not sure how to translate this exactly. But, basically, he's saying they will hit on you. A lot."

Carrianne looked down at herself. She was wearing jeans, hiking boots, and a baggy T-shirt.

This was flaunting herself?

"Tell him I'm not made of glass," Carrianne said. "I won't break that easy."

The translator shook her head. "I'm not going to say that. It would be considered rude to ignore his advice."

"His advice is ridiculous."

"In his own weird way, he's just trying to help."

"What does he want me to do? Wear a blanket over my body and hide from human contact?"

"I'm going to translate that as, 'With respect, what, in your considered opinion, is the correct course of action for me to take?' Is that okay?"

"Sure. Fine."

Ciarra spoke for a moment. Then, Inspector Yousef turned to Carrianne and began talking to her directly.

"He says he is very open-minded and doesn't have a problem with women himself. But he says if you meet other Egyptian men, you should tell them you have a husband. You should mention your husband before they ask. He says he is not responsible for what happens to you if you fail to heed his words."

There was more than a little menace in the last part. Once he was through, his eyes sank toward Carrianne's breasts, where they lingered for an overlong moment. Then, he dipped his head slightly.

"*Mae alsalama*," he said.

It was a standard Arabic farewell, but its full intention wasn't lost on Carrianne. It literally meant, "With safety."

"*Mae alsalama*," Carrianne repeated.

Without another word, Yousef pivoted and walked toward a small, grimy, tin can of a Jeep that was parked nearby. It started on its third try, then kicked up a cloud of dust as it drove off.

Carrianne introduced herself to the ESG liaison then said, "Now, would someone tell me what that was all about?"

"Well, as best I can tell, it started off as a shakedown," Javier replied. "But then it turned into the Bachelorette Season Twenty-Five. I think Mahmoud Yousef likes you."

Carrianne just shook her head.

"Other than my marital status, did the inspector find anything that was actually a problem we need to fix?"

"Let's see here. He started by breaking my *cojones* about PPE," Javier said, using the standard abbreviation for personal protective equipment.

"Yeah, what was that FFP2 thing he was quizzing you about?" Carrianne asked.

"Oh, it's nothing. It's a standard set by the Europeans for dust masks," Javier said. "Our masks pass."

"Great. What else?"

"Well, when you walked up, he was asking me if I had completed a full risk analysis for the diamond drill."

"Have you?"

"You want the honest answer?"

"Of course."

"No. Diamond drills have pinch points. Everyone knows that. A risk analysis basically comes down to, 'Yo, *amigo*, don't put your hand there if you like your fingers.'"

"Alright. Well, why don't you go online, find something that sounds a little more formal than that, get it translated into Arabic, and print it out. Make sure you show it to the new hires. Maybe even get them to sign that they've seen it? That way, if the good inspector asks again, we're covered."

"Sure," Javier said. "Although there is one problem."

"What's that?" Carrianne asked.

"You are so, so beautiful, I might be too distracted," Javier said in a comically bad Egyptian accent.

Then he grinned.

Carrianne just rolled her eyes.

"But seriously," Javier said, returning to his normal voice. "If we're talking about our own risk analysis, you might want to put that guy high on the list."

Don't worry, Carrianne thought. *I already have.*

After the loading of the core samples—and whatever supplies were underneath the white draping—A.J.'s so-called private jet taxied back out of the hangar and was soon on its way to Alexandria.

Jerry seemed anxious to make good on his promise to spearhead the hiring of locals for the crew. So, when he asked if he could head into the city, Carrianne's only suggestion was that he ask Ciarra to join him.

From there, Carrianne made her way into the office, where she met the office manager, a younger man with thick glasses who greeted her politely and otherwise kept to himself.

He seemed unconcerned whether she was married.

For several hours, she buried herself in trip preparation, which mostly consisted of working her way through a series of checklists that Blue Diamond had prepared. She was relieved to discover most of the supplies they would need were already on-hand, just waiting to be loaded.

As the heat of the day cranked up, she could feel the jet lag weighing on her. It certainly didn't help that the office was cooled only by an ancient, sputtering window unit that was increasingly inadequate for its task as the mercury climbed past a hundred.

At precisely two o'clock, the office manager departed. This, Carrianne had learned, was typical in Egypt, where many bureaucrats and administrative employees worked six hours a day, six days a week. They didn't eat lunch at work; rather, they returned home to partake in their main meal with their families. Then, they laid low during the peak heat of the day.

Within a half-hour, she was starting to see the wisdom of this. She was sweating enough that her arms were sticking to some papers on the desk.

When the power in the office went out—just as A.J. had warned it might—she retreated to the residential quarters, where the hum of the HVAC unit was drowned out by the chattering of the generator that kept it going. Otherwise, all was quiet as she entered her bedroom.

Egypt was seven hours ahead of Kentucky. She called Meemaw to let her know she had arrived safely. Meemaw fussed over her for a few minutes then hurried her off the phone because she heard that foreign "sin cards" were expensive.

"*Sim* card, Meemaw."

"Well, whatever. You just be a good girl and go wrangle some gold for that company so they keep you on, y'hear?"

"Yes, ma'am."

"Love you, baby girl."

"Love you, too, Meemaw," she said.

As she hung up, Carrianne became aware of a commotion coming from the hallway. She opened her door to find two men who looked to be in their late twenties. They had buzzcut brown hair, jutting ears, and the kind of lobster-ish hue that suggested both extreme physical exertion and a lack of awareness that sunscreen had ever been invented.

Both were panting heavily.

"You're just mad because I beat your ass," the first one was saying.

"You did not," the second replied.

"What part of me touching the warehouse first made you think you won?"

"You didn't win anything. You cheated."

"I said 'C'mon, let's go. First to the warehouse.' How is that cheating?"

"Because I hadn't even agreed to it before you took off. If you race someone, you have to give them more warning than that."

"You still chased after me. You had every chance to catch me. It's not my fault you didn't."

Their dispute was interrupted by the steel door opening and Dave Martin coming through. He was topless and glistening with perspiration that had soaked the waistband of his gym shorts. Carrianne began counting his abdominal muscles but stopped when she'd reached eight. Obviously, her previous thoughts about his fondness for sit-ups were accurate.

He was winded. But not nearly as much as he should have been.

"Oh, hey," he said when he saw Carrianne. "These two knuckleheads are mine. Joshua and Joseph Mason. Also known as Thing One and Thing Two, or Team A and Team B. They're both ex-Marines, so keep your hands away from their mouths at feeding time and you should be fine. They're also brothers. Obviously."

"Yeah, but we're not twins, or else I'd look like an asshole," Joseph said.

"Whatever. You're so ugly that instead of breastfeeding you, mom said, 'Let's just be friends.'"

"Where'd you rip off that joke? Reddit?"

"No. That's classic Rodney Dangerfield."

"If you're going to insult me, at least be original."

"Fine, you're so ugly—"

"Okay, okay. Knock it off," Dave said. "Meet our new boss. This is Carrianne Kaucher. She's running the show for Blue Diamond once we're out in the field."

"Ma'am," Joshua said as Joseph just nodded.

Carrianne was still trying to make sense of their choice of recreation. "You guys were out jogging? In *this* heat?"

"The bad guys don't quit when it's hot, so we can't, either," Dave said. "Now, if you'll excuse me, I'm hitting the showers before I flood this place."

Sure enough, there was already a puddle forming underneath where he had been standing.

It was a small hallway. He still passed closer to Carrianne than it felt like he needed to, as if he wanted to make sure she was treated to the full magnificence of his chiseled torso.

Joseph piped up. "I'm first in the shower."

Joshua quipped, "That's fine, since you weren't first at anything else."

This prompted a curse from the younger brother. The two disappeared into the room across the hall, where Carrianne heard their continued bickering through the door.

She went back into her room and worked until she couldn't keep her eyes open any longer. After succumbing to a nap, she awoke feeling a little bewildered—but also refreshed.

There was noise coming from the shared kitchen down the hall that suggested dinner preparations were underway. Carrianne looked at herself in the mirror and decided her bun was a hopeless cause.

She removed the bobby pins and replaced it with a hastily gathered ponytail.

When she entered the kitchen, she found a scene of domestic tranquility. Javier was standing over a wok, poking at its contents. It smelled like stir fry. A pot of rice simmered on a back burner.

Dave was chopping vegetables for a salad. Ciarra was elbows deep in the sink, keeping up with the dishes.

Joshua and Joseph were sitting at the table, playing cards. Jerry was leaning back, watching them.

"Hey everyone," Carrianne said. "What can I do to help?"

"We're good," Javier said. "You can just chill."

Carrianne noted that the table wasn't yet set, so she began scouting around for utensils and napkins.

"How did it go with hiring today?" she asked Jerry as she puttered about. "Find anyone promising?"

Ciarra shot Carrianne a glance from the sink. Jerry's bushy mustache twitched.

"Not really," he said.

"What happened?"

"We went up to the Aswan Governorate offices and struck out."

"That's where the regional unemployment bureau is," Ciarra clarified. "Jerry thought that would be a good place to find people who are looking for work."

"Skilled people," Jerry clarified. "We could always go to where the day laborers hang out and come home with a truck full. The problem is, most of those people don't have proper paperwork. That's the sort of thing that would get us in trouble with that EMRA inspector."

"Of course," Carrianne said. "Good thinking."

"Well, not so good, since none of the people at the Governate office seem to want to work for us."

"Why not?"

"Because of some silly curse," Jerry said gruffly.

"What do you mean?"

"When they heard about the area where we were going, they said that part of the Western Desert is cursed. Ciarra translated it as 'The Curse of Dust.' It's something about some ancient god being angry. Supposedly, people go out there and, poof, they disappear. The dust swallows them up. They're never heard from again. Their bodies aren't even found. Or so the story goes."

"And this ... happens a lot?"

"Often enough, I guess. We were talking with a guy who swore his second cousin's great-great uncle was lost to The Curse of Dust 100 years ago."

"But I thought people here are Muslim," Carrianne said. "Why should they care about a curse from some old god that no one believes in anymore?"

"Well, that's not quite true," Ciarra said. "They *are* Muslim for the most part, but there's been a revival of the old religion that's been spreading in Egypt since the seventies. I studied it in school. For some people, it's just superstition or a fun tradition—a bit like horoscopes for us. But other people take it pretty seriously. They worship the old gods in their homes. Academics call it neo-paganism. The people themselves will refer to it as Kemetism. 'Kemet' is what the ancient Egyptians used to call themselves."

"You ask me, it's all bunk," Jerry said. "They're just making like this is dangerous duty to drive up wages."

"I don't know, Jerry," Ciarra said. "Those guys we were talking to looked legitimately scared."

"Nonsense," Jerry huffed. "There's no such thing as a curse."

Carrianne noticed Ciarra seemed to be holding her tongue.

She didn't look so sure.

Chapter Five

That evening after dinner, Carrianne worked through the plan for the next day.

If they were going to leave in thirty-six hours—as Anthony and A.J. Sebastian were pushing for—they had a lot to accomplish.

Hiring local crew members was the top priority. In addition to Javier's equipment operators, they needed a cook and a cook's assistant; a driver to ferry core samples to Aswan and then bring any needed supplies back to camp; and two laborers to help with setting up and taking down camp, carrying equipment, and any other tasks that needed extra elbow grease.

Carrianne and Ciarra quietly put their heads together and decided there had to be a better way of finding workers than Jerry's random, old-world method of trying to bump into people.

In short order, they discovered a jobs app that was the Egyptian equivalent of Indeed. Within minutes of posting their openings, they were contacted by interested job seekers.

The candidates all seemed to live near downtown Aswan, which wasn't particularly close to the airport. And since many of them didn't have cars, the women realized they would have to go into the city if they wanted to interview applicants in-person.

They decided to establish a screening location at a coffee shop near Sharia as-Souq, the open-air marketplace that served as a gathering point in Aswan for locals and tourists alike.

By the time they were ready to turn in, they had already booked a few appointments, with the hope that more people would see their posting come morning.

Following a night's sleep that felt like it restored her powers, Carrianne awoke early. There were still a few remaining team members who wouldn't get in until later that day, so Carrianne sent everyone an email saying they'd gather for a full meeting after dinner.

She became aware Ciarra and Jerry were moving about, getting ready, and they were soon ready to roll out. For the sojourn into town, they selected one of the Ford Broncos from Blue Diamond's fleet of vehicles the group would be taking into the desert.

Dave Martin insisted on joining them, claiming it would be best if he drove. It was unclear to Carrianne whether this was out of concern for their safety or out of a desire to escape Joseph and Joshua's constant squabbling.

She was mostly just trying to ignore that he kept checking her out. She figured he would eventually get tired of staring.

As they neared the city center, Carrianne started to understand why Dave wanted to be behind the wheel. This wasn't like the highway from Cairo to Alexandria. To drive on surface streets in Egypt definitely required an aggressive military mindset. At some intersections, there were traffic lights or octagonal red stop signs, though motorists seemed to treat those like suggestions.

Elsewhere, right-of-way was determined by whoever had the loudest horn. Near misses were considered common courtesy. Observing the three-second rule for following distance was to invite another car to merge with your front bumper.

When they arrived at the coffee shop, Carrianne didn't need any caffeine. She was plenty awake already. It was eight thirty. Their first appointment wasn't until nine, so she told the others she was going to have a quick look around the marketplace.

Sharia as-Souq was located along Saad Zaghloul Street, which was named for the statesman who helped start Egypt on its way to independence from British rule. It was still coming to life, though Carrianne could feel it getting busy fast as people tried to beat the heat of the day.

The shops were as appealing as they were varied. On makeshift kiosks and weathered tables, vendors displayed food of every sort: fruits, vegetables, colorful grains in heaping piles—the bounty of the Nile arrayed for purchase.

From one booth, there sprang the smell of freshly baked halawa. Another was selling heaping portions of koshari, which was considered Egypt's national dish.

There was also clothing. And baskets. Rugs. Pottery. Live animals in cages. Dead animals on strings. Cheap tourist trinkets. Fine art. Lotions. Powders. Oils.

It was a fascinating mix of the modern and the ancient. Within a few steps of each other, you could find electronics that hadn't been available as little as two years ago next to textiles that hadn't appreciably changed in centuries.

The shopkeepers were aggressive, though they seemed to know how to stop just short of assault. Carrianne figured out quickly enough that this was really just a game. And the rules were easy enough to understand.

If she slowed down for even the briefest moment, if her eyes lingered on a display, if she swerved in the direction of a shop—even inadvertently—she would be deemed a potential customer, ripe for approach.

"My friend, my friend, you come over here ..."

"Special deal, just for you ..."

"I have the best, the best. You just look ..."

It was a feast for the senses, a smorgasbord of commerce; and Carrianne was so immersed in it she didn't notice the donkey cart bearing down on her. The light jangling of the bells attached to the animals' harnesses blended in with the other sounds of the souq.

And she definitely couldn't understand the driver hollering at her in Arabic to get out of the way.

By the time she became aware of it, the collision was already unavoidable. A slab of solid wood rammed itself into the side of her back.

The cart couldn't have been traveling more than about ten miles per hour, but the impact still sent her sprawling toward a nearby shop, where the first thing she struck was a table filled with brightly colored woven hats.

She knocked several piles of them onto the ground, where she soon ended up herself.

"Princess, Princess, are you okay?" she heard.

She looked up, dazed, at a wiry man who was suddenly kneeling next to her. He appeared to be in his thirties, with olive skin and a smooth, shaved head. His button-down shirt contained a knockoff Ralph Lauren logo whose polo player was slightly larger than the horse underneath him.

Carrianne went to prop herself up, but the man gently pressed on her shoulder.

"No, no. You had a hard fall. Just stay down for a moment," he insisted. "Are you sure you're alright? Nothing broken?"

Carrianne performed a brief check-in with her limbs and extremities, all of which seemed to be in working order.

"Just bruised, I think," she said.

"How about your head?"

"I didn't hit that. The table broke my fall. I think I'm okay."

"Still, you should take a moment, Princess. Just relax. My name is Ahmed. Ahmed Hassan. I will stay with you until you're ready."

"I'm Carrianne."

"Pleased to meet you, Princess."

She looked up and around for the driver of the cart, but he and his donkeys were already long gone. This was a hit-and-run.

"Who or what was that?" she asked.

"We call him *Magnoon* Babu—Crazy Babu, you would say. He is an old man, blind as a bat, dangerous as a Nile hippo. Unfortunately, you are not his first victim. He's not supposed to drive his cart around here. It's a pedestrian zone. But the police just throw their hands up and say, 'Oh, it's *Magnoon* Babu, what can we do?' If they threw him in jail, he would just annoy all the other prisoners."

Carrianne's hand went to her back. There would be a welt there, for sure. She could already feel it forming.

Nearby, the shop owner, a man in a flowing off-white thobe, a traditional dress in many Arab countries, was chattering in excited Arabic. He seemed, if anything, angry at Carrianne—as if it was her fault the cart had hit her.

Ahmed rose to his feet and shot back several terse phrases at the shop owner. The man did not seem particularly mollified. He walked away, muttering to himself.

"What's his deal?" Carrianne asked.

"He's just a grouch," Ahmed said. "Now, let's get you on your feet. Easy now."

He offered her a hand, but she rose quickly without taking it.

"I'm fine, really," she insisted. "Thank you, Ahmed."

"You are quite welcome, Princess. If I may ask, what brings you to Sharia as-Souq today?"

There seemed no harm in explaining that she was in town to hire several key positions for a geological expedition in the Western Desert.

As she finished, Ahmed lit up. "Well, in that case, I think this meeting is fate."

"How so?"

"I grew up in the Dakhla Oasis. It is one of the seven oases of the Western Desert, in the New Valley Governorate. I have a large family and many of them are still out there. I travel there several times a year. I know the ways of the desert better than anyone. And you say you need a driver?"

"Yes."

"Well, then, it's perfect. I am a professional driver."

"Are you now?"

"Well, my formal education is in the law. But there isn't much need for lawyers when the economy is in such terrible shape and the law means so little. I can make more money driving a taxi and showing tourists around. That is the pitiable state of my country. But my wife and I would like to start a family, and I do not want our children to starve. I do what I must."

Carrianne studied the man. She could hear Jerry warning her to watch out for cons, but Ahmed seemed completely lacking in guile.

In addition, he was kind enough to help a stranger in need. His English was clearly excellent. He was educated far beyond what she needed ... though there would be worse things than having a lawyer around, especially if Inspector Yousef came back and started inventing infractions.

"If I may ask, how much do you make as a taxi driver?"

He spit out a number. Carrianne did some quick math in her head to compute that it came out to about one hundred dollars a week. She was authorized to pay her driver three times that. When she mentioned what they would be offering, Ahmed practically swooned.

As far as Carrianne was concerned, there was really only one more test he needed to pass.

"Knowing the Western Desert as you do, are you familiar with The Curse of Dust?"

He made a face.

"People believe in many things," he said.

"What about you?"

"I believe in a paycheck."

"Ahmed, how would you like to come meet some of my colleagues?" she asked

He smiled broadly. "I would be honored."

None of the other driver candidates compared to Ahmed—in experience, intelligence, or enthusiasm. Hiring him was the easiest decision they made.

Some of the other calls were a little more difficult. They kept Ahmed around as a kind of impromptu consultant. He steered them away from obvious problem cases.

Within a few hours, they had rounded out their team and were headed back toward the airport. Carrianne tried to downplay her excitement, but inwardly, she was feeling triumphant. She had never hired anyone before, and now here she was, making important decisions that she felt good about.

Her optimism only increased when she returned to the hangar and met the guys Javier wanted to bring on.

The former ExxonMobil drill operator was named Jamil Gamal. He was a slender man with long lashes over his striking green eyes.

The excavator operator was named Mirza Ibrahim. He was short and stout with a heavy five o'clock shadow—even though it wasn't yet noon—and a ready laugh.

A little while later, the Blue Diamond plane came in from Alexandria and disgorged two more passengers.

The first introduced herself as Kimberly Taylor, a geophysicist who would serve as Jerry's assistant. She was medium height with light brown hair and looked to be half Jerry's age. Carrianne already wondered how their dynamic was going to work out. Kimberly was as spirited as Jerry was crabby.

The second, Keith Henderson, was the final member of Dave Martin's squad. He was another husky sort, though there were useful muscles under his extra layer of padding. He was a bit older than the other soldiers, maybe in his forties. He had a large drab olive duffel bag slung over his shoulder and two cigars in the breast pocket of his Hawaiian shirt.

One of the Mason brothers—Joseph, no Joshua—was already sizing him up and said, "Nice kit bag. Were you Army?"

"First Cav," he said.

"Well, you know what Army stands for right? Ain't Ready to be a Marine Yet."

"That's not bad for a crayon-eater," Keith shot back. "Hey, what do you call a Marine with an IQ of 150?"

He waited a moment then said, "A platoon."

They were grinning, and there were likely more putdowns on the way, except they were interrupted by a seriously malnourished mutt of a dog with half its left ear missing and a tail that was wagging on serious overdrive.

It ran up to the group and inserted its snout into Keith's hand in such a way that he had no choice but to pet it.

"Whose dog is this?" Carrianne asked, looking at the dog's ribs, which were painfully close to its skin.

"Oh, sorry. He's mine," a man's voice said.

Carrianne turned and found herself face to face with its owner.

Men had never been particularly high on Carrianne's priority list. At Pike High School, becoming too involved with someone was a sure way to either get pregnant or get stuck in Pike County for the rest of your life—neither of which were part of her long-term plan.

In college and grad school, there were plenty of guys around, especially in her geology classes. She had just been too busy, too focused on school, perhaps a bit too guarded—and definitely not interested in any of the men there.

But her first thought—totally unbidden—when she found herself studying this guy was:

Wow, he's beautiful.

Chapter Six

It wasn't just the natural highlights in his long, wavy brown hair.

Or that he had cheek bones that looked like they were on loan from a sculpture.

Or the way his jawline seemed to suggest a smile.

Or that she felt drawn into the mystery of his brown eyes.

Or how his broad shoulders tapered gently toward his trim waistline.

It was the way it all came together.

He was a seriously good-looking guy. Best of all, he didn't seem to be aware of it. He was about Carrianne's age and dressed in the same unpretentious manner. T-shirt. Jeans. Hiking boots.

Though maybe his T-shirt hugged his deltoid muscles a little more snugly.

And maybe his jeans were a bit tighter in the seat.

He was grinning slightly, in a way that came off as confident but not cocky. He smelled like some intoxicating combination of sandalwood and fresh citrus.

Carrianne shook her head slightly, just to clear it. She couldn't remember the last time she'd had a reaction to a man like this.

Maybe never.

Which was, under the circumstances—just as she was trying to launch and lead the most important geological expedition of her entire life—totally inconvenient.

"Hi, we haven't met yet," she said, trying to recover her wits. "I'm Carrianne Kaucher."

"Hey. Ray Brooks."

She recognized the name from some of the paperwork she had been going through. He had a light Southern drawl, though Carrianne couldn't place it geographically—just that it didn't come from anywhere near Kentucky.

"Oh, you're our drone pilot, right? The guy from SkyKings?"

Anthony Sebastian had told her that they outsourced the operation of the drone to the company that made the equipment because it was so specialized they couldn't find anyone with the needed expertise; and training someone would take too long.

"Yeah, that's me."

"And who is this?" she asked, looking down at the dog with its still-wagging tail.

"I've been calling him Digger. I was going to ask if I could bring him along."

"Her," Carrianne said, pointing to the dog's underside, which was clearly female.

"Oh. Her." He laughed at himself. "That's even better. My mother is always telling me I need a woman in my life."

He smiled at his own self-deprecating joke. Carrianne let this beautiful man's implied declaration of singlehood pass without comment.

"And Digger is ... *your* dog?"

"Yes and no. I've been staying at an Airbnb about fifteen minutes east of here for the last week. The company wanted me to make a few tweaks on the drone, tinker with the software, then take some test flights. No one likes it when you fly a drone around an airport—it makes air traffic control nervous, and sometimes when they get nervous around here, they start shooting. It's an eighty-thousand-dollar drone, but it's not bulletproof.

"Anyhow, I was taking it on a test flight out near the dam earlier this week and there were some schoolkids nearby, having lunch or whatever. I wasn't really paying much attention to them. The next thing I knew, they were making a lot of noise, throwing rocks at something. I thought it was a snake or a rat or who knows. Then I saw this poor guy. Sorry, gal. I think maybe she had been begging for food, and they were trying to get her to go away. I told the school kids to knock it off, then I fed her some beef jerky I'd been saving for lunch. We've been best friends ever since. She's super friendly. C'mere girl."

Digger did as told, wagging her tail extra hard, as if to emphasize her companionability. She sat obediently at Ray's feet and looked up at him in blissful contentment as he rubbed behind the smaller of her two ear flaps.

"Believe it or not, this is what she looks like fattened up," Ray continued. "She's probably put on five pounds since I've had her. She's a lot less nervous now, too. I think she was just hungry. She's a total sweetheart. I was thinking she could be our expedition mascot. That's why I named her Digger."

"It wouldn't be the worst thing to have a guard dog," Dave Martin volunteered, inserting himself into the conversation. "Dogs' senses are way better than humans. Hearing. Smell. My squad had a dog at one point in Afghanistan. He literally sniffed out an IED for us, even though he wasn't a trained bomb dog. He just started barking at this spot in the ground. He probably saved at least four soldiers' lives."

Ray hopped back in. "If you're worried about food, I can just feed her from my rations. What do you say?"

He looked at her with this boyish *can-we-keep-her-can-we-keep-her?* ardency that Carrianne found impossible to resist.

"Yeah, why not," she said. "And don't worry about the food. We have enough. And I'm sure we'd have room for a bag or two of dog chow if you wanted to pack them."

She was half-expecting Ray to pump his fist, but he just fixed her with a smile that made Carrianne feel so shy she had to look to the side.

Since when did she react to *anyone* that way?

What the hell was going on?

The others were dispersing, moving on with packing, which was coming along apace. Ray stayed where he was.

"Hey, there's something I've been wanting to show you," he said, seemingly quite unaware he was having any effect on her whatsoever. "Do you have a second?"

"Uh, yeah, sure."

"It's on my laptop. Hang on," he said.

Digger fell in obediently at his side as he walked over to the wall of the hangar. He knelt and rubbed the dog's head as he rooted around in his backpack. Then he pulled out a laptop with a heavy case around it and returned to Carrianne.

"Where do you want to go?" he asked.

She was going to suggest the office. But just then, as if struck down by the gods, the power went out. Ray laughed.

"Uh, I guess we can go to my room," Carrianne said. Worried it sounded like a come-on, she added, "There's a generator back there."

"Sure," he said. "Lead the way."

Carrianne and Ray walked toward the back of the hangar. Digger, who was sniffing at something apparently fascinating on the concrete floor, did not join them.

When they reached her room, Carrianne gestured toward the desk. "You can set up there, if you like."

"You bet," Ray said.

Carrianne settled on the bed, because there was nowhere else to sit.

Ray pulled out the desk chair and got to work. He brought up what Carrianne immediately recognized as a 3D representation of data from a magnetometer, which measured the subtle changes in the Earth's magnetic field.

"You got this from the drone we'll have out with us in the field?" she asked.

"Yeah."

"It's good."

He thanked her then uncorked a question about data resolution. They wound up having an intricate, technical conversation about the speed of the drone versus the quality of the data it could take in. Basically, the slower the drone went, the better the quality.

They crunched the numbers and eventually figured out that if the drone flew along at two-meters-per-second—a little faster than a brisk walking pace—it could give them the data they needed. That meant it would take the drone about nine hours to complete its surveying each day.

That was fine with Ray, who said a fully gassed drone could stay aloft for eleven hours, if he used it judiciously.

He then showed her how he had gotten magnetic data to overlay with camera footage while the drone was in flight, which made it easier to quickly pinpoint exactly where they were getting higher or lower readings.

"Wow, cool," Carrianne said. "And you'd be able to do this in real time?"

"As long as I can plug in my laptop. This mode sucks down the battery super fast."

"That's no problem. We'll have a generator in the field," she said, still somewhat mesmerized by the footage. It was practically movie quality, and it was so smooth and steady she had a hard time believing it was shot from a device that was flying through midair.

"You're ... you're really something, flying that thing," she said.

Ray blushed a little. "Some people think you fly a drone like it's a small airplane, and that's not it at all. Drone piloting is all about the gentle touch. You have to quiet your mind, take in all the factors, and respond calmly. It's about feel as much as anything."

He was looking at her, not the computer screen, while he spoke. With where she was sitting, their faces were quite close. She caught a clean, wholesome scent coming from him that was like boy mixed with fresh laundry.

For a long, delicious moment, their eyes locked and neither spoke. Carrianne felt something in her stomach that was somewhere between thrilling and *uh oh*.

"Anyway, yeah," Ray said, a bit louder than was necessary, standing up for no reason. "So ... Glad we got everything settled. You all good?"

"Yes. Perfect," Carrianne said, hastily standing up herself.

"Good, good," Ray said. "Anyway, I should ... I have to ... I'm sure Digger is getting nervous without me."

"Sure," she said. "Thanks again for showing me the footage."

"Anytime. I like ... I liked showing it to you."

He smiled nervously, collected his laptop, and excused himself.

Once he was gone, Carrianne needed a few moments to compose herself.

Her heart seemed to be beating a little faster than necessary.

After a few minutes, she went back out into the hangar to find the power was still out. She retrieved her laptop from the office and brought it back to her bedroom, where she made a game attempt at concentrating on a packing list she needed to review.

Really, she did.

Except she soon had to acknowledge that the only thing on her mind was Ray.

He wasn't really *that* good-looking, was he? She must have been imagining it.

Maybe because of the heat.

She decided if she just found a picture of him online looking ordinary—and not quite so gorgeous—she would be able to return to concentrating on more important tasks.

Surely, he had to be on social media somewhere. She could

search for him quickly, find something, satisfy her curiosity, and be done with it.

She googled "Ray Brooks," and it turned out there was an English actor by that name. He was older by many decades—definitely not her Ray Brooks.

Not that he was *her* Ray Brooks. She immediately corrected herself.

She tried googling "Ray Brooks United States." But that didn't help much, either. There were a lot of Ray Brookses. An electrician in Arkansas. A plumber in Oregon. A podiatrist in Illinois.

Finally, she googled "Ray Brooks drone pilot."

This immediately brought up the Ray Brooks she was looking for. He had an Instagram page.

She immediately found herself frowning.

The profile name was @Playah69.

Thinking she had to be mistaken—that wasn't *really* his name, was it?—she went to her phone, opened her little-used Instagram app, and searched for Playah69.

Sure enough, there was a picture of Ray. He was younger. His hair was shorter. But it was definitely him.

His profile read, "I like drones and the ladies, but not in that order."

When she scrolled down, she was aghast.

His page was chock-full of memes from across the internet. And what they established more than anything was that Ray Brooks, a.k.a. Playah69, was a certified pig.

The first showed a well-endowed woman in a crop top that barely covered her breasts. "Hey, beautiful," it said. "My doctor says I'm lacking Vitamin U."

Then, it was a bikini-clad woman with an overabundance of lip filler and the text: "Are you religious? Because I think you're the answer to all my prayers."

She kept scrolling, out of horror as much as anything. She finally stopped when she got to one particular comment: "3.8 billion women on the planet ... you'd think it'd be cleaner by now."

The memes typically had a handful of likes and were accompanied by equally stupid comments, which only served to confirm that Ray's friends were every bit as idiotic as he was.

Carrianne scrolled down a little more to see if there was anything even remotely redeeming, but it was more of the same stupidity.

He seemed so nice in person. But, obviously, that was just a façade. He was what Paw would have called an Eddie Haskell—a guy who pretends to be nice around your parents but is really a hellraiser.

And, yes, a player.

Which was exactly what Carrianne looked to avoid.

She went back to her google search page just to close the window. Then she saw that, one down from Instagram, was Ray's Facebook page.

Unable to help herself, she clicked.

The profile picture was at least unoffensive—just a younger version of Ray, albeit with his arm around an attractive brunette.

Then she looked down to the "Intro" part, where the last line was, "In a relationship with Loretta Hamel."

So much for him claiming to be single.

Shaking her head, she clicked off the page and got back to work.

Chapter Seven

C arrianne watched with pride that afternoon as the team bustled about and made final preparations.

Most of the major gear and supplies had already been loaded. This was primarily detail work—tightening that one last screw, strapping in that extra backup battery, hardening everything for a desert that was one of the planet's least hospitable environments.

It was daunting. But the way everyone went about their business filled Carrianne with confidence. This wasn't a group of hesitant grad students, fumbling around, casting sideways glances, forever unsure of what to do next.

These were seasoned professionals. They knew exactly how they wanted things, because they had done it before.

Carrianne kept checking in with the various working groups on the team, making sure they had everything they needed.

All they did was reassure her.

She heard "We got this" more than once from the younger members of the team.

From Jerry, it was even simpler: "Relax."

The weather remained blistering. Once it passed a hundred,

Carrianne stopped checking the weather app on her phone. She didn't want to know. She just made sure to keep reapplying sunscreen.

At one point, she was walking past Javier as he was hosing dust and grit off the diamond drill rig—or, as he called it, "giving Bertha a bath." The water from the hose formed a few puddles on the baking concrete, and Carrianne swore she could see them evaporating in real time.

Still, no one complained—about the heat or the power, which kept blinking in and out. Nor did anyone seem to need any of the handholding Carrianne went around offering. Blue Diamond had hired the best.

As the sun lowered and worked its way toward setting, they gathered for a meal. There wouldn't be any fresh food once they got out in the field. Without the luxury of refrigeration, their food choices would be some combination of dried, preserved, canned, or vacuum-sealed in foil packets. They would all be getting their fill of preservatives.

So, for their final dinner before they entered the desert, they prepared fish with mango salsa—who knew Egypt was one of the world's leading mango producers?—along with a massive salad and baked sweet potatoes, which filled the kitchen with their honeyed aroma.

For dessert, it was ice cream topped with fresh peaches, another readily available Egyptian crop.

With everyone's bellies full and spirits high, Carrianne brought them to order. It was time for their final pre-launch meeting.

She started by going around the room, introducing everyone, and making sure their roles were understood.

The introductions began with the geophysicists—Jerry and his assistant Kimberly.

Next was Ciarra Colyer, the ESG liaison. A natural extrovert, she had already engaged in at least one conversation with everyone in the room.

Ciarra talked briefly about a visit she had made to a museum in Aswan and how it was important to respect the culture and history of their host country, whose riches had been repeatedly plundered by foreigners. She reminded them they had to be careful not to add to that terrible legacy.

They were here to help build a new and better Egypt, she told them, not tear it down.

Once she had finished, Carrianne moved on to the soldiers. Dave, Josh, Joseph, and Keith. Each nodded solemnly as their name was called.

Then it was Ray Brooks. He introduced Digger, who looked freshly bathed and ready to join the expedition.

Ahmed Hassan—the only one of the new hires to make it to the meal—welcomed everyone to "my beautiful country" and told them about his history in the Western Desert.

Last to be introduced were Javier, Jamil, and Mirza, the diamond drill guys, who were sitting together in the corner.

All told, it was thirteen people at the meeting. Carrianne also announced the four others who would be joining them in the morning: Ihsan Fayek, the head cook, and Bassel Fayek, his nephew; and Tariq El-Hashem and Hani Shahab, the two laborers.

It brought their party total to seventeen.

"Alright. So, some of you know parts of this and some of you know all of this," Carrianne said. "But since we've got folks coming in from all over and with varying levels of knowledge, I just want to get us all on the same page, since that's my job. Any questions before I dive in?"

Keith sheepishly raised a hand. "Can I ask a really dumb one?"

"There are no dumb questions."

"Okay, I realize I'm the not-geologist here, so it doesn't particularly matter how much of this I understand. But I always like to learn a little bit about what I'm guarding. And, besides, I'm curious. What are we going out into the desert to look for?"

Carrianne smiled. "Anything. Everything. Whatever is out there that Blue Diamond can determine is economically viable to exploit. Gold is the most obvious answer. Just because no one has found it in the Western Desert doesn't mean it's not there. But there might be silver, copper, lithium, or even far less sexy stuff. And don't discount good old phosphorous. People always need more fertilizer, and Egypt contains roughly four percent of the world's phosphate deposits. That's actually the exciting part of this. We don't know what we're looking for."

"I hear you," Keith said. "But one more dumb question for those of us who didn't go to school for this: Whatever we're looking for, how are we going to find it?"

"That's *definitely* not a dumb question. So, let me give you a super quick crash course in geology. Earth is a rocky planet with a lot of different metals mixed up in it. For example, aluminum makes up about eight percent of the Earth's crust. Iron is five percent. Magnesium is two percent. Titanium is half a percent—and on, and on, and on, until you get down to rare earths, some of which are actually not that rare. But others are so rare it's difficult to even express how unusual their occurrence is in numbers that are meaningful to the human brain.

"But let's talk about gold for a second. On average, gold is found at 0.004 parts per million. That's one of the reasons it's so valuable, because that's basically nothing. You could process a million pounds of rock and not even get one-tenth of an ounce of gold. That would be a huge waste of money. So why do we even bother? Why go looking for something that's not really even there?"

She threw in a brief pause before answering her own question. "Because the beautiful, wonderful, amazing thing about Earth is that all those metals I've just mentioned are not evenly distributed. They weren't perfectly mixed at the start, and then we've had geological processes that have been grinding, mashing, and throwing them all over the place for 4.5 billion years. It's made our planet an interesting place that's full of surprises. So, with any element, you'll get areas where there's nothing and areas where there's quite a bit. A geologist might get excited about a sample that's four parts per million gold, and that still doesn't sound like much. Except it means the gold is already a thousand times more prevalent than average, and that suggests to us that if we keep looking in that area, we might find gold deposits that are truly significant and worth going after.

"But here's what it all comes back to: in geology, as in life, nothing is ever even. You'll hear me and other geologists talk about 'anomalies' a lot. That's just a fancy word that means that there's something unusual or different going on. Even at the surface, there are subtle variations in magnetism, gravity, and conductivity that give us hints as to what might be happening underneath. And then we take samples—at the surface or, thanks to the diamond drill, at greater depths—that tell us more. It's all about finding one of those wonderful surprises Earth has hidden away. Does that make sense?"

"Yeah, thanks. I think even the Marines could follow you," Keith said.

"Huh?" said Joseph, who had been looking at something on his phone.

"You stand corrected," Dave said.

Everyone laughed.

Carrianne continued. "Now that we've got that settled, I'm going to talk about our approach to exploration, because it's a little different from what some of us—me included—may be used to. Anthony Sebastian calls it Lightning Geology. Normally, we'd do an aerial survey first, then move on to soil sampling, then get serious with the diamond drill. With Lightning Geology, we do it all at once. What that means is we're all going to have to talk to each other a lot. What are you getting? What are you seeing? Is there something we should be looking at more closely? We'll plan on having a meeting each night, but if something really promising pops up during the day, don't wait to tell me. We're all going to have to be agile and flexible, responding to each other. And, above all else, no one is allowed to be shy. I know that'll be a real problem for you, Jerry." She threw him a wink.

"Yeah, I'm a real shrinking violet," he responded.

Carrianne smiled then started passing out eleven-by-seventeen sheets of paper on which there was a relief map with grid lines overlaying it.

"I'm usually a screen person, so it goes against my instincts to print out anything," Carrianne said. "But we don't have a screen in here that's large enough for everyone to see and, besides, I know some people just like to be able to touch and feel stuff IRL."

"She's mostly doing this for the dinosaur in the room," Jerry interjected.

"True, but the dinosaurs at least had one thing going for them— they never had to worry about the power going out in the middle of their meeting," Carrianne said.

"Wait. I need to figure out how to plug this in," Javier said, holding up his printout.

More laughter.

When things settled down, Carrianne continued. "This is the map of our license area. It's just slightly north of here but mostly due west. As you can see, it's a big chunk of Earth—a little less than 200 square kilometers. For those of you who are Yankees, that means you could fit three Manhattans inside and still have room to spare. To make things a little more manageable and bite size, I've divided this into a grid with sixteen equal-sized quadrants, which I've named quadrants one, two, three, and so on. Each quadrant is twelve kilometers square, which means it's a little less than 3.5 kilometers on each side. Even with the rough terrain, you should be able to walk across the entire quadrant in about an hour if you hustle. Make sense?"

Around the room, heads bobbed.

"The plan is to spend two days in each quadrant. We'll set up camp in roughly the middle of the quadrant. Dave Martin and I have worked together to find plots that are flat enough and large enough for all the tents while still being suitable from a security standpoint."

"Call me old-fashioned, but I like the high ground," Dave said. "Better visibility, better field of fire. Just makes it that much less likely that any hostiles we might trip across will be bold enough to try anything."

"Setting up in the middle makes exploration easier for everyone, and it's a safety feature," Carrianne explained. "No part of the quadrant should be more than about 1.75 kilometers away. That's just a hair over a mile. It's important to stay close in the desert. At that distance, you should be able to see camp at all times. I know it's not sandstorm season yet, but I don't want anyone to have to wander too far."

Dave piped up. "It may not be sandstorm season, but it's always bandit season."

"Yes, of course," Carrianne said, remembering what Dave had said about travel advisories for the Western Desert. She wondered if she should mention something about them.

She quickly talked herself out of it. Everyone here already knew the risks. There was no reason to scare them further. The soldiers would keep them safe.

Or at least that was her quick rationalization.

The closer truth was that she knew she couldn't afford to lose anyone. If even one team member backed out at this point, it would lead to a delay while they replaced the person. And she didn't want to be the principal geologist whose first exploratory foray was held up by a case of last-second nerves.

"Anyhow, after two days in each quadrant, we'll pick up and move to the next quadrant," she said. "I hope you're all early risers, because we'll be up before first light so we can move in the early morning, when it's cooler. The hope is to get set up in the new quadrant before the heat gets too unbearable. If we're able to explore a little bit after we get there, great. If not, that's okay, too. We'll still have the next two full days to look around.

"Two days of exploration and one day of movement for each quadrant gets us to forty-eight days. Tack on a day to get out there and a day to get back, and you're looking at fifty days in the field. At that point, we'll all need a break. We'll come back here, take a little time off, regroup, and decide what merits further exploration. Make sense?"

More bobbing.

"Okay, now as I was saying earlier, we have a three-pronged approach—three separate units," she said, holding up three fingers. "I need to stress that each unit is equally important, so please don't ever think I'm playing favorites. Each unit is going to be providing vital data on different levels, in different ways, with varying limitations and levels of detail."

"Our most expansive view will come from Ray, who will be piloting the drone with the camera and scanning equipment mounted aboard. He'll be flying the entirety of each quadrant in lines that are 100 meters apart. This is going to form the basis of a detailed map we'll eventually be creating that will show us the aforementioned magnetism, gravity, and conductivity. But I'm also going to be analyzing those results in real time as best I can. So, if something is really popping, I'll let the other units know. Ray is going to be operating from camp every day, because his equipment needs power. So, yes, you can hate him a little bit because he'll have an air conditioning unit. But he's also going to have some pretty expensive equipment in mid-air at all times, so don't get too jealous of him because he literally can't let his focus drop for a second."

"Oh, you can still hate me if you want," Ray joked, which earned him a laugh from the group.

"Our boots on the ground are Jerry and Kimberly. They're going to be analyzing soil and rock samples on the surface. They've got the handheld XRF spectrometers that will be giving them results as they go. They'll be on foot a lot of the time. So, if you're giving an award for most steps, they'll get the prize."

"Don't worry," Kimberly said, holding up a foot. "These boots are made for walking."

"That brings us to the diamond drill guys—Javier, Jamil, and Mirza. They will be closer to the earth than any of us because they'll be burrowing down into the middle of it. They'll be digging out core samples that Ahmed will be driving back to Aswan every few days so they can be flown up to the lab in Alexandria. The diamond drill rig is our heaviest piece of equipment. We'll have the excavator to clear out some obstructions for it, but it still won't be able to reach every part of the quadrant. So, they're the most limited in some ways. At the same time, if anyone is *literally* going to strike gold, it would be them."

"Yeah, baby!" Javier hooted.

"Okay, I know we've just covered a lot, but that's the overview," Carrianne said. "Any questions—dumb or otherwise?"

This time, no one spoke.

"Great," she said. "Good meeting, everyone. We're starting early tomorrow, so you best be hitting the hay. I'm excited for tomorrow, and I hope you are, too. We are being given the rare opportunity to adventure into the unknown. What we find could change the course of a lot of people's lives—our own, but also the hundreds of people who will have stable, good-paying jobs when it comes time to extract the resources. I have every confidence we've assembled the best team possible. Now, let's go out there and make ourselves proud of the work we do."

Javier led a round of applause, which Carrianne joined in. It was a rousing way to end things, and the group soon started breaking up—except for Ray, who seemed to be hanging around like he wanted a private audience with the principal geologist.

Carrianne pretended to ignore him as she gathered her things and prepared to depart. But when she went to leave the kitchen, Ray was half-blocking her path.

"Hey, sorry to bother you," he said. "I just wanted to say I thought you handled that meeting really great. I can see why Blue

Diamond picked you for this job. You may be younger than everyone, but you're also smarter."

"That's nice of you, thank you."

Not bad for one of the 3.8 billion who doesn't know how to clean up, she thought.

"I'm really looking forward to working with you," he added, laying on the Eddie Haskell extra thick.

"Thank you," she said. "Have a nice night."

And then she squeezed past him and disappeared into her room.

Playah69 was going to have to look elsewhere for his Vitamin U.

Chapter Eight

The sun had yet to crest the eastern horizon when it came time to roll out the next morning.

There had been little conversation. Carrianne felt like she had said her piece the night before, and no one else had set their alarms at such a gasp-inducing hour so they could stand around gabbing.

Throughout the journey—and for the next seven weeks—they would communicate primarily via walkie-talkies they had been instructed to keep clipped to their belts at all times. Once they reached their license area, they would be far from cell reception. The one satellite phone they had would be for communicating with the home base, not for intergroup communications.

As such, Carrianne only had to click one button and talk into a mouthpiece to address the entire team.

"Okay, let's head out," she said. "Stay close, y'all. I don't want anyone wandering off."

The convoy consisted of a half-dozen vehicles, led by the diamond drill rig, because it was the slowest and heaviest. While its twin tracks would prevent it from getting mired down in the soft sands of the desert, they did so at the price of speed.

Even with an experienced driver like Javier at the wheel, and with Jamil urging him on from the passenger seat, the rig topped out at forty miles an hour on pavement. It was lucky to do half that while driving cross-country.

The next in line—and the next most cumbersome combination—was the super duty pickup truck that hauled the excavator, which was chained down to a gooseneck trailer. Mirza was driving the truck, and he kept his speed down because he knew he'd risk jackknifing if he did anything too crazy.

All the remaining vehicles were Ford Broncos that had been outfitted for desert travel.

Dave, Joshua, Joseph, and Keith rode in one, trailed by a flatbed that carried their guns, the portable watch tower they would set up once they reached camp, and other equipment.

Ihsan and Bassel, the meal crew, were in the front seat of the next Bronco. Tariq and Hani, the laborers, sat in back. They were hauling a 1,600-gallon fuel tanker that more than likely contained enough gas to sustain the trucks and generators for fifty days. Though they could always have Ahmed refill it during one of his trips to Aswan if they ran low.

The Bronco hauling the 1,600-gallon water tanker came next. Its passengers included Jerry, Kimberly, Ciarra, and Ray, who made noises about there being enough room for Carrianne. He said Digger —who had enthusiastically bounded into the SUV and was now curled up in the third-row seat well—would be lonely without her.

But, no, Carrianne had insisted she wanted to be at the rear of the convoy, in a Bronco being driven by Ahmed. All of its rear seats had been removed to make room for the long core sample boxes that Ahmed would be regularly transporting back to Aswan.

It also had a flatbed trailer with more equipment, including the tents, the tent platforms, and several hard-sided suitcases that contained the drone and its attachments. Carrianne had seen Ray tugging on the straps securing the cases at least four times, making sure they were snug.

Ahmed made it clear he was pleased to have Carrianne in his Bronco. "I am chauffeuring the Princess!" was how he put it.

Everyone's personal gear had been tossed in the back of Broncos, with good-natured scorn heaped on Ciarra and Dave, who had the largest bags and were therefore deemed to have been the most egregious packhorses. Carrianne took quiet pride in having packed the lightest.

Most of the food and the remaining camp gear were strapped to the Broncos' roof racks.

For the first twenty or so miles of the trip, they traveled along the paved road that connected Aswan to Luxor, the next major city to the north. Traffic was sparse. Every few minutes, they'd pass a car coming the other way or get passed from behind. But that was it.

They made good time, covering the distance in a little more than a half-an-hour.

Then, finally, it came time to leave civilization.

Carrianne was a geocaching nerd who was well-accustomed to navigating via longitude and latitude, which was how their license area was defined. She had done her best to plot the best route to Quadrant 1, using a combination of topographic maps and satellite imagery to avoid steep grades, cliffs, rocky outcroppings, deep gullies, washouts, and other impassable obstacles.

As careful as she tried to be, she knew there were times when she was just guessing. They wouldn't know for sure until they got there. She just hoped they wouldn't have to backtrack too much.

Carrianne kept an eye on her GPS as Ahmed motored along the roadway. When they reached a certain point, she got on the walkie-talkie and said, "Okay. This is where we get off."

There was nothing more to it than that. They simply turned off the pavement.

The ground was a mix of rocky soil and sand. It was mostly devoid of vegetation, except for a few inconsequential clumps of dried grass that had managed to establish roots—nothing that would challenge the progress of the Broncos, much less the larger vehicles.

They spread out into a V-shape. They were still fairly close to each other, as per Carrianne's final instructions, but this way no one would have to eat anyone's dust. They began bouncing along through the desert, headed due west.

It was around this time that the long orange-yellow rays of the sun began reaching out from behind them and caressing the tops of the rock outcroppings beyond. The rocks themselves appeared to be glowing.

"Welcome to the new day, Princess," Ahmed said.

"And what a day it promises to be," she replied.

As beautiful as it was, Carrianne still felt a stirring of anxiety. The sun—the source of light, life, and energy on the planet—would also be one of their chief antagonists over the next fifty days.

The Western Desert was a notorious furnace, and they were in the midst of a hot spell that showed no signs of abating. At this point in September—at the tail end of another long, dry summer—all the moisture had been baked out of the world. And nothing could stop the daily climb of temperatures to brutality.

Carrianne had been advised that once it reached 110 degrees Fahrenheit, Blue Diamond's policy was to cease all exploration activities. This was important for the humans, who could suffer dehydration, heat stroke, and other perils. But it was also critical for the trucks, which became more susceptible to broken drive belts, tire blowouts, and engine failure as the mercury soared.

Any such calamity could bring the expedition to a sudden halt.

That meant today's journey out to Quadrant 1 would be a race against time.

Now that they had left the pavement, it was sixty miles as the crow flies to the license area. But the terrain wouldn't permit them to travel in a straight line. By Carrianne's calculations, the various twists and turns made their route more like eighty miles.

Her hope was that they could average at least ten miles an hour. Maybe a little better. Since it was now a little after six o'clock, that should put them at the Quadrant 1 campsite by two o'clock at the latest.

The heat would be brutal by then but, she hoped, still under the 110-degree threshold. Her plan was for them to hastily erect some shelter and hide in the shade until later in the day, when it cooled enough for them to finish setting up camp.

Not reaching the campsite was unacceptable in her mind for at least two reasons. One, it would mean they wouldn't be spending a full two days exploring Quadrant 1, which felt like starting off the expedition with a loss.

Two, she and Dave had put a lot of care into picking out sites that he felt good about from a security standpoint. Hunkering down at some random spot in the desert just didn't feel safe.

Whether they would be able to make it in time was really up to the weather, which she had no control over, and Javier's abilities behind the wheel of the diamond drill rig. It was their least maneuverable vehicle, meaning he would essentially be setting their pace.

She eyed Ahmed's speedometer. The needle was above ten but not quite to fifteen.

That was fine. Good enough.

After a surprisingly short amount of time, they could no longer see the roadway they had left, nor could they make out any other human-made structures.

There was nothing but desert in every direction.

As if he was on the same wavelength, Ahmed cleared his throat and said, "My grandmother always liked to tell me the desert has no memory."

"I've heard that before," Carrianne said. "I'm not even sure what it even means."

"Because right now we are leaving tracks, putting our mark on the land, but it will not last. Nothing we do out here lasts. The wind blows. The sands shift and cover over everything. Before long, there will be no evidence we were ever here.

"Or look at the pyramids. For thousands of years, my people built the mightiest structures the world had ever seen. Some have been found, yes; but there are others out there that have been covered over and may never resurface. They have been swallowed whole by the desert with no memory. It is so powerful that even history itself can be wiped away."

He reached into his knapsack on the floor behind him. Without taking his eyes off the path ahead, he rooted around for a moment and pulled out a bag of nuts and dried fruits.

"Are you hungry, Princess?" he asked. "My wife packed it for me this morning. She is always saying, 'Ahmed, you forget to eat. You must keep up your strength!' She is good to me. This is why I must work hard for her and provide for her. When you find a woman like I have, you hold onto her."

Carrianne suddenly realized the energy bar she had jammed down when she first awoke was no longer tiding her over. So, when he offered her the bag, she accepted it and scooped out a handful of the mixture.

She passed Ahmed the bag, and they chewed in silence for a while. The dried dates practically exploded with flavor in Carrianne's mouth. They were the best she had ever tasted.

The Bronco plowed ahead, unchallenged by the landscape so far. The speedometer needle had crept up a little, touching fifteen a few times. She wished they were taking advantage of the wide-open conditions to cover more ground while they could.

Then, she reminded herself to be patient. Go too fast, hit an obstruction, or plow into a hole, and the broken axel would throw a major wrench into her carefully constructed itinerary.

There weren't exactly any tow trucks she could call.

After an hour or so, they'd reached the first feature Carrianne had worried about: a long mesa that stretched for more than a mile through the heart of their route. As they approached it, she saw it was every bit as insurmountable as it had appeared to be on the topo maps, with sides that were very nearly sheer walls.

Carrianne had routed them around the south side because the north side contained what appeared to be a dried riverbed that she was less certain about.

It turned out to be the correct call. There was a bit more loose rock than Carrianne had perhaps realized, which slowed their speed to the single digits for a little while. But soon enough, they had navigated around the mesa and were back onto an open, flat plane.

As their journey reached its third hour, the sense of remoteness really began to overwhelm Carrianne. She had grown up in a part of Kentucky that was considered rural, and she had worked in parts of the American West that felt pretty empty.

But it didn't compare to this—to being able to drive, and drive, and drive, and still know there was nothing, *nothing*, in any direction for many more miles yet to come.

"We're really on our own out here, aren't we?" she said.

"In many ways, yes," Ahmed said. "You know the first thing we were taught in law school about the desert?"

"No, what?"

"In the desert, there is no law."

He let that sit for a moment then added, "Or maybe it's just that everyone makes their own. Some people choose to abide by the social contract. Other people ..."

His voice trailed off as he squinted into the distance. Then, he resumed. "There are no rules to govern our behavior out here, just our own consciences and individual moralities. To me, this is where you learn about the true nature of humanity."

"And? What do you think? Is it good? Bad?"

"I think it's ... unpredictable. And that, in some ways, is the worst of all. If it was all good or all bad, we could plan accordingly. But the truth is, you just never know."

Carrianne laughed. "No, I suppose not."

"There was a time, maybe ten years ago, when I broke down in the desert. I was young and driving a car I had bought from a friend that turned out to be very unreliable."

"The car or the friend?"

"Both," Ahmed said, and now he was the one laughing. "I was going home to visit my family in Dakhla when my radiator sprang a leak. The temperature gauge immediately went to red, and I had to pull off to the side of the road before I destroyed the engine. It is an eight-hour trip, and I was only about halfway there, so this was the middle of the desert. Much more remote than we are now. There had been no one coming in either direction, and it was thirty or forty miles to the next town—too far to think about walking. I barely had any water. Like I said, I was young.

"I was trying to figure out what to do when a group of Bedouins came up on me. You know the Bedouins, yes?"

"They're nomads, right?"

"Yes, exactly. They came up on me in this old camper that had bedsheets in the windows and chickens strapped to the top. The camper was so packed with people that some were hanging off the sides because they didn't all fit. There were at least fifteen of them and only one of me. Do you understand what I'm saying?"

"You were outnumbered."

"Yes, but not just outnumbered, Princess. I was also unarmed and undefended. I had not considered that I would have to confront anyone. I was just going home to see my family. The Bedouins, they could have done anything to me—robbed me, killed me, whatever they wished. There would have been no witnesses. There are stories of Bedouins murdering travelers just so they can drink their blood."

"Do you believe that?"

"No more than I believe The Curse of Dust. People like to make up stories, especially about people who are not like them. But I was still scared as the Bedouins approached. I was at their mercy. And you know what they did?"

The question was rhetorical, so Carrianne just waited for Ahmed to resume.

"They pulled out some heavy tape and patched the hole in my radiator. Then they gave me water and coolant and helped me restart my engine and get back on my way. When I offered to pay them—not that I had much—they refused. They said it was almsgiving and wished me well by the grace of Allah."

He let that sit for a moment then said, "Not everyone out here is a threat."

Just then, the walkie-talkie squelched out a burst of static followed by a voice.

"Carrianne, it's Dave. You hearing me?"

"Loud and clear."

"Look to your left. Do you see that?"

Carrianne peered beyond Ahmed out the driver's side window. There was a plume of dust rising in the distance.

"Yeah, what is that?"

"Well, it's not a sandstorm, so the better question is 'who is that?' Whoever it is, they've been following us for a while. It's hard to get a good look while we're moving. If it's okay with you, I'd like the caravan to stop for a second or two so I can check it out."

Carrianne willed herself to think clearly. She didn't want them to get off schedule when the roughest terrain was still to come. Even a small delay might cost them the chance to reach their destination.

At the same time, it hardly seemed wise to ignore a request from her chief of security.

"Okay," she said. "We're about to reach the top of that mound up ahead. Let's stop there and have a look."

"Roger that."

"Everyone else hear that?" Carrianne said. "We're stopping in a moment or two."

The walkie-talkie was soon filled with the sounds of the other team members voicing their affirmatives.

Carrianne put the device down, turned to Ahmed, and asked, "What do you think?"

"Well, it's like I was saying, not everyone out here is a threat," he repeated. "But some people are."

Chapter Nine

As soon as the caravan came to a halt, Dave hopped out of his Bronco.

With surprising grace for a man of his size, he vaulted himself onto the vehicle's hood then clambered up to its roof.

He brought a pair of binoculars to his face and peered at the dust plume in the distance, very much in ex-Navy Seal mode.

Carrianne had walked over to the side of his Bronco. It was only nine-thirty, so the air was still cool. This was the paradox of desert sand. It did a very poor job holding and transferring warmth, so mornings could be quite pleasant, even chilly.

But it also heated very quickly, and Carrianne could already feel the sun beating on her face. The great desert bakeoff was underway.

She looked up at Dave and asked, "Well? What are you seeing?"

"Three bogeys. They're pickup trucks—old, beater, piece-of-crap pickup trucks. Damnit."

"What?"

"Well, I was hoping against hope that maybe it was the government or an oil company or I don't know what. But they're definitely bandits."

"How do you know?"

"Because those trucks look like they're held together with spit and paperclips. They probably double in value every time you fill the gas tanks. That's strike one. Strike two, we're a long way from the nearest road or anything else worth visiting. No one comes out here for a nice drive through the desert countryside. Strike three, I picked them up about a half-hour ago, and they've been paralleling us ever since."

"But how did they find us? It's not like I registered our trip plans with the local authorities. This part of the desert is, what, 100,000 square miles? Two hundred thousand? I don't even know. It's huge. How did they get onto us so fast?"

"Oh, who knows?" Dave said. "There's not exactly anywhere to hide out here. If you think they're kicking up a lot of dust, you should see what we're doing. It might as well be a big, bright, shining beacon saying, 'Here we are! Come and get us!'"

"And you're sure they're bandits?"

"Come up and have a look for yourself," Dave said, holding out the binoculars to her.

Carrianne studied the Bronco for a moment. She had watched Dave scale it like it was no more challenging than a child's jungle gym. She wasn't sure she could replicate his agility, and she was quite certain she didn't have his strength.

But Ray, Jerry, and some of the others had also gotten out of their trucks, and she didn't want to look inept in front of her team.

The Broncos came equipped with front grill guards, so she was able to use one to hoist herself onto the hood. From there, she accepted Dave's outstretched hand and let him pull her up next to him.

Without a word, he handed her the binoculars.

They were high-end Zeiss lenses, surprisingly heavy for their size. She raised them to her eyes. With the autofocus feature, the trucks immediately snapped into view. She was shocked by the level of magnification and the sharpness of the image.

She could clearly make out the drivers.

Just a little bit.

But enough to see that their faces were wrapped in bandanas.

She sucked in a quick breath. The rational part of Carrianne's brain told her it was just because of the dust. Beater pickup trucks didn't come with the kind of sophisticated cabin filtration systems that kept the air inside the Broncos so pristine. In the absence of that, a face covering was just a necessary and prudent piece of PPE.

But it sure made them look like bandits.

"Oh sugar," she said, trying to quell the panic she felt rising inside.

"Yeah, I might have used a stronger word than that."

"That's because you've never met my Meemaw."

Dave chuckled dryly. Carrianne kept studying the men, switching from one, to the next, to the next.

It may have been her imagination, but she felt like the one in the lead was slowing down. She kept careful watch on him and, yes, he was definitely decelerating. He appeared to be gesturing to the other drivers to do the same.

"I think they're stopping," Carrianne said.

"Because they're realizing we've stopped, and they don't know where to go next."

Carrianne kept the binoculars against her face to the point where she realized she was pressing so hard it was making her eye sockets hurt. As she eased off the pressure, the lead pickup truck came to a halt, as did the two others.

The lead driver got out.

So did the other two.

They congregated for a moment. There was a brief but animated conversation. Then one of them reached back into his truck for something.

The next thing Carrianne knew, there was a flash of light where the man's face had been—a glinting of glass reflecting the rapidly rising sun.

The man was looking back at her through his own binoculars.

She almost dropped the Zeiss lenses.

"He's ... he's looking at me," she said, feeling this sense of ... what was it, exactly?

Fear, for sure.

No.

More than that.

Vulnerability.

Violation, even.

She suddenly knew what it was like to be hunted. There was now no doubt in her mind these men were bandits, and they were stalking the Blue Diamond caravan.

"Let me see," Dave said.

She handed him the binoculars.

"Hey, buddy," he said as he looked through the lenses. "You wanna play? Is that it? You really think you want a piece of this?"

Maybe the bravado was intended to be reassuring, but Carrianne did not feel much comfort.

"Alright. What now?" she asked. "Do we turn back or—"

"No, no, nothing like that," Dave said, lowering the binoculars so he could look at her. "This is what we're trained for. It's why you hired ETS and why we've got all that gear back there. Three hajis in pickup trucks don't stand a chance against the SAWs. If they make even the slightest move toward us, we'll shred them. It's a nuisance, something to keep an eye on, nothing more."

"If you say so."

They clambered down from the roof of the Bronco. When they were back on the gritty ground, he put on a cocksure grin.

"Come on. This is part of the experience," he said. "When you go to the amusement park, you have to try out all the rides."

As they resumed their journey, so did their shadow—that ominous, menacing, distant dust plume.

It remained unnerving. But Carrianne was at a loss to do much about it.

As Ahmed had explained, that was the law of the desert: there was no law.

Just shy of ten-thirty, they had reached their first stretch of hamada landscape. This was a common feature in the Western Desert—and, really, across the Sahara.

In some ways, it was the opposite of sand dunes, because most of the sand—and even the pebbles and tinier rocks—had been scoured away by strong winds.

What that left behind was a flat, barren-looking plain consisting of sharp, bare rocks jutting up from the earth without much cushioning from smaller particles.

It wasn't completely unpassable—just perilous. Some rocks were too large or too pointy to safely drive over, so they would have to be driven around.

There were two main dangers here. The first was that one of the trailers—Carrianne particularly worried about the fuel tanker—would get stuck or, worse, overturn on a particularly jagged bit of terrain. She could easily imagine all 1,600 gallons of their precious gas leaking out onto the rocks below.

The other threat was punctured tires. The Broncos had been outfitted with sturdy off-road tires that were, at least in theory, puncture resistant.

But they weren't impenetrable. And Blue Diamond didn't use run flats because they came with their own set of issues that, in the estimation of the people who did the purchasing, weren't worth the tradeoffs. So, if someone blew a tire, the entire caravan would just have to stop while it was replaced with a spare.

That would be precious time lost.

Even without a flat tire, though, it would be slow going. Carrianne knew from her satellite imagery that this particular band of hamada was about five miles wide, stretching across their path like a scythe. There was no getting around it—the blade was too long. They just had to get through it.

As soon as they entered the field, progress felt like it ground down to almost nothing. She didn't even bother looking at the speedometer. It would have been too disheartening. They were seldom traveling above five miles an hour as Ahmed carefully picked a path over the treacherous surface.

Carrianne didn't bother saying anything to him. She could tell it required all of his concentration just to get through the next ten meters, then the ten meters after that.

The soil—what little of it there was—had a red tinge. This, the geologist in Carrianne knew well, was from the iron oxides.

But between that and the bleakness of the topography, it made her feel like they were traveling across Mars.

The vehicles had fanned out further into a long, uneven straight line. While they were still easily within sight, this afforded each of them room to maneuver around the more dangerous rock formations. Each truck was locked into its own battle for incremental advancement.

It was simply tedious. The dynamic of the caravan shifted. The diamond drill rig was actually making better time. Its wide, steel-reinforced tracks were well-suited to this challenge. And it's not like Javier had to worry about a flat tire.

The other vehicles had their struggles. More than once, she watched as a Bronco reached a point where it couldn't find a safe way through. At that point, it had to back up and hope to find a better path in some other direction. The only thing more difficult than driving forward with a trailer was reversing with one.

Carrianne's eyes kept shifting toward the Bronco with the fuel tanker. It was being driven by the cook, Ihsan. She knew he had a driver's license—he had shown it to her when she was verifying his employment status—but did that mean he had the skill needed to drive across stuff like this?

Did anyone?

Even Ahmed, who was raised in the middle of the desert, was clearly under duress. His knuckles had gone white from gripping the steering wheel too hard as they rattled along.

She could only hope that the bandits were also struggling; and maybe even that they had given up the chase, since their vehicles surely had flimsier tires.

There was no way of knowing. Now that everyone's speed was so diminished—and the sand was mostly gone—no one was kicking up any large dust clouds anymore.

It took more than an hour and a half to pass over the hamada. Carrianne felt like she was holding her breath the entire time.

Eventually, however, they returned to a more accommodating landscape—this being relative. They still weren't setting any land speed records.

Carrianne already felt like they were behind where she'd hoped they'd be by this point. Traversing the hamada had been more difficult than she had imagined.

But maybe not difficult enough.

The bandits were still off to her left, kicking up dust.

All the while, the temperature outside continued its relentless climb. The desert was shimmering as the sand heated faster than the air above it.

The Bronco had a temperature reading on its dashboard. At high noon, it was already ninety-two degrees.

And it would only get hotter.

She had, of course, been keeping track of their progress on her GPS the entire time. By her best reckoning, they still had twenty-seven miles to cover. Ahmed's speedometer was holding between ten and fifteen for the most part.

Unless the ground beneath them turned into something more like a roadway—there was no way they were going to make it to Quadrant 1 by two o'clock, as she had so ambitiously planned.

She said a silent prayer for the heat to hold off long enough for them to make it and kept monitoring the temperature reading. At a little after one, it hit triple digits.

From there, it just kept going.

102.

105.

107.

Carrianne's teeth ground together harder with every degree. There were still fifteen miles left.

They were never going to make it.

An hour—and eleven more miles—had passed when a squelch from the walkie-talkie broke the tense silence inside the Bronco.

"This is Jerry," he said. "Our thermometer just hit one-ten. If you're going by company policy—"

"I know what the policy is," Carrianne said. "Drivers, please look at your temperature gauges. Anyone seeing any problems?"

"Bertha is doing fine," Javier said.

"This is Mirza," came a heavy sounding voice. "I'm running hot."

That made sense. Mirza was hauling that big, heavy excavator. Carrianne looked at the Bronco's temperature gauge. Still near C.

"How hot?" Carrianne said. "Is the needle at H yet?"

"No."

"How close is it?"

"Three-quarters of the way."

"Okay. Keep an eye on it and let me know if it gets too much closer. Same for the rest of you. Otherwise, we're pressing on."

Jerry came back with, "Are you sure that's—"

"Yes," Carrianne snapped. "Keep driving."

The bandits weren't going away. The last thing she wanted was to spend the night in a place where they would be even more vulnerable.

Dave's high ground had suddenly taken on paramount importance.

She braced herself for an argument. But Jerry just said, "Okay. You're the boss."

The walkie-talkie went silent. For a moment, the only sound was the Bronco's air conditioner, shooting cool air at them.

Ahmed gave her a wary glance.

"What?" she said in a challenging voice.

"Nothing, Princess," he said. "Nothing at all."

They pressed on. Carrianne told herself this was a calculated gamble. She knew the risks from the heat. The danger from the bandits felt greater.

Still, her stomach roiled as the number on the dashboard grew.

111.

113.

114.

It was after two o'clock. They were definitely pushing it.

But she felt like the dust plume to her left gave her little choice.

Chapter Ten

Carrianne poured her concentration into the GPS, as if that would enable them to get there faster and without catastrophe.

She knew what the Quadrant 1 campsite looked like—or at least what she imagined it looked like from her study of the available satellite data. It was a flat rock formation that jutted up from the surrounding desert. Only accessible on one side, it would provide a clear view of everything below.

From overhead, it looked like a teardrop. Its distinguishing feature was a chunk of hard Nubian sandstone that must have been more resistant to erosion over the last several million years because it towered above the middle of the rest of the rock by a good thirty feet.

Nervously, she eyed the temperature reading on the Bronco.

It was holding steady, dead middle.

But, of course, that wasn't the vehicle she was really worried about.

She looked toward the excavator for signs that the super duty truck was laboring. It was plowing steadily onward just like everyone else.

Nonetheless, she was already questioning her decision. Was this reckless? Was she pushing too hard? Should she radio Dave to start scouting around for a suitable spot for the night?

She looked down at the GPS, then back up.

They were traveling down the middle of a long, dry gully with banks on both sides. She could no longer see the dust plume, though that might have just been because their visibility was now limited. You didn't need military training to know this was a terrible place to stop.

She exhaled nervously.

The gulley soon emptied into a flat, open plain.

She looked to her left. The dust plume was gone. Had they really lost the bandits? Maybe this heat was an unexpected blessing that had caused one of the bandits' vehicles to break down?

It certainly seemed possible. The temperature outside had climbed to 115. If it was challenging to late-model, well-maintained vehicles like the kind Blue Diamond had provided, it had to be hell on beater pickup trucks.

Maybe if the caravan could just hang on a little longer, this would prove to be the right call after all.

What it really came down to was this: if they made it—and lost the bandits in the process—she was a strong leader who made a gutsy decision that paid off.

If something went wrong, it was all her fault.

Welcome to being in charge.

More desert passed under their tires. She checked in with everyone on the walkie-talkies and heard only positive reports.

They were going to be fine.

She just had to believe.

Then, she saw it, rising in the distance: that thirty-foot-high chimney of rock that up until now had only existed for her in two dimensions.

In all three, it was even more spectacular—especially under the circumstances.

Better yet, it was only about three miles off. At their current pace, they would be there in less than twenty minutes.

Best of all, there was still no sign of the bandits.

Carrianne had the coordinates of the license area etched in her brain, so she knew it the instant they crossed the eastern boundary of their claim.

She clicked on the walkie-talkie and said, "Great news, everyone. We just entered our claim. From here on out, everything under our feet is ours to discover."

This announcement was greeted by a burst of shouts and hurrahs over the airwaves.

"Our destination is dead ahead," she said. "Just a little farther."

Ahmed grinned. "Shall we lead the way, Princess?"

"Onward, Ahmed."

He goosed the engine, and they spurted into the lead. The campsite was within sight, so she no longer had to worry about losing anyone or getting separated.

When they reached the spot she and Dave had picked out, she told Ahmed to come to a halt. Anxious to let everyone know this was the spot, she hopped out of the truck.

She almost immediately regretted it. As soon as she was upright, she was hit by a wall of heat that took her breath away.

Quite literally. Intellectually, Carrianne knew that hotter air had less dissolved oxygen in it. She had just never experienced it quite like this before.

There was no air in this air.

The sun was striking her with what felt like physical force. Whatever sunscreen she had applied in the morning already didn't feel like enough. Between her hiking boots, layered shirts, jeans, and the baseball cap that corralled her ponytail through its back opening, she'd left precious little real estate for the desert to claim. She tugged her cap lower all the same.

One by one, the other vehicles came to a stop in front of her, with their radiators hissing and popping. She knew she had pushed the trucks hard. Probably too hard.

But she had gotten away with it.

As soon as everyone had piled out, Carrianne called out, "Okay, we're going to set up the main work tent, the generator, and the air conditioner. Then, we're all sheltering inside, no exceptions. Everything else can wait until it cools off. Good plan?"

There was quick agreement, and the team went seamlessly to work.

Everyone just wanted to get out of the heat.

The main tent, like all the others, was pitched atop a lightweight platform that elevated it six inches off the ground.

This wasn't merely a luxury being afforded to them by their generous employer. It was a necessity. Scorpions were a significant hazard in this part of the world. And several of the more dangerous species made their homes by burrowing under the desert to hide during the heat of the day. Then, they emerged at night to hunt.

Unwittingly planting a tent with a thin, nylon bottom directly on top of a scorpion's home was an excellent way to put yourself in a world of hurt.

Or worse. Carrianne had read that venom from an Arabian fat-tailed scorpion could cause respiratory arrest or heart failure in less than an hour—making it just one more thing out here that could kill you.

Shaking off that thought, Carrianne directed a quick unpacking of the needed equipment, keeping a careful eye on everyone.

All the jokes about it being a dry heat only helped so much. 115 degrees—or whatever it was by this point—was enough to put anyone in distress.

The only member of the team who wasn't laboring at least a little was Digger. She was sniffing out every corner of their new home, wagging her tail wildly, apparently pleased by what she was finding.

Carrianne had asked that a carton of dog biscuits be packed

amongst the kitchen supplies. She rooted around until she found it then slipped one to Digger, whose tail now wagged even more vigorously in appreciation.

On the other end of the spectrum, Jerry, who was older than everyone else by at least two decades, was struggling. But when Carrianne quietly approached him and suggested he take a breather, he just waved her off.

It took a half hour before everything was set up and all seventeen people were able to clamber inside. Powered by the generator, the air conditioner roared out welcome relief.

The tent was far from airtight, so it wasn't going to approach room temperature in these conditions. But before long, it was at least twenty degrees cooler inside.

Carrianne felt like she could breathe again. Jerry had positioned himself directly beneath the vent and had his eyes closed in some combination of meditation, prayer, and exhaustion.

For the next few hours, they just hung out. A raucous game of cards, led by Ahmed, had broken out in the corner. Carrianne wasn't sure what the game involved, except that it occasionally resulted in bursts of excitable Arabic. Ciarra was translating for Ray, who seemed to want to join but couldn't figure out the rules.

Kimberly, who was showing signs of being the most tech-savvy member of the team, had set up the satellite internet. They had rules about not using their limited bandwidth for anything frivolous.

But when Joshua and Joseph busted out Clash Royale on their phones, Carrianne deemed it a necessary use of internet resources from a morale standpoint. Naturally, the brothers weren't in the same clan. They took turns sacking each other's bases then talking trash about how much treasure they had looted.

Carrianne estimated it would take another hour to unpack everything else and set up the remainder of camp. Her goal was to start that sixty-minute window when the sun was just about down, which would allow them to get everything done while it was somewhat cooler—but before it became too dark to see.

When that time came and they emerged from the tent, a light breeze was stirring, which made conditions feel bearable.

As everyone set to their tasks, Carrianne noticed the soldiers seemed to be moving with the most urgency.

Their first task was to erect the portable watch tower. They then set up a series of solar- and battery-powered motion sensors that would establish a perimeter 1,000 yards out from camp so no one could sneak up on them in the dark.

Dave had explained the sensitivity was set so that it wouldn't be triggered by insects or small mammals, but if anything larger than a desert fox was out there, whoever was on night watch would be alerted immediately.

Carrianne asked how that person would warn everyone else if there was a threat.

"Simple," Dave said.

He'd just start shooting, and no one would be sleeping for very long.

As Carrianne predicted, everything was more or less done within an hour. Ihsan and Bassel had already started dinner preparations and said they'd be serving something soon. The others had moved on to getting their cots and other personal gear arranged in one of the five sleeping tents that had been set up.

The only member of the team who didn't seem to be settling in was Digger. She had taken up position at the edge of camp, where she was facing into the breeze and growling toward a bluff in the distance.

Ray's efforts to comfort her didn't seem to be helping, and Carrianne eventually wandered their way.

"What do you think is bothering her?" she asked.

"I don't know," Ray admitted. "But not even beef jerky could settle her down, so I know it must be serious."

Ray gave Digger's chest a scratch. She looked up at Ray for a moment, whimpered, then returned to growling at the bluff.

Carrianne looked toward the bluff but couldn't make out

anything ominous. Twilight was nearing its end. It would soon be fully dark.

"You think maybe it's an animal or something?" she asked.

"I could find out if you really wanted."

"No. It's too late to go out there now."

"Not out," Ray said. "Up. I already got the drone unpacked so it would be ready to go first thing in the morning. I could send it up with the camera and have a look."

"You think the camera would be able to see anything in this light?"

"Oh, I can switch it over to the thermal setting. It'll show us an image that looks like one seen through night vision goggles."

"Okay. Give it a shot, I guess."

Ray left Digger and retreated to his tent.

He came out a few moments later with his ruggedized laptop, a small briefcase, and a handheld controller that was the length and width of a license plate. It had two stout antennae sticking out of the top.

Carrianne trailed him to the main tent, where he set the computer and controller down on a folding table.

He then returned outside with the briefcase and walked over behind one of the flatbeds, where the drone was already unpacked.

This was the first time Carrianne had seen it out of its containers. It looked like a huge flying spider, with eight propellers extending from eight arms to form an octagonal perimeter.

The body of the drone was roughly two feet long and two feet wide. Its chassis was supported by four legs, one for each corner, that allowed it to sit elevated off the ground.

With the arms, the entire package was roughly six feet long and just as wide. It looked like something that would have been very comfortable lowering itself from an alien spaceship.

Ray opened his briefcase to reveal a stout-looking digital camera. With practiced flair, he knelt and attached it to the underside of the drone. He checked his work once, twice, and then stood, seemingly satisfied with his work.

"Okay, let's take her up and have a look," he said.

They returned to the tent. Dave was in there, soaking up the air conditioning, having just finished setting up the perimeter. He was drenched in sweat, with his shirt sticking to his chest and abs, though he seemed to be in good spirits.

He asked what was going on, and Carrianne quickly filled him in.

Ray had already powered up his laptop and connected it to the controller. He fiddled with a few settings then looked up at Carrianne.

"You want to give me a countdown to blastoff?" he asked.

"Ten, nine, eight—"

"Too slow," he said with a grin.

From behind her, Carrianne heard a powerful whirring sound as the drone came to life. This was not the high-pitched buzz of some weekend warrior's favorite toy. It was lower in register. Carrianne could feel the vibration in her chest and heard small rocks and pebbles being scattered by its downwash.

As the drone lifted, her eyes went to the laptop screen. It was almost entirely black.

How was Ray piloting this thing when he couldn't see? Carrianne didn't want to distract him with the question. His attention was fixed on the controller, and he seemed to know what he was doing.

The buzzing from the drone elevated and then became more distant. Carrianne could only guess its speed. But it was a lot faster than the two-meters-per-second, brisk walk Ray had talked about for its scanning speed.

When it wanted to, this drone could *move*.

It wasn't too much longer before Ray announced, "Okay, we're up over that bluff right now. Let's see what we've got. Lights, camera ..."

He pressed a button. The screen went from black to shades of bright green.

The image was excellent—high definition with sharp contrast.

Which is why Carrianne had no problem making out three pickup trucks, each with a human form resting in its flatbed. One of them was very clearly cradling a rifle.

So much for having lost the bandits.

Chapter Eleven

S leep largely eluded Carrianne that night.

Dave had tried to reassure her that this was little more than an annoyance—a housefly in need of swatting, nothing more.

He had the night watch divided into thirds. Three men would each take a three-hour shift, starting at nine o'clock and going until six in the morning. The fourth man would be given the evening off as a way of keeping fresh.

He assured her they were accustomed to this schedule, that this was his worry and not hers, and that she should put the threat out of her mind.

But that was like someone telling you not to think about pink elephants. From then on, the only thing in your head is rose-colored pachyderms.

Or, in this case, bandana-wearing bandits.

After tossing and turning her way past midnight and into the early morning, she was grateful when she finally became aware the sky was brightening. Yes, it would mean the sun would soon be beating down on them with all its savagery, but at least she'd be able to distract herself by getting to work.

As she stirred, she realized she was not the first to wake. Ihsan and Bassel already had coffee percolating and were in the midst of making several breakfast offerings.

Everyone else was soon moving about, too.

They were eager to get going while the day was still cool.

Carrianne had identified several interesting spots for Javier to tap into with the diamond drill. Jamil was clambering around the rig, and Mirza had already started the super duty truck.

Jerry and Kimberly were preparing to set off on foot with the XRF guns. Jerry had several ideas about the areas he wanted them to explore over the next two days, and Carrianne was quick to make it clear she respected his wisdom on the subject.

He didn't strike her as the kind of guy who'd take well to second-guessing.

Dave had declared that the bandits were unlikely to make a direct approach on camp during the day, when they'd be easy targets, but he still worried about Jerry and Kimberly wandering around without a vehicle.

There had been kidnappings of foreigners for ransom in this part of the world.

They agreed it made sense for Keith to take a Bronco and join Jerry and Kimberly as an escort. Keith had said he would further ward off the bandits by smoking a cheap, smelly cigar.

That left Carrianne and Ray with the drone in the main tent, which was pleasantly cool after overnight temperatures in the sixties. Carrianne had slipped Digger a dog biscuit when Ray wasn't looking, and the dog was soon curled up asleep at her feet.

Ray was all business as he got the drone up and working. He would be starting in the upper left corner of Quadrant 1 and would be flying it back and forth across the entire area over the next two days.

Once he switched on the autopilot, he leaned back and stretched his arms above his head.

"Okay, we're up and running," he announced.

Carrianne had mostly been ignoring how good-looking he was. Still, she couldn't help but notice that when he tied his hair back in a low ponytail, it made his brown eyes pop.

And, yes, he was an Eddie Haskell. But since he was still part of her team—and they would be working together closely during the coming fifty days—she decided she might as well make nice.

"So," she said, "what got you into flying drones?"

"Oh, I don't know. I've always been mechanical. My mother had to holler at me to stop me from getting into stuff in the house. I can remember one time when I was eight or nine, the neighbors put an old vacuum cleaner out on the curb. That was like Christmas for me. I spent hours taking that thing apart, putting it back together—the whole thing. Or, you know, those fan boats? The kind they take around the Everglades?"

"Sure."

"Well, that's where I grew up. I would see them all the time, and I thought they were really cool. So, I fixed up an old leaf blower and attached it to my skateboard. Me and my friends would go for rides on it."

"You sure you didn't grow up in Kentucky?" Carrianne teased.

He laughed. "I was fourteen when I saw a drone for the first time. And, man, I was hooked. That was just *it* for me. I wanted to know everything about them. I was working at an auto repair shop after school and on weekends. They were paying me under the table. As soon as I had enough saved up, I bought myself the nicest drone I could afford, and that was pretty much all I did in my spare time— just fly that thing around. And then, pretty soon, I realized I could turn it into a business."

"What business?"

"Well, there I was in Everglades City, and there are a lot of gator hunters."

"Alligators? Is that legal?"

"Sure. Everything's legal in Florida."

Now it was Carrianne's turn to laugh.

"They do have a license system," he continued. "You're only allowed one gator a season. That was actually the basis of my business. If you're limited to one, you want it to be the biggest, baddest gator around, right? It used to be the guides would hire some ol' swamp rat to go out and muck around until he found a twelve- or thirteen-footer, and they'd tell their best customer, 'Hey, I found a grandaddy for you.' Then, they'd go out and try to find it again, and the gator would be gone. But with the drone, it was just..."

He made a buzzing noise with his mouth. "I could cover more ground than a swamp rat ever could, and I could tell the guides exactly where the gator was at any moment in time. Word got around about what I was doing, and the next thing I knew I had a thriving business. So, I dropped out of school and that's what I did for a living."

"You dropped out of school to hunt alligators," she said flatly, trying not to sound judgmental.

"Yeah."

"What did your parents think of that?"

"Oh, I was on my own by then. My dad had gotten a job up in Tallahassee, and my mom went with him. They said I could come with them if I wanted, but I was pretty much a swamp rat myself. Plus, I had all my friends in Everglades City. I didn't want to leave. It wasn't like some big traumatic thing where we had a fight and stormed off. They went their way; I went mine. I've basically been on my own since I was sixteen. Hang on."

He checked on the drone quickly. Carrianne had been keeping half an eye on the data being reported back, but there was nothing to see. They were just flying over a stretch of flat, uninteresting desert.

"Anyhow, I did the gator thing for a while, and I was doing okay for myself—at least by Everglades City standards. The guides knew I was delivering for them, and they'd throw me a little extra if a client gave them a big tip. And I was still working at the auto repair shop on the side for extra money. But I think I knew there wasn't really a future in it. My idiot friends were getting high or drunk every weekend, like that was somehow the point of life. And I just thought there had to be more out there.

"I knew about SkyKings, because they're pretty much the best. They're located in Orlando, and their ads would pop up all the time. I would click over to their site and dream about what it would be like to fly one of their drones, but no way I could afford one. Then, one day I was like, 'You know what? Heck with it. I'm going to call them.' I was thinking maybe they'd let me do a test flight or something. Next thing I knew, I was talking to a salesperson who was telling me they were hiring pilots. I went up to Orlando for a tryout, and the rest is history. Here I am, four years later."

He shrugged.

"What about you?" he asked. "How'd you get into geology?"

Carrianne seldom talked about her past. Whenever she did, it started to sound like a sob story, and she didn't want people looking at her like they were sorry for her.

Her policy when asked was to say as little as possible and change the subject as quickly as she could.

"Oh, you know, I just always liked rocks," she said. "I majored in it as an undergrad, went to grad school for it, and now here I am."

"Well, you must be pretty good at it for Blue Diamond to give you this job."

We'll see, she thought.

"Speaking of ..." she said, nodding toward the screen. "Everything still good up there?"

"Oh, yeah, sure. Still going on that first pass. We'll turn her around in a little bit. How's the data looking? Everything okay?"

"Yep," she said. "Just nothing to see."

He pretended to fiddle with the controls even though Carrianne could tell he wasn't doing anything.

Then, the walkie-talkie clipped to her belt made a sound.

"Carrianne, it's Javier."

"Go ahead."

"There's a problem with Bertha," he said. "She has a stomachache."

Carrianne excused herself from Ray and Digger, hopped in a Bronco, and drove toward the drill rig.

It wasn't exactly hard to spot. It had a school-bus-yellow boom that, when fully extended, stretched twenty-seven feet into the air like a giant finger, pointing the way to it.

The boom in that position should have meant the diamond bit was noisily chewing its way into the ground. But when she pulled up and disembarked, all was quiet.

Javier had a side panel on the rig open and was staring absentmindedly into its insides. A case containing tools sat on the ground next to him.

"What's the matter?" she asked.

"Bertha is overheating, and I'm not sure why."

"I thought you tested it out before we left," Carrianne said.

"I did. She was working just fine. But obviously I didn't run her long enough to trigger ... whatever's happening."

Carrianne looked at the rig for a moment, every bit as stumped as Javier. The air reeked of grease and frustration.

This was definitely part of the principal geologist's job she was not prepared for. How was she supposed to know why the rig wasn't working?

Jamil and Mirza were sitting nearby in the pickup truck. Jamil had his feet up on the dashboard. Mirza was slumped against the door. Neither seemed interested in helping out with this issue.

It wasn't their problem.

As Javier went to check something in the rear of the rig, Carrianne saw one of the Broncos rolling up. It was Keith, with Jerry riding shotgun and Kimberly in back.

The truck stopped nearby, and Jerry popped out. He ambled up, and Carrianne immediately sensed a grouch in full bloom. He was delighted that something was broken because it afforded him the opportunity to be annoyed about it—and to offer his opinion about what was wrong.

"It's overheating, isn't it?" he growled.

"Yeah," Javier said.

"I guarantee you it's the filter. The filters on these damn things are notorious."

Javier was still in the rear, jabbing at something with a screwdriver. "I don't think it's the filter, *hombre*."

"Yeah, well, I first started horsing around with rigs like this one in Nicaragua in the nineties when you were still sucking your mama's tit, and nine times out of ten, it's the filter."

"I was bottle fed, and I put in a new filter right before we came out here. It's fine."

"Let me have a look," Jerry said, snapping together a pair of detachable reading glasses and peering through them.

"Suit yourself."

Jerry grabbed a wrench from the tool kit and immediately went on the attack. After a few minutes of swearing and grumbling, he pulled out a metallic cylinder and, waving it in the air, announced, "Ha! I knew it! It's the filter!"

To Carrianne, the filter looked absolutely pristine.

"It's not the filter," Javier said again.

Jerry took his case to Carrianne, bringing the filter over to her.

"See this?" he said, sliding a pinkie finger along block script letters that began with "T4."

"Yeah," Carrianne said.

"He put in the wrong kind of filter. This thing uses P17 filters."

Javier had come back over to them. "No, it doesn't. It uses a T4."

"I've been doing this for a long time, and I've seen this a thousand times before," Jerry fumed. "It uses the damn P17."

"You're wrong, *hombre*, it—"

"I'm wrong? *I'm* wrong?" Jerry snarled. "If I'm so wrong, why is your drill overheating?"

"I don't know, but—"

"Yeah, it's quite obvious you don't know."

"It's a brand-new filter," said Javier, shouting now.

"That doesn't matter when it's not the right kind."

"It *is* the right kind. You have no idea what you're talking about."

"Really? That's why this thing is purring like a kitten right now."

"*Puta madre,*" Javier said under his breath.

"You want to say that to my face?" Jerry spat.

The men were getting closer—and angrier. They were both big guys, and they seemed to be puffing out their chests. Carrianne worried what would happen if the confrontation became physical.

"Okay, okay," she said, sliding between the two of them. "Everybody, just cool it."

Javier grumbled something in Spanish—another insult, no doubt—but retreated to the side of the rig in stony silence.

Jerry turned to Carrianne and said, "We need a P17 filter. I'm sure there's one in the warehouse back in Aswan. If you send Ahmed in a truck, it'll take him a day to go out and a day to get back and we'll be dead in the water the whole time. Get A.J. Sebastian on the satellite phone. Tell him we need a P17 filter helicoptered out here ASAP."

"Blue Diamond has a helicopter?"

"No, but I'm sure he can find one."

"ETS has a chopper," Keith volunteered.

Carrianne briefly glanced at Javier, who shrugged a *whatever.* She climbed back into the Bronco and returned to the main tent, where she unplugged the satellite phone from its charger and dialed A.J.'s number.

He answered but didn't say anything.

"Hello? A.J.?" Carrianne said.

"Come back later, okay?"

"Uh, okay, I—"

"Sorry, I was talking to Tatiana. Anyhow, what's up?"

Carrianne explained the situation.

"So, let me get this straight: no filter means no core samples," he said.

"That's what I've been made to understand, yes. But if the helicopter is too expensive, I can send a truck back to the warehouse. It'll just mean some delay."

"No, no, let's get you that filter," A.J. said quickly. "We need those core samples pronto."

Chapter Twelve

It was a few hours later, a little after one o'clock, when Carrianne heard the thumping of rotors in the distance.

She had been with Ray and Digger in the main tent, where the air conditioner was now on full blast and the data being reported from the drone had continued to be unremarkable.

Maybe Jerry and Kimberly were getting better results on the ground. But, at least from the sky, Quadrant 1 was a bust so far.

When she emerged from the tent into yet another blazing afternoon, the helicopter was already low in the sky. It hovered over a spot several hundred feet outside camp, then slowly touched down, kicking up a huge cloud of dust and sand.

The pilot cut the rotors and, after a few minutes, emerged from the craft carrying a brown box.

Carrianne met the pilot at the edge of camp. He looked American and walked like he was ex-military, just like seemingly everyone at ETS.

"Special delivery for Carrianne Kaucher," he said in a Texas accent.

"Yeah, that's me."

"Thank goodness. It would have been a bad look for me if I couldn't find the right address out here."

Carrianne accepted the box from him. "I appreciate it."

"No problem," he said. "Hey, you know you got some company just on the other side of that berm, right?"

He jerked his head toward the bluff where the bandits were apparently still lurking.

"Yeah, I know all about the three stooges," Carrianne said in an attempt to sound nonchalant.

"Three?" he said. "Try five."

Carrianne felt a small wave of panic pass through her. Two more bandits must have snuck in.

There were now more bandits than soldiers.

"Oh," is all she said.

"I'll take a picture when I go back up and send it to you if you want. But yeah, they all came out and were giving me a hard look as I was coming down. One of them waved his pea shooter at me like that was supposed to scare me, though I was still at least a klick away. I'm pretty sure they were more afraid of me than I was of them. But it's definitely something to keep an eye on."

"Okay, thanks."

"You have Dave Martin with you, right?"

"Yeah."

"Then you have nothing to worry about," he assured her. "You're in good hands."

She thanked him one more time and walked back to camp. As the helicopter began its noisy exit, she climbed into a Bronco and turned over the engine.

The thermometer on the dashboard read 108. It would soon be time to call everyone back in. She wasn't going to push her luck two days in a row.

She drove back out to Javier, who had a stream of sweat pouring off his reddened face and a heavily dampened T-shirt to show for the effort he had been putting in. There were more tools spread out nearby.

Jamil and Mirza had become engaged in the repair. Jamil was on top of the rig. Mirza was on the ground underneath.

The area around the drill had become a small maze of seemingly random parts that had been pulled out of its middle.

The drill was still dormant.

"No luck?" she asked.

"Not yet, but we're gaining on it," Javier said. "I think there's a line clogged between the well and the pump, so the pump isn't getting the water it needs to cool off the drill. We're just having a hard time getting to the line. Everything is packed in here pretty tight."

"I've got that filter that Jerry asked for."

"Great," Javier shot back. "Give it to Jerry. Maybe he can use it for whatever he's smoking."

Carrianne stayed quiet for a moment. This was part of her new job she didn't relish—trying to juggle fragile egos.

Correction: fragile *male* egos.

The most brittle kind.

"I know Jerry can be a grouch," she said, gently. "But is it possible he's right about the filter?"

"No," Javier said.

"He *has* been doing this a long time."

Javier rolled his eyes. "I know. He keeps reminding us."

"Is there harm in trying the P17?"

Javier sighed. "Yeah, because he's wrong. Look, we're almost to the point where we can remove the line and unclog it. How about if my way doesn't work, then we try the filter?"

"How much longer will your way take?"

"We've got most of the stuff removed that we need to pull out already. Once we clean the line, we've got to put all those parts back in place. It's at least two hours before we can fire her back up and see."

Carrianne took in a deep breath. "I'm sorry, but you don't have two hours. You have to quit soon. It's already a hundred-and-eight."

"Believe me, I know, but we can—"

"No," she said firmly. "It's not safe. I appreciate that you want to get this working again, I really do. But it's not worth you dying from heat stroke. It's time to be done for the day."

He stared at her, mopping his brow with his sopping T-shirt sleeve.

"Please," she said simply.

"Alright," he said. Then, in a louder voice, he said, "Okay, boys. The boss says quitting time. Let's clean up."

He turned back to Carrianne and said, "We can't leave this out overnight. If the bandits decided to scavenge all this stuff, we'd have a hell of a time ordering all the parts we'd need to replace it. Bertha's engine still works fine. Can you give us a little time to collect everything? It shouldn't take long. Otherwise, we'd need someone out here watching this thing all night so nothing gets stolen."

"That's fine. Just keep drinking water and be as quick as you can."

"You got it."

Carrianne returned to camp. She got on the walkie-talkie and told Jerry to bring his crew back in.

Ray said he had about an hour left to go on his aerial surveying but that it wouldn't be a problem with the heat. He was fine inside the tent, and the drone could operate safely at temperatures up to 125.

Before long, everyone was back at camp, cooling off and rehydrating.

Jerry made a snide comment to Javier about the filter. Then, the two withdrew to opposite sides of the main tent—much to Carrianne's relief.

She was so exhausted after her restless night, she laid down in the corner for what she thought was a few minutes. Except, when she looked at the time on her phone, an hour and a half had passed.

The rest of the afternoon slipped away quietly. As the sun went down and the group started dispersing from the tent, Carrianne saw Kimberly approaching.

"Do you have a moment?" she said in a low voice.

"Yeah, what's up?"

Kimberly's eyes went to the entrance flap of the tent. "Can you take a quick walk with me?"

"Sure."

The women stepped out of the tent and walked in silence for about twenty yards, their boots crunching on the still-hot ground. Kimberly steered them until they were behind another one of the tents, out of sight of the main tent. Then, she turned to Carrianne.

"Jerry was going on and on all morning about the filters," she said quietly. "He's ... really sure of himself."

"Yeah, I noticed."

"Well, I went online this afternoon and was doing some research. The P17 filter was discontinued two years ago because everyone kept having problems with it. The T4 is now the recommended filter. See?"

Kimberly held out her phone. It contained a page from the drill manufacturer's website that corroborated what she had just said.

Carrianne took a deep breath and released it slowly. "So, he's wrong."

"Yep."

"Did you tell Jerry?"

"God no. He would just get pissed at me and I don't need that. I have to work with him. You tell him. And leave me out of it."

"Okay, thanks," Carrianne said. "I'll handle it."

Carrianne waited until she could get Jerry alone.

The last thing she needed was for him to lose face in front of the others, especially Javier. All she wanted was for him to back off about the filter. It wasn't necessary to wound his pride in the process.

There was no chance to grab him before dinner. But she realized there was a perfect opportunity for a quiet moment with him when she happened to look at the satellite phone signup sheet.

With seventeen people needing to share one phone—their only line to loved ones in the outside world—the sheet was a necessary organizing device. The phone was kept free for business use until five o'clock each day, but after that, it was available to be reserved for personal calls in ten-minute slots for the remainder of the night.

Jerry had signed up for the eight o'clock local time slot, which was eleven o'clock in the morning in Colorado.

At 7:58, Carrianne watched him grab the phone and shuffle off. She waited until ten after the hour then approached his tent, thinking she'd intercept him as he came out.

Instead, he was still in the middle of a conversation.

"... don't want to, but I have to," she heard him say.

There was a pause, then she heard him say, "Yes, I'm aware."

He waited to hear something else then said, "It's not ideal, but it is what it is."

Carrianne didn't mean to be eavesdropping. She was sort of just frozen in place. He wasn't supposed to be using the phone anymore. He should have been returning it by now.

"Look, you do realize how significant my shares are, yes?" he said tersely. "I've got *ten thousand*. It's basically my entire compensation for this project. I told Anthony I was looking for one big score so I could ride off into the sunset."

As Jerry talked, Carrianne gradually filled in the blanks in her own mind. Exploration projects like this were partially financed by the selling of shares to investors. Sometimes, exploration team members asked to be paid partly or wholly in shares, which could have tremendous value if they found recoverable resources.

Carrianne couldn't afford to do that—she needed the paycheck—but Jerry had obviously gone in a different direction.

"No, no, no," he said testily. "They're only issuing *one* million. I've got ten thousand out of a million. That *has* to be worth something. I'm not saying we're going to find another Sukari out here, but what if we do? My God, those shares would literally be worth a fortune. There's value here. We've just got to find someone who sees it and sell it to them."

Carrianne knew all about Sukari. It was a gold mine in the Eastern Desert, the most productive in the whole country. Its revenues were close to a billion dollars a year and it was expected to remain productive for at least another decade.

What was less clear to her was what Jerry was talking about. Was he really trying to sell his shares?

Almost despite herself, she leaned closer to the tent as he continued talking.

"Look, just tell them the truth—that I totally believe in the claim, but my wife is addicted to online shopping, and I need to cover some bills ... Yes, I've tried talking to her. And I've tried cutting her off from credit cards. She just gets pissed at me and applies for new ones. You know these damn credit card companies. They're happy to throw a drowning person an anvil."

He listened for a little while longer and sounded dejected when he resumed. "Okay, I hear you. I guess I'll just ... I'll let you know if anything looks promising. Just ... do what you can to drum up interest, okay? ... Okay, bye."

Carrianne heard his cot creak as he stood up. She took a few quiet steps away from his tent, then started striding toward it again as if she hadn't just been standing outside of it all along.

"Hey," she said brightly. "How's it going?"

"Fine," he huffed, and held the phone up. "Just talking to a business associate back in the States."

"Oh, good. Let's chat for a quick moment."

He stopped. What she had just overheard—Jerry looking to sell his shares out of apparent financial desperation—did not change her task here.

Leaving Kimberly out of it, as requested, Carrianne showed him the web page that recommended the use of T4 filters.

"Really?" he said, genuinely mystified for a moment before he recovered his usual gruffness. "Well, it's probably good they discontinued them. I told you those filters were always junk. Now, if you'll excuse me, I have to return the phone then hit the hay."

He stalked off with no acknowledgment that he had been wrong and no indication he planned to apologize to anyone about it.

Carrianne just shook her head.

The male ego strikes again.

She was, by that point, exhausted. The nap had only helped so much. She needed a real night's sleep.

With temperatures already cooling off nicely, she went to her tent. She changed into pajamas—really just cotton shorts and a T-shirt—and slid into her cot.

Sleep found her quickly.

But it didn't last.

She was somewhere in the middle of a dream when she was jolted awake by the sound of gunfire.

It was earsplitting and close. She sat upright in her cot and saw Ciarra and Kimberly doing the same.

Moments later, more gunshots split the night.

"What's happening?" Ciarra whispered.

"No idea," Carrianne said.

But it was already occurring to her: *I'm the principal geologist. It's my job to know.*

"Just stay here," she said.

She quickly jammed her feet into her boots, grabbed her flannel shirt, and exited the tent, looking around wildly.

There was another burst of gunfire. She could now tell it was coming from the watchtower. A figure was up there—Joseph or Joshua, judging from the jutting ears, but it was impossible to tell which one in the dark. Whoever it was had the SAW mounted on a tripod and was moving it around in search of targets. The air smelled like burned powder.

Carrianne saw Dave standing at the base of the watchtower. He had a SAW at his right side, with its barrel pointed toward the ground.

She scampered over to him and asked, "What's going on?"

"They're testing our perimeter," he said quietly.

"What does that mean?"

"It means someone out there set off one of our motion sensors. This isn't an attack. They're just probing our defenses, seeing what kind of response they get. They want to know how close they can come before we react and what the reaction will be. It's all fine."

"Fine?" Carrianne asked, realizing she sounded incredulous.

"Yeah. Fine. Sorry it's a little noisy. There's nothing I can do about that. Just go back to sleep."

"You're kidding, right?"

"No. I'm not," he said. "You've got a job to do, and so do I. I'm doing it. What's happening right now is just harassment. As much as anything, they're trying to unnerve us."

It's working, Carrianne thought to herself. *It's definitely working.*

Chapter Thirteen

The second day in Quadrant 1 didn't yield any more significant results than the first.

Ray's aerial data remained unremarkable, as did Jerry and Kimberly's soil sampling.

The only encouraging development was that Javier and his men were able to get the drill back together and operating.

It was a clogged line after all.

Nothing more was said about the filter. Carrianne didn't know if Javier was forgiving or forgetting. She was just glad he seemed to be dropping it, and Jerry certainly wasn't going to bring it back up.

A.J. checked in to ask if there would be core samples coming. Carrianne assured him they were now back in operation but explained that she wouldn't be sending Ahmed back to Aswan with any just yet. It just didn't seem worthwhile for him to traverse all that desert with only half a day's worth of samples.

She proposed he wait until there were enough samples to fill the back of the Bronco.

A.J. wouldn't hear it. He instructed her to send the Bronco with whatever samples they had. "We need those core samples pronto," he said—which was, word-for-word, what he had said the previous day.

Carrianne still didn't think it made sense. But she decided it was in her best interests to give her boss what he wanted.

At dawn the following morning, they folded up camp and prepared to move to Quadrant 2.

The packing took a lot longer than the unpacking had. Nothing wanted to fold properly or slide back into the narrow slot intended for it. Trailers that had been uncoupled were stubborn about being re-hitched. Valuable equipment seemed more difficult to secure.

Maybe it was her imagination, but she felt like all the dust, sand, and grit in the air had worked its way into all the small places—every hinge, every joint, every crevice. Objects that had once operated normally were now stiff, bloated, and creaky.

This, she realized, was life in the desert. Things that were easy in the warehouse would simply be more trying out in the field.

It was after eleven in the morning by the time they had everything squared away and ready to roll.

The next campsite wasn't far. Just a few kilometers.

It might have been a pleasant trip, except Carrianne was aware they weren't making it alone. They were still being shadowed by the bandits. Their vehicles remained out of sight, but they were kicking up a telltale trail of dust that was impossible to miss.

As soon as the Blue Diamond convoy arrived, Carrianne found Dave.

"They followed us," she said, without needing to specify who *they* were.

"Yeah, we're not exactly in stealth mode here," Dave said, gesturing at everything.

"But how did they know we were moving? It seemed like they were ready to roll the second we rolled."

"They've got binoculars, too. They probably saw us packing. Plus, they don't exactly have a lot of stuff to pack themselves. It takes us all morning. It probably takes them twenty minutes."

"Yeah, I guess so," Carrianne said. "How long until they get tired of following us around?"

Dave shrugged. "Hard to say. My guess is we're the biggest whale out here by far and they're trying to figure out how to overrun us and get their hands on everything. If you look around and start putting dollar signs on things, I mean"—he began pointing at various trucks and equipment—"there's fifty grand, there's twenty grand, there's a hundred. The drill rig? That thing is probably worth half a million. Even if they got twenty cents on the dollar for this stuff on the black market, it would be a huge, huge score. Bear in mind, these are people who think five thousand bucks is a fortune. I'm afraid we're stuck with them."

"Is there anything we can do to scare them off?"

"You mean, go on offense?"

"Well, yeah, I guess."

"As much as I would love to, it could get us in trouble. Not just lose-our-license trouble. I'm talking rotting-in-an-Egyptian-jail kind of trouble."

"But they're—"

He was already shaking his head. "Look, *we* know those guys are dirtbags. And the authorities know they're dirtbags, too. But what they're doing is not technically illegal. They're just out for a drive in the desert. From a legal standpoint, anything we did to them could be viewed as an unprovoked attack. Let's say we killed one of them by accident. It would be murder."

"But they wouldn't hesitate to kill all of us if they had the chance."

"I realize that. Unfortunately, in the eyes of the law, that doesn't justify a preemptive strike on our part."

"So, we have to play by the rules, but they don't?"

"I'm afraid that's what being the good guys is all about," he said with an apologetic smile.

Carrianne knew he was right.

She still didn't like it.

By the time they were done unpacking, the heat of the day was on them, and they went to their usual resting spots.

That evening, Carrianne used her ten minutes of satellite phone time to check in with Meemaw, who spent most of the call talking about how she was doing battle with the HVAC unit, which kept conking out and leaving her sweltering in the Kentucky heat.

It made Carrianne all that much more eager for payday to come. If she sent her entire first check home to Greasy Creek, that would be enough to keep Meemaw in cool comfort with a brand-new unit.

The rest of the night passed quietly, which was a welcome relief. Carrianne desperately needed the sleep.

As soon as dawn arrived, everyone slid easily into their tasks. The sense of routine was starting to set in.

For Carrianne, that meant being in the tent with Ray and Digger. They usually concentrated on their work—when there was work to be done—though they had taken to chatting quite companionably during quieter moments. It was typically just superficial stuff: likes and dislikes, tales from other job sites, that sort of thing.

There had been a few times when he had made attempts to steer the conversation to more personal subjects, and Carrianne had deftly redirected him each time.

This morning felt different. Maybe she was getting more comfortable with him—despite her own reminders to herself that beneath his seemingly polite exterior, he was still Playah69, still "in a relationship" with Loretta Hamel. Maybe it was something about Digger's presence that made the tent feel homey and safe.

Or maybe Carrianne was just lonely. So, when Ray mentioned that he had overheard her talking to Meemaw, Carrianne started babbling about Meemaw's air conditioning woes.

He listened well, like he really cared. She knew she was saying too much, yet she couldn't seem to stop herself.

At one point, he said, "You worry about your Meemaw a lot, don't you?"

"Uh huh."

"Is that who raised you?"

"Well, her and my Paw. But he passed away a year ago."

"Oh, sorry. What about … what about your parents?"

Ordinarily, this would have been a no-fly zone for Carrianne. But there was something so earnest about how he was asking. She knew he wouldn't judge—what with his parents essentially abandoning him when he was only sixteen.

So, she just came out with it.

"My dad died when I was twelve," she said.

"I'm so sorry. Were you close?"

"Yeah, I guess you could say I was a daddy's girl. He was a locksmith, and he used to take me out on calls with him and let me help him out. He taught me all about how to mentally see inside a lock and how the tumblers worked and all that. I just loved driving around with him. He'd let his arm hang out the side of the truck, and he'd play John Denver's greatest hits album over and over. He always sang along to 'Thank God I'm a Country Boy' and talked to me about how lucky I was to grow up in such a beautiful place. He taught me to love those hills."

"Did he get sick, or—"

"No. It was just a big, dumb accident. He was a volunteer firefighter, because most of the men in Greasy Creek are. It was sort of a social club more than anything. Anyway, he was inside this house one day, responding to what was supposed to be a routine kitchen fire. What no one knew was there was a meth lab in the basement. The place blew sky high."

"Oh, God."

"Yeah, it was rough. Twelve is a pretty bad age to lose your dad."

"Any age is a bad age to lose your dad."

"True. Anyhow, after that, my mom fell apart. Dad was kind of her world, and without him she just drifted along for a while. I think she needed a man to organize herself around. Then, she met this new guy. He was older, and his family had owned a big mining operation at some point, so he had a decent amount of money, at least by Eastern Kentucky standards. Mom was real pretty—is real pretty, I guess I should say. And he was really into her. He was a big Parrot Head, if you know what that is."

"You mean a Jimmy Buffett fan? Yeah, we got a lot of those in Florida."

"Oh, right. Anyway, he had a house on the beach in the Outer Banks in North Carolina, and he wanted to waste away in Margaritaville with my mom. He didn't want some over-serious teenage girl taggling along and ruining their fun. So, Mom asked Meemaw and Paw if they would take me in, and then she just took off. It was probably for the best. Meemaw and Paw were a lot more reliable than she ever would have been. They'd do anything for me."

He was nodding along, seemingly entranced by her story.

"They sound like good people," he said.

"They are. Paw is the real reason I got into geology. He was a coal miner his whole life. I think all miners are amateur geologists to a certain extent. He was really proud of the work he did. Coal gets this bad rap, and I guess it is pretty dirty stuff, but to him, coal was ... it was life. It was warmth and energy and prosperity, not just for his family but for every family in Appalachia. He was always amazed you could just go in and pull something that important out of the earth. I kind of caught that bug from him. He was always pointing out different strata of rock and talking about the millions of years it took to form them. I just loved listening to him and wanted to learn more."

"And your mom, did you stay in touch?"

"Not really. I visited her for a week in the Outer Banks the summer I was fourteen. She took me to the beach, and she would wear these little bikinis. Her new husband—they had gotten married by that point—was just all over her, touching her and ... it was just stuff a kid didn't want to see. Then, they'd start drinking at four or five every day, and he'd play his Jimmy Buffet. And they were pretty happy, I guess. They had their own life, and I could tell neither of them really wanted me to be a part of it, and that was fine, honestly. I never visited her again. She came back to Greasy Creek once, when I graduated high school and was giving the valedictorian speech. She didn't make it to my college graduation. Her husband was getting a hip replacement, and she said he needed her at home. These days, she texts me now and then. That's it."

Ray was staring at Carrianne with an intensity she found unsettling. Rather than return his gaze, she stood up and gestured toward the controller.

"Anyhow, enough of my sob story," she said, pointing toward the controller. "I think this pass is almost over. Time to turn around, isn't it?"

"Oh, yeah," he said, finally taking his eyes off her. "I guess so."

Quadrant 2 turned out to be no better than Quadrant 1—at least not from the air or on the surface.

It would be a few days before they'd know whether the core samples were returning anything of note.

After two days, they moved on to Quadrant 3.

It, too, was a bust. Even rock formations that seemed like they might be interesting proved to be ordinary.

Carrianne did her best to keep everyone's spirits up, though the weather certainly wasn't helping. The heat was showing no sign of letting up.

Jerry, in particular, started slowing down. He came back each day looking like he was on the verge of having a coronary episode, his red face contrasting with his white mustache. He would then practically collapse in the tent. And no matter how much water he drank, he always seemed to need more.

Naturally, he kept insisted he was, "fine, totally fine."

Another two days passed, and they traveled to Quadrant 4. The bandits were still present, though they had not made any more nighttime forays past the perimeter.

Maybe Dave was right. Maybe they would continue to be nothing more than a nuisance.

Still, he remained on alert. Their first night in Quadrant 4, Joseph fell asleep sometime during the midnight to three o'clock shift. And anyone in camp who wasn't a heavy sleeper knew it because, at 2:57 a.m., the silence was broken by Dave chewing him out.

"Wake your ass up, Team B!" he yelled. "This isn't nap time!"

He then added a few more colorful descriptions of Joseph's seriously lacking watch skills.

Joseph grumbled that he had only dozed off for a second and insisted he would have been wide awake the moment an alarm sounded.

Carrianne couldn't help but find Dave's response chilling.

"By then," he said, "it might be too late."

Thankfully, the rest of the team was functioning better. Javier and Jamil had the diamond drill humming; and Mirza was surprising them with how well he was able to clear the way with the excavator, allowing them to access places they didn't think they could get to.

Ahmed was having no difficulty making trips back and forth to Aswan with the core samples.

With Kimberly gently urging Jerry on, soil sampling efforts continued. Carrianne was confident that if there was anything out there worth discovering, they would find it.

Ray kept the drone in the air for nine hours each day, remaining steadfastly upbeat about the work they were doing.

"One of the gator guides I used to know always said, 'You gotta kiss a lot of frogs before you find a prince,'" Ray said at one point. "We just need to kiss more frogs."

And then he looked at Carrianne in a way that made her think it wasn't a frog that he *really* wanted to be kissing.

The next day, they moved onto their Quadrant 5 campsite. Dave started grumbling the moment he saw it, and Carrianne recalled they had struggled to find a suitable spot here. The middle of Quadrant 5 just didn't have many flat areas large enough to accommodate all the tents and equipment.

What they had chosen had its weaknesses, and it didn't take Dave's military training to see them. There was a large hill to the east of them that, to Carrianne, was shaped like a coffin lying on its side.

Back home in Greasy Creek, she was sure someone would have just named it Coffin Hill and cooked up a story about old miners being buried there. It sloped gently down toward the campsite in a way that was almost like an easy access ramp.

The ridge that ran along the top was perhaps three-quarters of a mile off—far enough that Dave wasn't worried about small arms fire coming from up there. But it still gave anyone up there an unobstructed view down into the camp.

Yet the western part of the quadrant had a number of smaller hills and rock formations that an enemy could have easily hidden behind, making anything nearby unsuitable.

They would just have to make do with what they picked.

Much to everyone's excitement, there were a few clouds in the sky as they unpacked—a first in their week and a half in the desert— and the temperature cooled so that the high was "only" 97.

Still, relative to what it had been, that was sweet relief.

Spirits remained buoyed the next morning as they got settled in for their first day of exploring the new quadrant. Ray had the drone up in the air, and Carrianne was studying the data, like usual, when Dave entered the tent.

He had the Zeiss binoculars in one hand and a SAW in the other.

"Hey, sorry to bother you," he said. "But there's something you need to check out."

"What is it?"

"More bogeys."

Chapter Fourteen

Carrianne emerged from the tent just behind Dave. He was already walking north.

Toward what, she couldn't tell.

Was it more bandits? She knew they were somewhere nearby because she had seen the dust being kicked up by their pickup trucks as they traveled to the new campsite the previous day.

The sun, low in the sky and blinding, was just coming up over the ridge of Coffin Hill. It forced her to narrow her blue eyes to squinting slits.

She passed Ahmed, who was just about to depart with the core samples from Quadrant 4. His pattern had been to leave for Aswan on the morning of the first day in a campsite, then return the second day to load the new core samples. He was then available to help as needed on moving day.

He gave Carrianne a hard look as she passed, like he could read the concern on her face.

"What's the matter?" he asked.

"I don't know. Dave says he sees something out there."

"Should I have a look?"

Dave, who was already well ahead of them, didn't turn around. He just said, "Couldn't hurt."

Carrianne and Ahmed continued following Dave as he trekked across gritty hardpan toward the camp's thousand-yard perimeter. He had just passed one of the motion sensors when he pointed to his left.

Just beyond a rock outcropping that had kept them hidden from view, maybe a mile and a half away, there was a small band of people.

"Meet our new neighbors," Dave said, passing Carrianne the binoculars.

She brought them to her face and was soon looking at an encampment of maybe fifteen or twenty people. They were dressed in flowing off-white and beige robes with headdresses that were more colorful. They had no cars or trucks. Just camels.

"Bedouins," Ahmed said, without hesitation, and without needing the binoculars. "Those are Bedouin tents."

Carrianne studied the shelters, which were supported by poles. They had taut ropes stretching from them in six directions, though it wasn't their structure that really struck Carrianne. It was their color. They were a dark chocolate brown, trending toward black.

"Why would you want a brown tent in the desert?" she asked.

"That's goat's hair," Ahmed said. "There's something about the hair and the way it's woven together that keeps out the heat during the day but also stays warmer at night. The Bedouin are famous for their goat-hair tents."

"Wow," Dave said. "You really could hide anything in those things."

"What are you talking about?" Carrianne asked.

"Oh, it's just something I read once in a book about military history. During World War II, British forces in North Africa used all kinds of tricks to deceive Rommel. They'd cover a tank in boxes to make it look like an ordinary cargo truck. Or they'd stick artillery in tents. I remember reading that, thinking, 'How could you hide a gun that size in a tent?' I used to think maybe they were just talking about small portable mortars, but now I get it. You could fit a couple of howitzers in those things, no problem."

Carrianne laughed. "You've got a weird mind, you know that?"

"Sorry. This is how they teach you to think in the military. Nothing is as it seems. Everything might be a Trojan Horse."

"Well, I don't think they're attacking Troy anytime soon," Carrianne said. "But what *are* they doing out here?"

"They're probably just passing through," Ahmed said. "There's nothing out here for them—nothing they want or need, anyway."

"I'm just surprised they can even survive," Carrianne said. "What do they do for water? I can't imagine a camel could haul one of those big 1,600 gallon tankers like we have."

"Oh, the Bedouin are experts at finding water, Princess," Ahmed said. "They literally get it from the rocks."

"What? They just squeeze really hard?" Dave asked sarcastically.

"Not exactly. They have this way of propping stones that makes condensation form on the undersides at night. It drips down to the bottom, and then every morning they collect the water. It's really quite ingenious."

"Huh," Dave said. "How about that."

"They also know that certain types of sandstone have water seeping through them. Or they dig in places that, to you and me, look like nothing—a canyon bottom, a dry riverbed. But they find water hiding underground. They know all the secrets of the desert."

"Yeah, I think I'll stick to our tanker if it's all the same to you," Dave said. "Mind if I have the glasses back?"

Carrianne handed them over.

"I'm still trying to assess the threat level here," he said. "Did you see any weapons? I haven't yet, but they must have some. I can't imagine anyone wanders this desert unarmed."

"Especially not the Bedouin," Ahmed confirmed. "They have an honor code known as 'muruwah.' I think the best word for it in English might be 'manliness.' But it's more than that. To them, it means having courage in battle and being willing to risk your life to protect the tribe. Part of that is that a Bedouin man is expected to defend himself. Long ago, that meant daggers—they still have the most beautiful daggers. You'll see them for sale in antique stores. In modern times, they have guns, even rocket launchers."

"Rocket launchers?" Dave said. "Get out."

"Oh, most certainly," Ahmed said. "In the Sainai Peninsula, the Bedouins are even known to be arms smugglers. Egypt shares a border with the Gaza Strip, you know. How do you think Hamas got its weapons? There are stories of Bedouin burying arms shipments in the desert and then digging them back up when they find a buyer."

"Great," Dave said. "One more thing to worry about."

"You think those guys are smuggling weapons?" Carrianne asked.

"They could be, Princess," Ahmed said. "The Bedouin are never lacking in surprises."

That night, several hours after the sun had disappeared, Carrianne found herself walking in the darkness out toward the edge of camp.

She had already made her call to Meemaw, but she wasn't quite ready to go to sleep. For the first time since they had gone out into the desert, she didn't feel completely exhausted.

It helped that the heat had broken a little.

As much as it surprised her, as someone who came from greener parts of the world, she was starting to get used to the desert. Perhaps she was even starting to appreciate it. For as frightening and forbidding as it could be, it could also be beautiful, almost shockingly so.

Like right now. There was no moon, and the sky overhead was putting on a spectacular show. In any place she cared to look, there were more stars than she could have counted in a lifetime. They were glittering and dancing and winking at her from across an unfathomable stretch of space.

It always blew her mind that the photons raining down on her from the heavens at any given moment might have been traveling toward her since the age of the dinosaurs.

How improbable that her eyeballs should happen to be there to receive them at that precise moment.

How wonderful.

Directly overhead, the Milky Way was a vivid white sash of celestial radiance. Carrianne thought that growing up in Greasy Creek had put her far away from light pollution, but it was nothing compared to this, sixty miles from the nearest streetlamp or porchlight.

She was totally lost in her thoughts, having forgotten herself and her worries, when she heard a voice with a gentle Florida twang say, "It's really something isn't it?"

Ray was somewhere just behind her.

"Sure is," she said.

"Kind of reminds me of the Everglades."

"Oh yeah?"

"People don't think of Florida as being wild, but that's just because they haven't been to the right parts. I don't know if you've ever seen a satellite image of Florida at night. The edges are all lit up. So is this band across the middle where Orlando is—thank you very much, Walt Disney. But down at the heel, there's this big dark patch. That's the part where I'm from. And once you get yourself out in that, it looks ... well, sort of like this."

He paused on that thought, then laughed as he added, "With a lot more bugs."

Carrianne said nothing, just watched as a meteoroid briefly burned its way through the upper atmosphere, leaving behind a thin streak of yellow.

Ray's breathing sounded like it was growing strangely short.

"You know ... maybe it's cheesy to start this when we're out under the stars and it's all romantic and all that, but I've been trying to find the right time to say this and ... You're ... You're really pretty, you know that?"

Okay, here goes, Carrianne thought to herself. *Playah69, making his move.*

"Thank you," she said tersely.

"Uh oh. Have I offended you?"

"No. It would just be inappropriate for anything to happen between us. We work together," she said, hoping that would be the end of it.

"Well, sort of. But not really. I'm employed by SkyKings. You work for Blue Diamond. And, actually, if you want to get technical, I signed a contract with SkyKings, so I'm an independent contractor. Which means I can do whatever I want. There's really no problem there."

She turned to him. "Look, it's not that. I'm just ... I'm not into guys like you."

"Guys like ... what? Guys from the Everglades? Guys who didn't go to college?"

"No, that's not—"

"Because I've actually been taking classes online. It's a little slow-going and I'm paying for it myself. But I've already got, like, seventy credits and I'm—"

"It's not that."

"Then what is it?"

Even in the darkness, she could see him looking at her with that earnestness that she had to remind herself not to find endearing.

But was that just part of his game?

Was she falling into the trap of allowing herself to become Playah69's desert booty call?

Then, she reminded herself it didn't matter. Whatever he was pretending to be right now, he was "in a relationship."

Finally, she just spat out, "Look, Ray, you're good at seeming like you're a nice guy, but I know your deal."

He looked genuinely mystified. "And what's my deal?"

"Playah69," she said. "Your Instagram profile. C'mon. Don't play dumb. I googled you."

His eyes had gone wide. "Oh, lord, those morons are still doing that?"

He shook his head and laughed.

"I don't think it's particularly funny," Carrianne said.

"No, no, no. You don't understand. That's not ... that isn't me. Playah69 is this thing my idiot friends started in high school. They all had the password to the account. The whole game was to dig up the most offensive, racist, sexist thing they could find. They didn't want to post it to their own accounts, because their mothers or girlfriends or teachers might see it. So, they invented 'Playah69.' Then, they thought it would be even funnier if they made it out so that *I* was Playah69. The whole joke was that I *wasn't* a player. I was like the opposite. I was this strait-laced grind who didn't smoke weed and didn't drink at parties and worked all the time. They just thought the whole thing was hysterical. I had no idea they were still doing it. But you have to believe me—that isn't me, wasn't me, and never has been me."

He was talking so fast Carrianne could barely keep up with what he was saying. Her brain was having a tough time absorbing this new data point.

Ray wasn't a pig?

He didn't like the ladies and drones, in that order?

"Okay, but even if that's true, it still wouldn't be right, us getting together," she said. "You have Loretta."

"Loretta?"

"Loretta Hamel. I have no interest in being the other woman."

"Oh, my lord. I haven't seen Loretta Hamel in ... I don't even know when. Like, three years, at least? I swear. Last I heard, she was married with a kid—not mine, by the way."

"Then why does your Facebook say you're in a relationship with her?"

"Because if I haven't seen her in three years, I probably haven't been on Facebook in five. At least. Loretta was my high school girlfriend. We were definitely pretty serious—that's one of the reasons Playah69 was such a joke. They used to tease me about how whipped I was and how I was the only sixteen-year-old middle-aged married man they knew.

"Anyway, she went off to college and met some guy. She came home at Thanksgiving freshman year and broke things off, and that was pretty much it. I forgot she was even mentioned in my status. I'm not much of a social media guy. I'm as single as can be. Swear to God."

He held his right hand toward the stars above him.

Carrianne didn't reply.

"Look, I'm not perfect, and I might not always say the right thing, but I'm sure as heck not Playah69, and I'm definitely not in a relationship," he continued. "I just ... I think you're gorgeous, okay? Gorgeous and smart and driven and ambitious and all the things I really admire. And I just ... I want to get to know you better, that's all. We can take it slow. We can take it fast. We can take it however you want. As long as I get to be with you, I don't really care about anything else."

Carrianne risked a look into his eyes. He was staring straight back at her with no hint of deceit.

She still didn't know if she could trust him.

Chapter Fifteen

They left it that she would think about it.

That night, with all still quiet, Carrianne went back to the main tent and looked a little closer at Ray's accounts.

He said he hadn't been on Facebook in five years. It was actually more like six.

And when she looked more carefully at "his" Instagram, she noticed the posts were being commented on by the same six or seven people, all guys, all of them clearly in on the joke. They were mostly just egging each other on and cheering their own obnoxiousness.

Where did that leave her?

With a recognition that she had been wrong.

And that she needed to reevaluate.

She hadn't even been open to the idea of a relationship with him. But now ...

Well, it was something to consider.

If she'd only judged him for how he had been with her—and not what she had seen online—she had to concede that he had been nothing but kind, attentive, and warm-hearted. He was the sort of guy who took in stray dogs, for goodness's sake.

And he did look awfully nice in a T-shirt.

If only she didn't have to spend the next five weeks sharing a tent with him for nine hours a day. Relations would get seriously awkward if things between them didn't work out.

Then, there was the boss factor. Yes, technically, he was an independent contractor. But would the higher-ups at Blue Diamond see it that way? If she pursued a relationship with him, would she be putting her job in jeopardy?

It was a lot to consider.

As morning rolled around, she had made no further headway, and it was time to get started in the main tent. Digger was already there, thumping her tail madly.

Carrianne had made a habit of tucking a few dog biscuits into her pocket and sneaking them to Digger throughout the day. It was a routine that had bonded human and dog quite nicely, and Carrianne once again greeted Digger with a biscuit and a scratch behind her half-missing earflap.

Ray came in a few moments later. The moment he saw her, his face flushed, which Carrianne found adorably charming.

"Hi. I didn't see you at breakfast, so I thought maybe you had ... Uh, never mind," he said a little too quickly. "It doesn't matter, I guess. Because I'm here. And you're here. Obviously. I bet you even knew that already."

He grinned nervously.

This was when Carrianne realized things were going to be seriously awkward no matter what.

"Anyhow, did you ... Did you sleep okay?" he asked. "Not that I, you know, think about you sleeping or anything. Sorry. That wasn't meant to be a creepy did-you-sleep-okay. It was just a very neutral, non-sexual, 'Did you sleep okay, Grandma?' kind of question."

He caught himself and clarified. "Not that I think of you like a grandmother. I mean, I think you might be, like, a minute and a half older than me. I was just—"

"It's fine," she said in an attempt to save him from himself. "I slept fine, thank you. How about you? Did you have good, non-creepy, non-grandmotherly sleep?"

"Oh, me? Yeah. Great. Thanks. Love that cool desert air."

He took an exaggerated inhale then said, "Anyhow, let's get to work."

Digger had positioned herself between the two of them and was looking back and forth like she couldn't figure out what to make of their exchange. But as Ray began fiddling with the drone controller, she decided he was more in need of comfort and curled up at his feet.

Ray poured his concentration into the laptop screen. They would be starting in the northwest part of the quadrant and working their way down through hundred-meter-wide passes, working left-to-right, just like usual.

Once the drone was up in the air and on autopilot—usually the time when they'd start with their low-stakes chatter—he instead ignored her and kept fiddling with various settings that even Carrianne knew didn't need to be adjusted. She could feel him ginning up the nerve to say something.

But he must have decided against it, because they ended up passing most of the morning in uncomfortable silence, saying little beyond the bare minimum.

It was a little after one o'clock. when the walkie-talkie squawked to life.

"Carrianne, it's Javier."

"Go ahead," she said.

"I'm down here at one of the areas you told us to check out. It's in the western part of the quadrant, about even with camp north-south wise. We got something weird happening with the drill. I'm not sure what exactly. You might want to come out and see."

"Okay, I'll be right there."

She looked apologetically at Ray. "Sorry, I—"

"No," he said immediately, making a shooing motion. "Go, go!"

Carrianne exited the tent and hopped into a Bronco. Even at a crawling fifteen miles per hour across the uneven terrain, she reached the rig within minutes, approaching from behind.

It was sitting atop a large domed mound that stretched for several hundred yards. Other than Coffin Hill, which was also on her list, this was one of the more interesting features in the quadrant.

As she pulled up, the drill was chewing noisily into the ground. The excavator was nearby, with Mirza in the driver's seat and its engine still.

Carrianne walked up to Javier, who was staring at the spot in the ground where the drill was plunged in. He looked up as she approached and gestured to Jamil to cut the engine.

He pulled out his earplugs and said, "Thanks for coming. Okay. So, here's the deal. It's something that's happened in two spots, and I'm trying to see if it happens in a third. We get about ten yards down, and then the drill bit just drops."

"What do you mean, 'drops?'" Carrianne asked.

"I mean, it's churning through rock, bringing up cores, doing its usual thing and then, boom, nothing."

"Nothing?"

"Nothing. As in, no more rock, no more cores. Just air. It's empty."

"Empty like—"

"Like a cave. A cavern. Whatever you want to call it. There's a big open expanse under the rock."

Carrianne could feel her excitement growing, even if she was a bit confused. Caves were almost always created by water—specifically by rainwater, which was made slightly acidic by its trip through an atmosphere that contained carbon dioxide. That slightly acidic water then seeped down through small cracks and slowly dissolved the carbonate minerals it found, like limestone.

But had there really been enough rain in the desert to create a large cave? She knew this region hadn't always been so dry. Go back

10,000 years, and the Sahara was a green grassland filled with lakes and rivers. Had the cave formation occurred under those circumstances?

She walked over and studied the cores that Javier had laid out, expecting to see the familiar white or light gray of limestone.

It wasn't limestone. This rock was darker.

But maybe that just meant the lighter color rock had all been eroded away?

Still, the possibility of water—even an underground place that formerly had water—was tantalizing. Carrianne once had a professor who liked to say that water and gold were like peas and carrots: you often found the two mixed up with each other.

The reason for that was simple chemistry. Gold didn't react with other elements very easily. It was also much denser than most other rocks. So, when small amounts of gold were eroded out of rock by water, the other rock washed away, carried off by the water, while the gold just sat at the bottom and collected in what were known as placer deposits.

In California, the gold rush of 1849 was created by such deposits. The first Europeans to explore the Sierra Nevada mountains literally found streambeds lined with clumps of gold that the native populations had been walking past—and ignoring—for thousands of years.

Was there something similar waiting for them underneath where they were standing?

Certainly, if there had been limestone at some point, that was another potentially promising sign. The Carlin Trend in Nevada, which contained some of the world's richest gold deposits, had a fair amount of limestone.

She went back to Javier.

"Okay, why don't you keep drilling and see if you hit air again?"

"You got it," he said.

He motioned to Jamil, who set the drill chattering again. Perhaps five minutes later, Javier started yelling.

The bit had hit air again.

"What do we do now?" he asked.

"I don't know, exactly. I think this might change our plans, though. First, I want to call this into A.J. to see what he thinks."

"And what do you think?" Javier asked.

She couldn't help but grin as she echoed Anthony Sebastian's words from weeks earlier: "No one knows what might be lurking beneath the sands."

———

Carrianne returned to camp, went to the satellite phone, called A.J., and delivered the exciting news.

"That's fantastic," he said when she was done.

"Well, we don't know what it is," she cautioned. "It still might be nothing. But it's definitely the most promising thing we've found out here by far."

"I agree. How can I help?"

"I guess I wanted to talk strategy with you. We have this three-pronged plan in place, each team focusing on their own area. But my instinct is to say let's focus all our resources on this. This isn't random exploration anymore. We now have a target. That's Lightning Geology, isn't it?"

"You're right. Absolutely. This should be your sole focus until we know what we have, good or bad," A.J. said. "In the meantime, I'm going to call dad and let him know you might have something."

"Isn't that ... a bit premature?"

"Not at all. Don't worry. He's done this before. He'll keep it in perspective. But he's been under a lot of pressure from investors who are asking if this whole Western Desert thing isn't just a huge mistake. He needs some good news to share."

"Okay, if you say so."

"Let me know how things go."

"Of course."

"And definitely let me know if you find something."

"Will do," she assured him.

Once she had ended the call, she took a few moments to collect herself. Then, she clicked on the walkie-talkie, announced what was happening, and began reassigning everyone.

She instructed the soil sampling team to focus on the mound and even train their XRF gun on the core samples, just to get a better idea of what was happening down there. The guns wouldn't be as precise as a full assay done in a lab, but they would at least provide some information.

Next, she asked Javier if he could try to find the outlines of the cave. Was it shaped the same as the mound? Was it larger? Smaller?

Finally, she returned to the main tent, where Ray and Digger both turned toward her expectantly.

"Okay, what's the plan?" Ray asked.

There was no hint of the faltering, embarrassed, blushing boy from earlier. He was locked in again.

"We can call off the search grid for now. Can you knock off the autopilot and take the drone over to where the diamond drill rig is?"

"Absolutely," he said. "I'm going to switch to camera view so we can both see what's up—get the overhead view."

"Great."

Ray gripped the controller, banked the drone at a sharp angle, and increased the speed until the desert below was practically a blur.

Less than a minute later, the drone was hovering roughly a hundred feet above the mound. The drill had moved to another spot and was again boring through the surface. The Bronco carrying Jerry, Kimberly, and Keith was just pulling up.

"You want to switch to electromag sensors now?" Ray asked.

"Actually, before we do that, could you just take me for a little spin around the whole area? I want to get a better sense of what we're dealing with."

"Of course," he said.

"You can keep it at walking speed. No need to rush this."

"You got it."

The drone began a slow canvas of the mound, moving around it in a clockwise motion. When it reached a spot in the northeast corner —roughly two on the clock—Carrianne noticed some ground that looked different from the surroundings and unusual within the context of the desert. It was at the base of the mound.

"Hold it there for a second," she said. "And maybe even bring us down a little bit. I want to have a closer look."

Ray quietly did as instructed, decreasing the altitude until they were more directly over a rubble field the likes of which Carrianne hadn't seen before.

It was a collection of small boulders, each roughly the size of a laundry basket. They almost looked like they had been placed there deliberately and didn't seem to match the other rocks nearby.

There could be any number of explanations for how that had occurred. Maybe they had been deposited there during a flood in those long-ago wetter times.

Still, geologists were trained to look for anomalies. And this was definitely anomalous.

There appeared to have been a fair amount of erosion in the area recently—"recently" in geologic terms meaning the last few decades.

She remembered what Anthony had said about how that was part of what led him to the Western Desert in the first place, how certain features had been brought closer to the surface as winds scoured away sand deposits that could have been massing there for thousands of years.

Was this another one of Anthony's SWAGs that proved to be correct?

"Those rocks are ... interesting," she said.

"You want me to get closer?"

"No, I'm going to check it out in person."

She left the tent and returned to where the rest of the team was hard at work. She parked up on top of the mound, where the other vehicles were then followed the slope down to the boulder field.

It was definitely unusual, like nothing else she had seen during her weeks in the desert. It occurred to her that maybe the water had entered the cave this way, through these very porous rocks.

Then an even better idea came to her.

If this was how water had first entered the cave, maybe—with a little help from the excavator—people could get in that way, too.

Chapter Sixteen

I t was nearing two o'clock in the afternoon. Everyone had been working since six in the morning.

As eager as Carrianne was to discover if she was right about this boulder field serving as a door to a cave, she also didn't want to push her people too hard.

Even though it was "only" 95 degrees, that was still plenty hot enough to tax the system.

Then there was the matter of the bandits. Just say she did have Mirza bring the excavator here and start clearing away the boulder field, and it did, in fact, lead to a cave. By the time he got it open—if he got it open—it would probably be nearing dark, and they would have to retreat to the safety of camp.

In that case, they'd either have to leave a guard behind—who would be vulnerable to a sneak attack without the benefit of the perimeter. Or they'd risk the bandits getting first crack at the cave.

It struck Carrianne that if there really was some kind of opening down there, it had been there for millions of years.

They could wait at least one more day to discover it.

She ran her thinking by Jerry who was, as usual, fading fast and happy for the relief. He agreed her logic was sound. They packed up and returned to camp, where Carrianne called A.J. and told him there was no news. Yet.

That evening, there was a lot of excited chatter about the possibilities that might be awaiting them. Carrianne guessed she wasn't the only one who had a tough time getting to sleep.

The next morning, she burst out of her tent and made a little more noise than usual. Her selfish rationale: the sooner they got to work, the sooner they would get answers.

Everyone else must have shared her impatience, because they, too, were up and about earlier than usual. Jerry, who probably had more to gain than anyone financially, was particularly edgy.

Though that also meant he was thinking ahead. He insisted they pack flashlights—"Just in case we have something dark and spooky to explore," he said.

As engines began roaring to life—Mirza in the excavator, Javier in the drill rig, she and Keith driving Broncos filled with other team members—Carrianne felt the thrill of the unknown.

This was the life-changing discovery they had been sent out to the desert to find. She could feel it.

They rolled out toward what they were already calling "the cave," even though they weren't even sure if that's what it was.

As everyone else got set up on top of the mound, Carrianne guided Mirza to the area down below where she wanted him to dig. It was at the bottom of the mound's slope, where it met the flat ground of the rest of the desert.

She was glad Ciarra had joined because, while Mirza had decent English, it was nice to have instructions and responses translated so nothing was lost in a language gap.

Mirza nodded throughout. Ultimately, the basic idea wasn't difficult: he should start at the top of the area of loose stones, try to work horizontally as much as he could so he was digging into the hill as well as down, and keep going until he found something.

Once she was through giving her instructions, he set up the machine in front of the rubble and got to work. The excavator had a long arm and a sturdy bucket, so it was plenty capable. Still, the rocks were large enough that Mirza was picking out one at a time and then moving it to the side.

It was slow going.

There was little Carrianne could do to help him speed up, so she returned to the top of the mound.

Once there, she directed Javier over to the side of the mound where Mirza was. She didn't want him too close to the edge because Mirza would be making that area less stable, and she didn't want to lose her diamond drill if the ground suddenly collapsed under its weight.

But she still wanted to establish that her theory of the cave's formation was correct—that if water had gotten in through the boulder field, it would have started its slow and steady excavation there.

In other words, she wanted to make sure Mirza wasn't digging in the wrong spot.

Javier was on board with the plan, and the drill was soon chewing through the ground.

While that got underway, Carrianne next went to check on Jerry and Kimberly. They were shooting the cores with the XRF guns and having a hard time containing their excitement.

"We're getting a lot of quartz," Jerry said, and he didn't need to elaborate why that was putting pep in his step.

Gold deposits were often found mixed in with quartz. It wasn't a guarantee. Quartz, which was made of silicon and oxygen, was the most common mineral on Earth's surface. So, there were plenty of places where there was quartz and no gold whatsoever.

Still, gold and quartz were considered complementary on a molecular level.

The presence of gold was another promising sign.

All the while, Carrianne knew Ray was hard at work because the drone was buzzing overhead.

She radioed him about the data he was seeing. Sure enough, the area around the mound was getting low conductivity ratings. This made sense, since quartz had high resistivity and was considered a good electrical insulator.

Another encouraging data point.

Ultimately, however, Carrianne knew that all these things were merely teases.

What mattered most was Mirza and the excavator.

With this in mind, she returned to monitoring the progress of his digging. He looked like a man in the zone, patiently and persistently clearing a growing gouge in the side of the hill.

Carrianne stared at the rocks, wishing all the while she had X-ray vision. There was still no end in sight to the rubble field.

How deep did it go? How long would it take? Were they even digging in the right spot?

Even with all the equipment they had, she didn't have immediate answers to any of those questions.

An hour later, Javier called her over. After ten yards, the drill bit had once again dropped and started spinning through air.

Which meant Mirza was on the right track.

She didn't dare push Javier any further east because it would put him too close to the edge. Instead, she sent him north to see how far the cave extended in that direction. She was still trying to establish its approximate dimensions.

It was definitely big, though. They now knew that for sure. The distance from where he had created this new hole to the middle of the mound, where he had been making holes the previous day, was several hundred yards.

As Javier went to his new spot, the sun continued creeping higher in the sky. She thought it felt marginally cooler—that had been the trend—though that might have just been wishful thinking.

By noontime, she was getting the sense that everyone was spinning their wheels. Javier had punched a few more holes through the roof of the cave, but that wasn't helping them find a way inside. Ray had passed the drone over the area multiple times and was getting no new data. Jerry and Kimberly weren't really learning anything new from the XRF guns, either.

It was really all coming down to the excavator, and everyone knew it. They were cheering its progress with every rock removed.

At Javier's suggestion, they gave Mirza a break, letting him eat some lunch and hang out in the air conditioning of one of the Broncos for a while.

Javier took over the excavator during that time so they could keep making progress. He wasn't quite as smooth with the machine, but he made up for it with sheer determination.

As the afternoon wore on, Javier and Mirza continued taking turns at the controls while everyone else watched on.

No one even mentioned quitting for the day. They were all too interested in where this might lead.

The hole grew wider and deeper. Carrianne was worried that they would soon run out of the boulder-sized rocks to dig through. If they reached bedrock or hard sediment, they could always try to blast their way through with dynamite, though that had its uncertainties and dangers.

It was also just messy.

On the other side of the spectrum, they'd have trouble if they reached smaller stones or, worse, sand. Because, in that case, the sides of the hole would not remain stable. They didn't have materials on hand to reinforce it. They would be risking a cave-in.

Three o'clock became four o'clock. It was hot—around 95 degrees again—but compared to what they had been dealing with, that felt tolerable.

Just when Carrianne was starting to wonder if she should be the sensible one and declare them done for the day, Mirza removed yet another rock. Suddenly Kimberly was pointing toward the hole and gesturing at Mirza to stop.

"What's going on?" Carrianne asked over the chatter of the excavator's engine.

"Look," Kimberly said. "There's an opening."

Sure enough, Carrianne peered downward. The hole was like an extra-wide V, and at its bottom, a dark space had appeared. It was roughly round, maybe three feet in diameter.

Mirza was looking toward Carrianne, and she held up two hands, telling him to stop. He raised the excavator bucket and stopped it in mid-air.

Kimberly grabbed a small rock and tossed it toward the hole.

The rock sailed clean through.

They conferred briefly.

The area around the opening looked quite stable. The rocks on all sides of it were large, and none of them appeared to be perched at angles that suggested they would be going anywhere soon.

Just to make sure, she had Mirza bang the sides vigorously with the excavator bucket to see if anything would dislodge.

Everything stayed in place.

The next question regarded timing. It was nearing five o'clock. They had already passed the peak heat of the day, and temperatures were now cooling ever-so-slightly.

The greater issue before long would be darkness. They had another hour-and-a-half until sunset, plus another hour or so after that when it would still be light enough to move about.

No one thought it was a good idea to be outside the perimeter and down in a hole beneath the ground when it was pitch black.

But, ultimately, they decided there was time to at least go down and have a look.

Mirza, Javier, and Keith volunteered to stay topside with the equipment. Keith had already lit a cigar and seemed quite content up there.

Everyone else was game to explore underground.

Since they were younger—and smaller—Carrianne and Kimberly led the way, clambering down the rocks. There were one or two spots where the footing was a little tricky, but, all things considered, the grade was gentle and the climbing was easy. It reminded Carrianne of riprap that had been placed alongside a river or bay for erosion control.

When they got down to the bottom, they shined their flashlights into the darkness. Carrianne was expecting to see either more boulders, or a long drop into a deeper chasm.

What she found instead looked more like a tunnel. It appeared to have been chiseled out of solid basalt rock on all sides and sloped gently downward.

It reminded Carrianne of an abandoned mining shaft she had once visited with Paw back in Kentucky.

Kimberly was studying it, too, and seemed equally puzzled by it.

"This is weird, right?" Carrianne asked.

"Yeah," Kimberly said.

"It doesn't look like it was made by underground water erosion."

"Nope," Kimberly confirmed.

"So, what did this?"

"I don't know. Maybe a long time ago it was exposed? So, this is normal weathering that then got covered up?"

"Could be."

They left it at that.

"You want to go first, or should I?" Carrianne asked.

"I'm smaller. It probably makes sense for me."

"Okay, go ahead."

Kimberly eased through the opening with room to spare. She was soon crouching on the floor of the tunnel, shining her light farther down.

"There's more," she said.

"Okay, here I come."

Carrianne put one foot into the hole, then the other. Gripping both sides of the rock, she gently lowered herself down. Kimberly had gone deeper into the tunnel to make way for her.

There was plenty of room for two people. Maybe even four or five. And there was definitely more tunnel ahead. It sloped down and away, leading in the direction of the middle of the mound.

"What's going on in there?" Jerry called from just outside the hole.

"Why don't you get down here and look?"

Jerry grumbled as he slid through the opening in the rocks. It was a tighter fit for him, but he still had just enough room to clear.

As soon as he was through, he pulled out his flask of water and thirstily took a swig.

Ciarra and Jamil joined next. Neither had much trouble negotiating the short drop.

The five of them began descending through the tunnel. Carrianne was still studying the walls of it, trying to decide how it had come to be.

Erosion was tricky. It was sometimes hard to say why certain rocks had disappeared while others remained because the ones that had vanished were no longer around to be studied.

It might have just been a vein of minerals that were more chemically reactive, which made them easier to break apart. Or it was a strata of rock with a structure that made it more susceptible to wear and tear.

The footing was easy enough, though. The floor of the tunnel was smooth, like it had been worn by a gentle stream through the millennia.

No one was in much of a hurry as they walked down the tunnel. They were all swinging their flashlights around, taking in their surroundings. The quiet scuffling of their feet bounded off the walls.

After about twenty feet or so, their surroundings abruptly changed.

The tunnel opened into a massive chamber—so large their flashlight beams could not begin to reach the end of it. This was the feature Javier had kept punching into with the diamond drill. The roof arched high above them like a jagged, rocky cathedral ceiling.

The space was huge. And it was unlike any underground opening Carrianne had seen before. In every cave she had explored in the wetter parts of the world where she lived, dripping water had left behind calcium carbonate deposits, which formed stalactites and stalagmites.

Neither was in existence in this cave.

Yet if water hadn't created this space, what had?

Jerry, who was just behind Carrianne, let out a whistle as he reached the end of the tunnel. "Holy smokes, look at this place," he said.

Jamil said something softly in Arabic, and Ciarra laughed.

"What's so funny?" Kimberly asked.

"He said, 'Praise be to Allah' … and he didn't know Allah had a shovel this big," Ciarra said.

"More likely it was a small shovel, but He had a lot of time to dig," Jerry said.

Ciarra translated and Jamil said in English, "Yes, my friend."

"Okay, so what's our plan here, boss?" Jerry asked.

Carrianne realized the question was directed at her.

She glanced at the time on her phone.

"As I see it, we've got about a half-hour before we need to head back to the surface and start packing up to go back to camp. Let's just take that time to have a look around. We don't exactly have breadcrumbs to mark our trail, so stay within voice range and you won't get lost. If you come across another tunnel or a smaller area to explore, just do your best to remember where it is. We can do it tomorrow when we've got more time. Good plan?"

There was general agreement, and they split up.

Carrianne turned south and followed the wall of the cave, keeping her hand on its rough surface for balance. She was primarily looking for signs of water—or where water used to be—knowing that was where interesting deposits were most likely to have formed.

It was actually her nose that told her there was no water left. A cave with water in it would have smelled a little damp, perhaps musty. This one just smelled dusty. Her boots kicked up small clouds of fine, dry sand with every step.

She was working her way through the cavern slowly, deliberately, trying not to miss anything while also being careful to watch where she was going. The space was so vast that her light disappeared quickly when it didn't have anything to bounce off.

After fifteen minutes of slow progress, she had traveled no more than a few hundred feet. She sensed there was still plenty more to explore.

Then, from another part of the cave, Kimberly called out. "Hey guys," she said. "You might want to come over here. I think I've found something."

Chapter Seventeen

Carrianne followed the sound of Kimberly's voice. As she closed in, she watched the other flashlight beams converge on the spot where Kimberly was standing, which was near the cave wall to the north of the tunnel opening.

She was aiming her light at a spot in the ground.

"I feel like someone should be filming this," she said. "This could be important historically."

"What are you talking about?" Jerry said, his breathing slightly ragged as he approached.

"I'm talking about *that*. Look," she said, keeping her light steady.

Carrianne could finally see what Kimberly was pointing toward. There was a slightly convex metal disc lying partially buried in the ground. The visible portion was wider than a standard household door frame—call it three and a half or, max, four feet—and oval shaped, broader than it was tall.

It was unquestionably human-made.

Nature didn't make shapes like that. Which meant whatever this cave was, they were not the first people to have been down here. Just, perhaps, the first in a very long time.

The metal disc was covered in a heavy layer of dust and grit that looked like it had been accumulating for many years. Fifty? A hundred? More? It was impossible to say.

"Well, okay. Start filming if you want to start filming," Jerry said. Then he grumbled, "You kids and your cameras."

The beam from Kimberly's flashlight was soon joined by an additional light coming from her phone.

"I'm now filming," she said. Then, she recited the date, time, and place, like she was conscious of this being for posterity.

"Alright, Madam Director," Jerry said. "I'm gonna clean this thing off so we can see what it is, if that meets with your dramatic sensibilities."

"I feel like that should be Carrianne's call," Kimberly said, sounding very formal about it. "This is her expedition."

"Well?" Jerry said, turning to Carrianne.

She stared at the object. The camera had made her self-conscious to begin with, and now she felt like she was being put on the spot. What if this was a truly significant archaeological find? Should they leave it where it was? Call in the experts?

She was frozen with indecision.

"Oh, for the love of God, this isn't King Tut's tomb," Jerry said. "This is probably some rusty old piece of junk left behind by a nomad."

"How did the nomad get in?" Ciarra asked.

"How am I supposed to know?" Jerry shot back. "It's a cave. There's probably another entrance somewhere. Anyhow, let's get on with it."

Jerry tilted his water flask over the leading edge of the disc, poured a stream of liquid on it, and cleaned away the remaining dirt with a handkerchief.

Carrianne felt like she couldn't breathe as she watched him rub, revealing a highly polished yellow metal.

Then, she gasped.

It wasn't a rusty old piece of junk.

And the disc wasn't just any metal.

It was gold.

"Holy mackerel," Jerry said.

Everyone stood there gawking at it for a moment.

"Is that what I think it is?" Ciarra asked.

"Well, it's not made from melted tin cans, if that's what you're asking," Jerry said, pointing his flashlight at the spot he had cleaned off, then panning it down to where the rest of the disc disappeared into the ground. "Whatever it is, there's more of it. Here, help me dig."

Any instinct Carrianne had toward restraint was quickly replaced by the desire to know what this thing was. She joined Jerry, Jamil, and Ciarra in carefully clearing away the sand and dirt that had long encased the object.

Kimberly kept filming the whole time.

What gradually emerged was the top portion of a statue of a woman. She was smaller than life-sized, but still several feet tall. The disc was part of a helmet she wore that seemed to serve as either a mirror or a reflector.

Other than the helmet, she was nude, though her legs were rather demurely squeezed closed. In her right hand, she was cradling what appeared to be a kitten.

The entire piece was gold, or at least gold-plated. The metal alone had to be worth millions. Tens of millions, perhaps. And that didn't take into account the historic, cultural, and artistic significance of the piece.

Whatever the case, it was enormously valuable.

And ancient.

They would need someone more learned in Egyptian sculpture to estimate how old, exactly. But to Carrianne, this looked like something that could have been in a pharaoh's tomb.

"My God," Jerry said, when the entirety of the sculpture was uncovered. "Isn't that something?"

Before Carrianne even knew what he was doing, he had bent down and was trying to pick it up.

"Stop, stop!" she cried. "Don't do that!"

"Oh, come on," Jerry said, ignoring her. "I'm not going to hurt this thing. It's as solid as can be. It must weigh eighty pounds at least."

He had lifted it just a little off the ground, but then immediately set it back down—owing, apparently, to its heft.

They all stood around it in silence for a few moments. Even if they didn't understand its full significance, they knew it was something extraordinary.

Carrianne was feeling like her brain was slowly coming back online. She needed to start asserting herself again and giving them some direction. She took another glance at the time on her phone.

"I hate to say this, but we really need to be heading back up," she said. "We can't get caught outside the perimeter after dark. It's not safe."

"What are we supposed to do, just leave this thing here?" Jerry asked.

"I don't think it's going anywhere," Carrianne said. "And even if we did feel like lifting it up and carrying it with us, it's not going to fit through the opening to the cave that we squeezed through to get here. The oval part at the top is too wide."

"Fair point," Jerry conceded.

"It's been here a long time. If it's gold, it's not like we have to worry about it rusting now that it's more exposed to air. And there's nothing else down here that's going to harm it. We're leaving it here. For now. We can talk it through more once we're back at camp."

"Okay, good plan," Kimberly piped up quickly. "Let's go before we run out of daylight."

They started moving back toward the tunnel. They were almost to the mouth of it when Ciarra, who was a few steps behind Carrianne, let out an odd sound that was halfway between a gulp and a shriek.

"What's the matter?" Carrianne asked.

"Uh, look," she said, pointing her flashlight at the wall.

To Carrianne's astonishment, there were hieroglyphics carved into the rock.

"Oh my God," Carrianne said.

Everyone had stopped again. Carrianne ran her flashlight along the pictographs, feeling a sense of awe.

She had done her research. The age of the pharaohs had ended more than 2,000 years ago, when Egypt was conquered by the Roman Empire. The use of hieroglyphics went into decline until it was banned outright roughly 1,600 years ago.

Which meant this writing—just like the sculpture—was very old, indeed.

"What do you think it says?" Carrianne asked.

"I don't know, but I can find out," Ciarra said. "When I went to that museum in Aswan, I downloaded an app that translates hieroglyphics into English. Supposedly it works offline. Hang on."

She drew her phone out of her pocket, aimed its camera at the wall, and snapped a photo. She stared at the screen for a few moments while the app churned.

"It's a curse," she announced. "The Egyptians were big believers in curses—in magic of all forms, really."

"What does it say?"

"That anyone who leaves this cave will face certain death."

"Anyone who *leaves* the cave?" Carrianne asked. "Are you sure?"

Ciarra held out the phone so Carrianne could see it. "Yeah, why?"

"It's just weird. I thought Egyptian curses were about scaring people away from *entering* places—to deter tomb raiders. Why would they care about someone *leaving*?"

Ciarra just shrugged.

It was one more mystery they would not be able to solve without help.

"Well, let's keep going," Kimberly prodded. "We can come back in the morning and look around more. Maybe there's other writing nearby that will help us make sense of this."

"Right," Carrianne said.

They walked with haste up the tunnel, then took turns hoisting themselves back up through the small opening in the rocks where they had entered.

The sun was just about down as they rejoined Javier, Keith, and Mirza by the excavator. Carrianne briefed them on what had been found below.

She finished by saying, "So I know it sounds weird after we went through all the trouble to make the hole in the first place, but why don't we place a few rocks over the opening? That ought to keep the tourists away, at least until morning."

"Good plan," Javier said.

Ciarra translated for Mirza, who already seemed to get the gist.

It only took him a few minutes to strategically replace enough rocks to obscure the entrance to the cave. Carrianne wasn't kidding herself that they had rendered it impenetrable. It would certainly do for overnight.

Then, as twilight began, they hopped into their vehicles and made the short trip back up to camp. Carrianne's mind was whirring the whole time.

She had just arrived and hadn't even gotten the door to the Bronco open yet when Dave approached. She rolled down her window.

"We have a visitor," he said.

"What are you talking about?"

He just jerked his head toward a mustachioed man in an unmistakable yellow reflective jacket.

It was Inspector Mahmoud Yousef.

A.J. Sebastian's words were now rushing back at Carrianne.

They find something wrong with how you tie your shoes ...

They can cancel the license because they don't like the way you look at them ...

That mild-mannered nerd with a pocket protector can put us out of business and kick us out of the country with one stroke of his pen.

She felt her mouth going dry already.

What was Inspector Yousef doing here?

What did he want?

Was it just a coincidence that he had shown up the same evening they had discovered the cave? It had to be. Up until about two hours ago, they didn't even know what they were going to find themselves. And he had to have been traveling for longer than that to get here.

Still, how did he even know where they were? Their claim was huge. And where had he come from? They were a day's journey across treacherous desert from anywhere. She noticed his Jeep—the rickety thing that took three tries just to start—parked nearby.

Had he really come in that thing? And had he really traveled all this way just to shake them down for more bribe money? How much of an "inspection" was he about to subject them to?

There were no obvious answers. Yousef was just standing there in the middle of camp with his pocket protector perfectly in place and his hard hat on, totally ready in case a meteor should happen to fall out of the sky.

He turned as Carrianne stepped out of the Bronco. She smiled nervously back at him, held up her index finger—*one minute!*—and scrambled over to Ciarra, who was just getting out of the backseat of a different Bronco.

"Hey," Carrianne said and pointed toward their guest. "I need your help."

Ciarra didn't ask questions; she just joined Carrianne and walked up to Yousef.

"*Asalam alaykum.*" Peace be with you.

She bowed a little, even though she wasn't even sure if that was a thing in Arab culture.

"*Wa-alaykum salam,*" he replied. And upon you be peace.

"It's nice to see you again, Inspector Yousef. How can I help you this evening?"

Ciarra translated her boss's words into Arabic then listened as a stream of words in reply came from Yousef.

"This is a routine inspection," she translated. "He is just coming by to have a look. He wants to know how things are going."

"Everything is going wonderfully," Carrianne said, forcing a smile.

Yousef's next query, according to Ciarra, was, "Have you found anything of interest? Anything that makes you think this license area has promise?"

"No," Carrianne said quickly.

She wasn't sure why she had lied so readily. Maybe it was just the instinct that, for whatever they had just seen, having the Egyptian Mineral Resources Authority more involved wouldn't help matters.

Jerry, Dave, Javier and some of the others were lurking nearby, clearly eavesdropping. She hoped they heard what she was saying and would back her up if Yousef started quizzing them.

The inspector was talking again. "He wants to remind you that the Ministry is to be kept informed of all potentially significant findings. As contractual partners, we are obligated to notify them if we believe we have encountered recoverable resources."

Carrianne had no idea if that was legally true, but she said, "Yes, of course."

"He would now like to see the core samples," Ciarra declared.

The core samples?

Carrianne felt herself go rigid. They had been so distracted by the cave—and the samples were so scant and incomplete compared to what they usually had by this point—they hadn't been cataloguing and collecting them like normal.

What few samples they had produced in Quadrant 5 were still lying on the ground at the top of the mound, not far from a gaping hole in the side of the hill that Carrianne didn't particularly want to have to explain to the Inspector.

"Tell him ... tell him we've been having problems with the diamond drill"—that was true, or at least it had been at one point—"so we have no core samples from the last two days. Our driver, Ahmed, took our last truckload of samples from our previous campsite back to the warehouse in Aswan yesterday. If he wants to inspect them there, he is welcome to—as long as they haven't been loaded on the plane and sent to our lab in Alexandria. But we have nothing to show him here."

As Ciarra delivered this information, Yousef's face cast itself into a frown. He didn't like this answer. Maybe he didn't even believe it.

Yousef's tone grew noticeably sharper.

"He says he needs to be able to inspect our labeling system to ... to make sure we're maintaining standards and tracking everything properly. It is a matter of national priority that the riches of Egypt are not mishandled. Sorry, I might not be saying that right. National pride. National importance. National something. The super short version is he's pissed, and he wants to see our core samples *now*."

Carrianne felt she had no choice but to stick to her story. There was little chance he'd catch her in this lie, so she just shook her head and said, "I can't show him what we don't have."

Ciarra's translation elicited another frown from Yousef. He seemed to take a moment to decide what to do. When he finally did, it was decisive.

"*Mae alsalama*," he said tersely.

"*Mae alsalama*," Carrianne replied, but she said it to his back.

Yousef was already stalking off in the direction of his Jeep. He climbed in, cranked its sputtering engine to life, and drove off.

Where was he going with darkness fast encroaching in the middle of nowhere in a dangerous desert?

It was yet another question Carrianne couldn't answer.

Chapter Eighteen

Carrianne told the Blue Diamond employees they would have a team meeting in the main tent at eight o'clock to discuss the day's events.

Then, needing time to process everything, she kept her distance from everyone as Ihsan and Bassel finished up dinner preparations.

They served tabbouleh, which was one of the dishes that had been in a rotation with a few others. It wasn't exactly a meal Carrianne had grown up with in Greasy Creek, but she had come to look forward to tabbouleh night. Considering the tomatoes had come from cans and the onions had been in jars, it was surprisingly tasty.

Or maybe Carrianne had just been in the desert too long.

After they ate, Carrianne decided to take advantage of the camp's portable solar shower to knock off the layer of dust that felt like it was ever-present on her body.

The shower came in its own molded plastic stall that reminded her of a large porta-potty, complete with the dial lock that showed red for occupied, green for unoccupied. Inside the stall, there was a dividing curtain that separated the changing area from where the nozzle was, so you could get undressed and redressed without your clothes getting wet.

Everyone had joked about how the "locked" changing area was the height of privacy in a camp that otherwise didn't have much of it.

Still, it was nice to know she was away from everyone for just a few moments. She treated herself not only to shampoo but also conditioner during her brief spritz. Since Ahmed would be returning with a newly filled 1,600-gallon water tanker the next day, she figured there was no harm in running the shower a little longer.

When she was done, she toweled off in the changing area, ran a brush through her still-wet hair, and put it up in a ponytail. There was no need to dry it. The desert was its own blow dryer.

Then she put on clean clothes—"clean" being a somewhat debatable term. Basically, it meant these were items that had been quickly rinsed and laid flat to dry in the sun.

That was about as good as she was going to do out here.

Still, as she emerged from the stall, she felt refreshed. She returned her dirty clothes to her tent, then went to the main tent for the meeting.

Ray was lingering outside when she arrived.

"Hey," she said.

"Hey. Mind if I join the meeting?"

"Of course not. Why would I mind?"

"Well, I'm not Blue Diamond."

"I know," she said. "But you're part of the team, Ray. If you want to join us, please do."

She smiled at him quickly, then did her best to quit it. Was she flirting? She didn't mean to be flirting. She didn't want to be leading him on when she still hadn't decided what to do about him.

It didn't matter. He was already looking at her with eyes that had gone a little soft.

"You look nice," he said quietly.

"Because I actually showered?" she said, trying to make a joke out of it, even as she worried she was still being too flirty.

He laughed then said, "No. Because you always look nice. You're just beautiful."

She couldn't help smiling this time. Guys in Kentucky only said you were beautiful when they were drunk and were hoping for an easy score.

Why are you so sweet? she almost said. But she managed to stop herself.

"Well," she said instead. "Meeting's about to start. Come on."

She entered the main tent, with Ray coming in behind her. Everyone else had either already arrived or showed up in the next minute or so. It wasn't like they had anywhere else to be.

"Okay," Carrianne said loudly enough that it got everyone's attention. "I know we're all excited about what we found today. I guess I just want us to be thoughtful and deliberate and get everyone on the same page about our next steps. We have found something that is obviously very old and very valuable. What do we do next?"

Ciarra was quick to jump in. "Is that even a question? I should have said something earlier today when we were down in the cave. Egyptian law is clear that any antiquities found in the country belong to the Egyptian people. We're not supposed to move them. We're not even supposed to *touch* them. We're supposed to notify the proper authorities immediately and then let them take it from there."

Jerry let out a laugh. "Yeah, because everyone around here follows the law."

"Just because there are bandits out here doesn't mean—"

"I'm not talking about the bandits on the other side of the hill," Jerry interrupted. "I'm talking about the bandits that run the country. You are kidding yourself—absolutely kidding yourself—if you think the Egyptian government is populated by rule-following Boy Scouts. I'll bet you all the donuts at Krispy Kreme that if we forked that thing over, it would get sold to a private collector, and the proceeds would end up lining some high-ranking government official's pockets. This regime is basically a kleptocracy."

"A kleptwhat?" Javier asked.

"Kleptocracy. It means the government are basically a bunch of crooks."

"If you ask me, homie, that's every government everywhere," Javier said.

"Yeah, but it's even worse here," Jerry said. "Ahmed was telling me stories about Hosni Mubarak. He never made more than about eight hundred bucks a month as president of Egypt, but when he died, his family's wealth was something like seventy billion dollars. That's Bill Gates money, and most of it was stolen. Don't be naïve enough to think that's not still happening on every level—*every* level. The Ministry of Tourism and Antiquities is no different. It's probably worse."

"Whether that's the case or not, we still have to follow the law," Ciarra said. "Egyptians are tired of having their treasures plundered by foreigners. There's been a huge push to get items that have been taken in the past returned, and the authorities are not going to let a new find like this be swiped out from under them. You're putting every single person on this expedition at risk—nationals and foreigners alike—if you steal that sculpture. We could all be arrested."

"Were not going to be arrested, it's not stealing, and we *are* following the law," Jerry said. "Look at our exploration license. It's very clear that whatever we find here is ours, fair and square."

"Whatever *minerals* we find," Ciarra clarified.

"Gold is a mineral."

"You can't be serious."

"I absolutely am."

"That's not—"

"I realize you're not trained as a geophysicist. I am, so let me help you out," Jerry lectured. "A mineral is a naturally occurring solid with a specific chemical composition. Therefore, gold is a mineral. What we found today is the property of Blue Diamond, period, end of story."

"You can't honestly tell me that finding a sculpture is the same as finding gold in the ground."

"Sure I can. And, let me remind you, we found this gold in the ground, too. We dug all day and then we hit gold. That sounds like the very essence of greenfield exploration to me, and that's what we're doing here."

"It's art. It belongs in a museum for everyone to enjoy."

"Art covered in a mineral, which we have full rights to."

Carrianne was just watching them go back and forth.

But, of course, Jerry was not exactly offering an unbiased opinion. He owned shares in this expedition. If Blue Diamond claimed this sculpture as part of the spoils of exploration, Jerry would benefit directly.

At the same time, she knew she had to be realistic that the law as written and the law as practiced did seem to diverge widely. She needed to look no further than Inspector Yousef, who had been skulking around camp with his hand out mere hours earlier.

"Okay, okay, everyone. Just stand down for a moment," she said. "Maybe this disagreement is a sign that this is a complicated issue and we're not the ones who should be trying to settle this. Let's let the Sebastians decide—A.J. and, ultimately, Anthony. What do we think of that?"

Javier was already shaking his head. "Yeah, you might want to hold off on calling them."

"Why?"

"Because of Big Foot."

There was laughter around the tent. Carrianne looked around, bewildered by the joke she was apparently not in on.

"What are you talking about?" she asked.

"He means you need to be careful about calling corporate because their first move might be to big-foot you off the project," Jerry explained.

Carrianne hadn't even considered this possibility. "They ... they wouldn't, would they?"

"They might," Jerry said. "You're the youngest principal geologist in the whole company. I don't mean that as a knock against you.

That's just the truth. If it becomes clear to the Sebastians that there really is something major out here, they could very well decide they need someone who's a little more seasoned. Even if they let you stay on, you'd be pushed to the side. There's definitely a chance of that."

"More than a chance," Javier insisted. "A few years ago, I was on a job up in Canada, in the Northwest Territories. We were a more junior-level team, and Anthony Sebastian pulled us out of the field and replaced us with the first string so fast it made our heads spin. Why? Because we'd discovered kimberlite pipes."

Carrianne didn't need to be told that kimberlite pipes were volcanic structures known to be associated with diamonds.

"That doesn't mean the same thing will happen here," Jerry clarified. "But it might. Either way, there's probably nothing you can do about it in the long term. All I'm saying is, don't be in a rush. What corporate doesn't know won't hurt it. Tell A.J. we dug all day and you're still not sure what's down there. That's basically true, and it buys us a little more time. We're the ones who found that cave. We should at least be the ones who get to finish the initial exploration, even if Blue Diamond eventually decides to replace us."

From a quick read of the room, Carrianne could see there was agreement in all corners.

And maybe it was just self-preservation. But they had worked hard, and no one wanted to be booted off a job when they were on the verge of something huge.

She turned to Ciarra. "Is that okay with you?"

"I guess so," she said. "As long as we follow the law eventually, that's what matters."

They kicked things around a little more but soon settled on a plan. They would return to the cave in the morning, give it a solid day's exploration, *then* tell A.J. the full extent of what they had found.

Carrianne made her call to A.J. and artfully stalled him, saying she hoped to have more to share soon. He was clearly impatient for news, but he also seemed to accept that there was none to share.

When she emerged from the tent, she looked up at the sky. Whatever sliver of a moon there might have been hadn't risen yet, so she was once again treated to the spectacular sight of all those brilliant stars set against an inky backdrop.

Without any specific plan, she meandered toward the edge of camp, putting space between herself and the main tent, with its lights and chattering generator. She told herself she was just giving her eyes a chance to adjust so she could enjoy the show above her a little more.

Though, if she was being honest, she was half-hoping Ray would find her out here, away from the others.

Maybe even more than half.

She lingered for a while, her ears tuned for the sound of approaching footsteps.

But the night stayed quiet.

After a few minutes, she thought more about what she was doing and chastised herself for being ridiculous. She wasn't some tentative teenaged girl who needed to wait around for a boy to ask her to a dance.

She was a grown woman. If she wanted Ray to look at the stars with her, she should go find him and invite him.

But *did* she actually want that?

No, she decided. She did not.

Maybe someday. But not yet. Not with everything going on.

With this decided, she retreated to her tent and started getting ready for bed. She pulled the tie out of her hair so she could run a brush through it one more time before she went to sleep.

Then, she looked around.

There was no brush anywhere.

She must have left it in the shower.

With a sigh, she hoisted herself off her cot, grabbed her flashlight, and trudged across camp to the plastic stall. The dial lock was green —unoccupied—so she shoved the door open.

Then, she yelped in surprise.

Jerry was in there.

Even as he quickly turned his back to her, the image of him momentarily frozen in her flashlight beam locked in her mind.

He was mostly clothed—thank goodness—but he had the hem of his shirt raised and had been jamming a hypodermic needle into his gut.

"W-what ... what are you doing?" she stammered.

"Nothing," he said quickly, still turned away.

But that image of him wasn't going away. She knew what she had seen.

"Jerry, sorry, but I'm the principal geologist, which means I'm ... I'm responsible for your health and safety, not to mention the safety of everyone else on this expedition. So, I have to ask: Are you doing drugs?"

"What? No!" he spat. "Jesus."

"Then what are you doing with that needle?"

With an outsized sigh, he said, "It's just insulin."

He turned back toward her and showed her a clear glass bottle that was clearly labeled as such.

"You're diabetic?" she asked.

But, of course, she already knew the answer. There were loads of diabetics where she grew up.

And, really, shouldn't she already have been able to guess? Jerry was in his sixties. He was overweight. He tired easily. He drank water like a camel but always seemed to be thirsty.

"Yeah, it's no big thing," he said. "I've been dealing with it for years now. It's just something I have to monitor, that's all."

She was staring at him and his glass bottle. "Isn't insulin supposed to be refrigerated?"

"It lasts longer that way, but you can keep it at room temperature if you need to. As long as you don't do something stupid and leave it in direct sunlight, you're fine."

"Still, Jerry, diabetes is … If you had a problem, you'd be in real trouble. There aren't exactly walk-in clinics around here. There's a reason Blue Diamond made us fill out those health forms saying we were in good enough shape to be a long way from medical care. If they knew about this—"

"They'd kick me off the expedition. I'm aware," he said. "That's why I'm not telling them. Look, I need this, okay? I don't like to talk about this, but my wife is … Let's just say our retirement savings aren't where they're supposed to be, and I'm at an age where I'm running out of time to fix that. If this expedition goes well, I can set everything right. But if I get pulled off, my compensation would be …"

His voice trailed off for a moment, and then he finished with: "Look, it would just screw things up for me. Big time."

"Jerry," she said softly. "I've seen you struggling. I … I know the signs and symptoms. You're not doing well. We both know that."

"I'm fine," he insisted. "I can take care of myself. There's no danger here—not to me and certainly not to anyone else."

"Jerry, I don't know, this is—"

"Look, we have enough issues already. We don't need another one. Just forget you saw anything, okay?"

Chapter Nineteen

C arrianne didn't like keeping secrets, and now she felt like she
was lugging around two of them. And as she tried to wrestle
down sleep, she couldn't decide which was heavier.

Was she doing the right thing on either front? She knew she had
taken the path that served everyone's needs—professionally and
personally.

She still wished she could talk to someone about it.

What would Paw have said if he knew the totality of the
situation? Oh, who was she kidding? She could practically hear him
from the grave. *Stick to the truth, Carrianne. It's the easiest story to
remember.*

At one point, she thought she heard Kimberly's cot creaking. Was
she having difficulty sleeping, too? Maybe she wanted to talk?

But, no. This wasn't a slumber party. And, besides, all was quiet
in Ciarra's corner. It wouldn't be fair to her to start a conversation in
the middle of the night.

. . .

Eventually, Carrianne succumbed to fatigue. The next thing she knew, it was morning. As she got herself ready for the coming day, she felt like things were spiraling out of control.

Perhaps instinctively, she locked her hair into a tight bun, using a few extra bobby pins to keep it in place. She put on a baseball cap and tugged it low over her eyes. Then, she put on a hoodie that made her feel like she was hiding even more.

Even still, as she grabbed a quick breakfast, she felt like she couldn't make eye contact with anyone.

No one seemed to notice. Soon, she and the others were pointed back toward the mound. There were three new additions to their group.

The first was Ahmed. He had returned from his trip to Aswan the previous evening. He joined the cave group because there were very few new core samples to load. And, as he put it, "I want to see this treasure with my own eyes, Princess."

Next was Ray. He had finished his survey of Quadrant 5 the day before, so he was free to help explore. Carrianne had asked him to remove some of the sensing equipment from the drone and bring it underground with them. She wanted to be able to use it to get a better sense of what might be down there.

Lastly, there was Joseph, the young ex-Marine. Dave said that, given the value of the statue, he liked the idea of having "one more gun down there." Keith would remain with the equipment at the surface, and Joseph could join them in the cave. Just in case.

Carrianne certainly wasn't going to object. She didn't want to think about the kind of battle they'd have on their hands if the bandits realized they were so near to a work of art worth ten million dollars—or maybe more.

When they arrived at the dig site, there was no sign anything had been disturbed overnight. There weren't even tire tracks or footprints to suggest the bandits had been curious.

The treasure remained safe.

It took Mirza about twenty minutes in the excavator to uncover the hole. Then, at Javier's suggestion, they had Mirza spend a little more time removing a few extra rocks, revealing the entirety of the opening, which was even larger than Carrianne had imagined. All told, it was about five feet wide and perhaps a little taller.

She once again found herself captivated by it. How *had* this entire structure come to be? She had been thinking hard about it overnight, and the only answer she had come up with was that this had perhaps been a lava tube. It would have been very old—there hadn't been active volcanoes in Egypt for a long time—but she knew of lava tube caves in California and Hawaii.

Maybe Egypt had some, too?

After the excavator had finished its work, they picked their way down. Once in the main cavern, Carrianne had them form teams. She didn't like the idea of anyone wandering in a dark cave by themselves.

Ciarra joined Jamil, since she could communicate with him better than anyone else. They went hard left, to explore along the south wall.

Jerry and Kimberly, for as different as they were, had gotten used to working together. They went hard right, to hit the north wall.

Ahmed and Joseph, both newcomers, agreed to pair up. They took a soft right, to explore the north half of the middle.

That left Carrianne and Ray. She tried to tell herself that the teams just worked out that way, and it wasn't a big deal. They made a soft left, to take the south half of the middle.

The going was slow. It had to be. Their flashlight beams illuminated no more than a few feet in front of them, and there was no telling if there would be another tunnel somewhere. Or if the bottom of the cave would suddenly drop out beneath them. Or if they would come across unstable ground.

After maybe fifteen minutes of careful trekking, Carrianne stopped and had Ray set up the equipment.

Ray had warned his laptop battery was only going to last so long —an hour, tops, before he'd have to recharge it. As he got everything booted up, she was already thinking about whether they might be able to haul the generator down here.

The thing was a bit of a beast; it took two people to get it on and off the flatbed when they moved camp. And as wide as the opening was, they wouldn't be able to get a Bronco down here to haul it.

But it was something worth thinking about.

Maybe tomorrow.

Before long, Ray announced he was ready to start scanning.

Okay, she thought, *here goes nothing.*

Except, the moment she saw the conductivity readings, she knew it *wasn't* nothing. They were high. Abnormally high. It was possible that the rock had metals in it that made it more conductive. But another explanation was a lot more likely.

Water. There just had to be. Whether it was groundwater, or a natural spring, or something else, it was nearby—not terribly far beneath them, if she was reading things right.

Forget a lava tube. Didn't that fit with what Carrianne had been thinking all along about this cave? But then why wasn't she seeing more signs of actual water?

She was just trying to puzzle her way through it when she heard Jamil's voice calling out in the darkness. He was speaking Arabic, but Ciarra was quick to provide a translation.

"Hey, everyone," she called out. "Jamil has found another sculpture. Come check it out!"

Ray and Carrianne looked at each other for a moment, but they didn't need words. *Of course* they were going to go check it out.

Ray closed his laptop. Carrianne helped him grab the rest of the equipment.

They backtracked toward where the flashlight beams were assembling. Jamil and Ciarra were on the south side of the tunnel entrance, in a spot that Carrianne had probably walked past the previous day.

When she arrived, she figured out why. It wasn't a distinctive round dome emerging from the sand and grit this time. It was just two tiny feet. Unless your light happened to catch them just right, they just looked like two more rocky protrusions in a cave full of them.

There was already an effort underway to dig the figure out by hand, so Carrianne just hung back and took in the scene. What slowly emerged was a woman, identical to the other they had found, right down to her golden veneer.

It struck Carrianne that they were as far along the south wall as they had been along the north wall when they found the other sculpture, which suggested at one point they had been placed there deliberately—equidistant from the mouth of the tunnel, on either side.

Were the women meant to be guardians of some sort?

Was this a tomb? Egyptians were certainly keen on those. Except they also believed in burying their dead with all the possessions they needed in the afterlife. If this was a tomb, where was everything else? Had it all been pillaged? That hardly made sense. Why would looters leave behind such valuable pieces? Unless they had also missed the sculptures in the dark?

Kimberly had once again taken to documenting the find with photos and videos. Maybe someday they would have more answers.

After they had finished revealing the second statue, they dispersed back out into the cave.

Over the next few hours, there were continued shouts of discovery. Jerry found what appeared to be old potshards. Then, Jamil discovered more in another spot. Ciarra identified what might have been clothing—a bit of woven cloth that appeared to be wool. Joseph came across what looked to be a stone mallet head whose handle had perhaps rotted away centuries ago.

It all suggested this cave had been inhabited at one point. But by whom? And how long ago? Was it the same people who had carved the hieroglyphic warning?

Or someone else entirely?

When noontime came, they were no closer to having answers.

Ordinarily, they would work until about two o'clock then call it a day. But since the temperature was not an issue belowground—and no one seemed to want to quit for the day—Carrianne called everyone to the surface for a lunch break instead.

This was when she first heard about a new tunnel, located at what appeared to be the other end of the main cavern.

Ahmed and Joseph had just started to explore it when she called them back. They reported that, at least initially, it sloped downward. But they said they had only traveled down it about ten or twenty feet, so, for all they knew, it would dead end soon.

Still, there was excitement about this new perhaps-passageway. At least in some parts of the team.

Joseph was eager to explore more. Jamil and Ciarra wanted to check it out, too, as did Kimberly.

Ahmed, on the other hand, seemed to be spooked by the whole idea of further underground exploration. He made noises about having a stomachache and needing to retire to his tent for the afternoon.

But Carrianne felt like he was just trying to cover up the real story: he was scared. Something he had seen underground seemed to have him spooked.

It couldn't have been the hieroglyphic curse. He wasn't the superstitious sort.

So, what was it?

Jerry also made it clear he wasn't feeling particularly adventurous toward deeper exploration. Carrianne let it pass without comment, but she was sure he simply didn't want to stray too far from the surface in the event that his blood sugar spiked and he needed more insulin.

Ray was harder to read. Or maybe he was a lot easier. He just seemed to want to go wherever Carrianne went.

With all those factors swirling in her head, Carrianne announced she was reformulating the teams for the afternoon. She was putting Kimberly in charge of a group that would include Ciarra, Jamil, and Joseph, who were tasked with exploring the new tunnel.

Jerry, Ray, and Carrianne would remain in the main cavern and see if they could pinpoint where any water might be.

Ahmed was heading back to camp.

Javier, Keith, and Mirza would remain with the equipment up top.

Carrianne's last instruction to Kimberly was to keep track of time and be back to the main cave no later than five o'clock. Carrianne didn't want any close calls with staying underground too long, especially when they had no way of communicating. The walkie-talkie signals needed a clear line of sight and couldn't penetrate solid rock.

Kimberly readily agreed. Since they were leaving around one o'clock, that would give them two hours to explore the tunnel, then two hours to backtrack to the surface.

As Ray slipped back to camp to get his laptop recharged, Carrianne and Jerry talked water-finding strategy. His geophysics background was a plus and, of course, he had relevant experience. He had once worked on a hydrology study of a mine in British Columbia.

Once Ray returned, they got to work.

The short version of their findings was that there continued to be water, water everywhere—at least in the readings they got from various portions of the cave—but not a drop to see.

As Ray's battery blinked out once again, Carrianne checked the time. It was five o'clock exactly.

Kimberly and the others had yet to resurface.

Carrianne tried to be optimistic and believe there was no reason to worry. They were responsible professionals who understood the need to be punctual. Maybe it just took them a little longer to get back than they thought.

Then five-fifteen came and went.

And five-thirty.

By this point, Carrianne was feeling a growing sense of foreboding. Something bad must have happened down there. She hoped it was something relatively harmless—someone had sprained an ankle, and it was taking them longer to hobble back up. Or something had happened to their flashlights, and they were groping along in the dark, moving much more slowly than anticipated.

But maybe it was much worse.

They had gotten lost and couldn't find their way back up top. Or someone had suffered a more severe injury. Or there had been a cave-in that had trapped them underground. Or—the ultimate nightmare —the tunnel had collapsed on top of them.

These were among the scenarios being discussed once Carrianne, Jerry, and Ray returned to the surface, where Dave had joined Javier, Mirza, and Keith.

But there was also another problem—one that was even more immediate than their missing team members. They were running out of time to close the hole for the night. Having made the hole larger than it had been the day before, Mirza needed at least an hour to move the rocks back.

They could hardly start that work while there were still four people underground. Sealing them in a cave overnight with no food, no water, and no decent place to sleep seemed cruel, if not unsafe. What if one of them really did need medical assistance? What if they couldn't get the tunnel back open again for some reason?

Yet they also didn't want to leave the cave wide open and allow the bandits to waltz in and steal the gold ladies overnight.

It felt like they were faced with nothing but wrong decisions.

"There is another solution, you know," Jerry said.

"What's that?" Carrianne asked.

"We bring the statues back to camp. That way, we know for sure they'll be safe for the night, and we can still leave the tunnel open for when our four last lambs decide to rejoin us."

This, Carrianne realized, was probably step one in Jerry's long-term plan, which was to have Blue Diamond claim the artwork as its own.

"But ... but Ciarra said we're not even supposed to touch those things. It's the law."

"I assure you the bandits wouldn't show similar concern for the rules and regulations regarding Egyptian antiquities."

"Fair point."

She still didn't like the idea. But, at least for the short term, it seemed like the best option.

Or maybe the only option.

"Okay," Carrianne said. "Let's do it."

It took fifteen minutes to locate the statues and another thirty minutes to wrap them in protective tarps, bring them to the surface, load them into the Broncos, and get them safely to camp. At eighty pounds each, handling them was a two-person job, and they had to exercise the utmost caution. No one wanted to be the person to drop a ten-million-dollar piece of art.

All the while, Carrianne kept her ears out for sounds of Kimberly and the others returning.

The cave remained utterly silent.

After they had moved the heavy equipment back to camp, Dave remained with Carrianne at the entrance to the tunnel to keep vigil. As the shadows around them grew ever longer, she felt increasingly hopeless.

At 6:33, the sun sank below the seemingly endless flatness of the desert to the west, and twilight began setting in.

Every so often, they went back underground and called for their missing team members.

They received no answer.

With increasing dread, they watched as the last long rays of a pink and red sunset bounced off Coffin Hill to the east. Darkness was coming on hard. There was still no sign of their missing comrades.

"We really have to get back to camp now," Dave said softly. "It's not safe outside the perimeter at night. We're too vulnerable out here."

"Fifteen more minutes," Carrianne said. "I *know* Kimberly will be here."

Dave just shook his head. "Having you and me get ambushed because we're down here waiting for them isn't going to help anyone," he said. "It's time. I'm sorry."

Chapter Twenty

T he headlights of the Bronco were still searching for the Quadrant 5 campsite when Carrianne felt the first pangs of a throbbing headache.

She might have told herself it was just dehydration—that she hadn't remembered to drink enough while she was out of the sun, but she knew better. It was the stress—a giant, unseen hand reaching out from the depths of her worst worries and crushing her skull.

"I hate that we're abandoning them," she said.

"They'll understand," Dave said. "They'd do the same if the circumstances were reversed. You have to put on your own air mask before you help other passengers."

"Yeah, except why do I feel like we're actually pushing them out of the airplane?"

Dave regripped the steering wheel as they bounced over a rock. "Our best hope is still that whatever trouble they're in, they'll work their own way out. They're professionals. Joseph has been trained not to lose his cool. Kimberly and Ciarra strike me as being levelheaded. And I'm sure Jamil can handle himself, too. We have to trust that they'll be resourceful."

"That hardly sounds like a plan."

"I'm not saying it is. Let's get back to camp and get our bearings a little and then we can start talking about what our search-and-rescue operation will look like. We'll come up with a real plan tonight and then return to the cave at first light tomorrow."

"And, in the meantime, they have ... how much water? I mean, I know they took some, but not enough. And I don't think they have any food."

"They won't starve to death."

"I know. I just ... I never should have let them separate from us without some way of communicating with them. It was irresponsible and reckless of me."

"It didn't seem like a terrible idea at the time. It only looks that way now because of how things turned out. That probably describes 99.9 percent of the decisions you'll make in life. This just happens to be the point one percent. Don't beat yourself up too much."

"I can assure you it's too late for that," she said.

They finished the rest of the ride in silence. Once they'd made it back to camp, Carrianne went straight to the main tent. She glanced at the statues in the corner—even though their presence made her nervous, they really were quite magnificent—and then pulled the satellite phone out of its holder.

She dialed A.J.'s number.

He answered enthusiastically. "Hey, I've been hoping I'd hear from you. What's the latest?"

"There's some good and there's some really, really bad," she began.

She unspooled both parts with what she hoped was sufficient detail without belaboring anything. A.J. took in the part about the sculptures without much comment.

Then, she moved onto the part about how four team members— two Blue Diamond employees, one mercenary, and one local contractor—were missing and perhaps in danger. When she was done, he was not as upset as she thought he would be—or should be.

"It's okay. People get lost underground sometimes. It happens," he said. "I'm sure they're fine. They're just not where they're supposed to be. That's not the end of the world."

"We're still planning to go in after them first thing tomorrow."

"Good. And they might just surprise you and come back tonight. But, in the meantime, I've been thinking you guys need some reinforcements, and this settles it. I'm going to get you more soldiers so you don't have to worry about those bandits quite so much and some better equipment for exploring underground. The mission has changed, and we need to respond accordingly. I'll run it by Dad, but I'm sure he'll agree. ETS has an emergency response team that promises it can mobilize in any of the countries where it operates within twenty-four hours. Can you make do between now and then?"

"Of course," she assured him.

"Okay. You're doing a great job out there. The key is not to panic."

That, Carrianne thought as they ended the call, was easier said than done.

And it became immeasurably harder when Dave burst into the tent a few minutes later, breathing heavily. With an edge to his voice, he announced, "Hey, we've got a situation."

"What?" she asked.

"It's the bandits. There are more of them out there. A lot more."

"What makes you think that?"

"Come and have a listen."

He led her out away from the noise of the generator to where a group of others had already gathered. Their faces were pressed with concern.

It didn't take more than a few seconds before she understood why. From the other side of Coffin Hill, she could make out the sound of engine noises—revving, idling, driving around.

She couldn't count how many, but it was more than the five trucks she knew about already. A lot more. It almost reminded her of a Friday night at the Pike County Speedway, where all the motorheads came to race muscle cars in circles around the dirt track.

"That's not good," she said.

"Yeah. I don't like it one bit."

"What should we do?"

"I'm not sure. Sometimes, the only thing worse than being able to see bandits is not being able to see them."

"Well, Ray can fix that for us," she pointed out.

They quickly found Ray in his tent. He was trying to comfort Digger, who was nervous about the sound of all the car engines.

"We need the drone to do some reconnaissance for us," Carrianne said. "How soon can you get it up in the air?"

"About as long as it takes you to ask the question," Ray said. "She's gassed up and ready to go right now."

Three humans and one dog returned to the main tent. They congregated around Ray's laptop.

While he had removed some of the sensing equipment for use underground, the camera was still attached and already set to infrared. As the drone buzzed its way to liftoff just outside the tent, the laptop screen showed the world beneath it in a greenish hue.

They could even see the outlines of their own body heat showing through the tent.

Ray brought the drone up to an altitude of maybe a hundred feet, hovered there for a moment, then gently pushed the throttle forward. The campsite disappeared from view, replaced by the darkness of the empty desert as the drone flew up the gentle slope of Coffin Hill.

The moment it passed over the top, two things happened in short order.

The first was that the bandit camp came into view. Carrianne felt her stomach drop when she saw its size and shape. It was massive. And sprawling. There had to be at least fifty vehicles. Their warm metal frames were easy to make out against the backdrop of the rapidly cooling desert sand.

So were the bodies swarming all over the area. There were

probably a hundred of those—some still in the cabs of their vehicles, others in their flatbeds, others just milling nearby.

Carrianne had not even managed to get the words of shock and alarm out of her mouth when the second thing happened.

The unmistakable sound of gunfire rang out.

"They're shooting at me!" Ray yelped.

He reacted immediately, sending the drone into a steep dive away from the bandits and jamming down the throttle simultaneously.

The laptop screen showed a chaotic scene as the angle of the camera and the speed at which the drone was traveling instantly went haywire.

"Are you hit?" Carrianne asked.

"I don't know," he said, his voice cracking slightly from the nerves. "I don't think so. If they did hit something, it wasn't any of the propellers or the ailerons. It's still responding to me just fine."

"Yeah, you do realize we have a much bigger problem than whether your boyfriend's toy is broken, right?" Dave said, with quiet urgency in his voice. "I know what a force looks like when it's massing for an attack, and it's exactly what you just saw on that screen."

Carrianne just stared at him for a moment, still unable to process all that was happening. "Alright, so what do we do?"

"It's three versus a hundred," he said. "There's no way we can hold off that many combatants. Especially if they spread out and come down from the top of the hill at the same time. That's how I'd do it if I were them. The SAWs might be able to pick off a few of them, but the rest would be on us in no time. We wouldn't be able to get all of them. We'd be overrun."

"What are you saying?" she asked.

"We have to evacuate. Immediately."

The word didn't even make sense to Carrianne at first.

"Evacuate," she repeated. "How?"

"We get in the Broncos and go. Now."

"But what about all our stuff?"

"We leave it."

"Even the diamond drill?"

"Especially the diamond drill," Dave said. "That thing couldn't outrun a frisky poodle, much less a pack of rabid bandits."

"But—"

"I'm sorry, we don't have a choice," he said sharply. "Everything stays behind. The drill. The excavator. The trailers. The tankers. All of it. We can take the statues. They'll fit in the back of a Bronco. But that's it. Those are our most valuable possessions now, anyway."

Carrianne just stood there with her mouth hanging open.

"I think I should call A.J. and—"

"*There's no time.* Look, I know this is going to cost Blue Diamond a pretty penny, but they knew the risks coming out here. Sometimes you just have to write things off as a loss. Maybe they have insurance, maybe they don't. Frankly, I don't really care. Anthony Sebastian can handle it. Right now, I'm not worried about the equipment. I'm worried about the human beings. This isn't a choice anymore. The choice has been made for us. We *have* to go."

Dave was already on the move, striding over to the corner. He lifted one of the statues and tucked it under his arm. Its weight was clearly manageable for a man of his strength.

"But what about Kimberly and the rest of them?" Carrianne asked.

"Wherever they are, it's probably safer than here," Dave said. "We'll just have to worry about them later."

"So, you're just ... you're just leaving?"

On his way back across the tent, he stopped when his face was a foot away from hers. "Yes. And you are, too. I can't stick around to defend the indefensible. Every second we waste right now increases the chance we all get slaughtered when they decide to come over the hill after us. If you don't get on the walkie-talkie and make the call, I will."

He didn't wait for her response; he just left the tent. Once outside, he shouted orders at Keith and Joshua to grab the SAWs and the ammunition box. Then he came back for the other statue.

Still in disbelief, Carrianne clicked on the walkie-talkie and made the announcement.

"Everyone, this is Carrianne," she said, trying to keep her voice calm. "There is a huge force of bandits just on the other side of the hill. Dave says there's no way he can hold them off if they decide to attack. We have to go. Now. Drop whatever you're doing and get yourself to a Bronco. We're leaving in two minutes."

As soon as she clicked off, Ahmed came on the air and repeated the instructions in Arabic.

Carrianne lowered her walkie-talkie and turned to Ray. "That means you, too," she said.

"I can't just let them have the drone," Ray said.

"Yes, you can. It's too late to save it now, anyway. It won't fit into a Bronco with the propellers still on. You'd have to disassemble it, and there's no time for that now. Just set it down wherever it is. Maybe we'll get lucky and they won't find it out in the desert and we'll be able to recover it if we're able to come back."

He didn't respond. All his attention was still on the drone controller.

"Ray," she said softly and put a hand on his shoulder.

The physical contact seemed to break whatever spell he was under.

"I know," he said. "Hang on."

It took him just a few more seconds to set the drone down on a patch of sloped desert.

"Let's get out of here," he said, then turned to Digger. "Come on, girl."

Carrianne grabbed the satellite phone on her way out so she could let A.J. know that they had to abandon camp and he should send help—if in fact, the help had a prayer of reaching them in time.

Outside the main tent, there was predictable pandemonium and a lot of shouting in two languages. But Carrianne was relieved to see everyone was moving in the direction of the Broncos, which is where she and Ray were now dashing to.

As she ran, she risked a glance up toward Coffin Hill. Its dark outline was no longer the smooth, unbroken line it had been. There were now jagged shapes at the top of it.

She had to suppress the urge to sob when she saw them. There would soon be trucks pouring down that easy access ramp of a hill and into camp.

Dave was right. They really had no choice but to run.

"They're coming," she shouted, swallowing the lump in her throat. "Okay, everyone in a Bronco. Go, go, go!"

She paused as she reached the rear door of one of the vehicles.

"Do we have everyone?" she shouted.

No one seemed to have even heard her. But when she looked around, she saw Ahmed, the two cooks, and the two laborers already in one Bronco. The three soldiers were in the one she was standing next to. Opposite the side she was on, Joshua had the window down with the barrel of his SAW sticking out and trained up at the hill.

Javier was the last person piling into a Bronco that already contained Jerry and Mirza.

Ray was at her side, as was Digger.

That made twelve humans and one dog. Plus her. Thirteen humans. There were seventeen in their party, total, but four of them were somewhere down in the cave.

"Okay, let's roll," she shouted as she dove into the soldiers' Bronco, with Ray and Digger just behind her.

As soon as Ray slammed the door, Dave jammed down the accelerator. They shot forward, leaving a cloud of dust behind them.

On both sides, the other Broncos were doing the same thing.

Carrianne's first focus was to get her seatbelt on. Then she pulled out the satellite phone and sent A.J. a text.

SOS. Bandits are attacking in overwhelming numbers. We are fleeing camp in Broncos. All personnel accounted for minus four in cave. All equipment likely lost. send help.

There was more to be said, but she didn't even know where to start. She just hit send.

Joshua still had the window down.

"They're coming," he yelled over the sound of inrushing air. "I can see them on the hill. Some of them have their dang headlights on, the arrogant pricks."

"Fire off some shots," Dave said.

"Boss, there's no way I'm going to hit them. They're too far away."

"It doesn't matter. I just don't want them to think they're getting into camp without any resistance whatsoever."

"Okay," Joshua said. "Fire in the hole."

He squeezed the trigger. Carrianne immediately put her fingers to her ears. The noise was still astounding. She had grown up around hunters and had been near guns all her life. None of them compared to an M-249 SAW set in automatic fire mode.

Joshua held down the trigger for five seconds, relaxed for a moment, then squeezed off another burst, eliciting a loud howl from Digger.

He only stopped a second time because the Bronco was bucking wildly over a patch of rough ground. In the back, the unsecured statues lifted in the air and came down with a heavy thud. If Carrianne hadn't been buckled in, she was sure her head would have hit the ceiling.

Dave was doing at least forty, which might not have felt all that fast on a paved highway. On uneven desert, it was murderous.

Still, they were putting ground between them and the campsite. At the moment, that's all that mattered.

They were already half a mile away. There was more gunfire, though it wasn't coming from Joshua. It was coming from somewhere behind them.

The bandits were returning fire.

Carrianne turned back and squinted in the distance. It was easy to see what was happening in camp because they had left the generator running and the lights on. Some of the bandit vehicles were already swarming around the tents.

But not all of them.

Some had passed straight through camp and were continuing their pursuit. In all the confusion, it was difficult to count how many. But even at a quick glance, Carrianne could make out at least twenty or thirty shapes silhouetted against the lights of camp.

"They're not stopping at the camp," she shrieked. "They're still coming!"

"What the hell?" Dave said. "They've got our stuff! The stuff is what they want! What do they want us for?" He swore explosively.

"I don't know, but they're still coming," Carrianne said.

He swore again, then clicked on the walkie-talkie.

"Everyone, head for the cave," he announced. "We're going to hole up in there."

"The cave?" Carrianne said. "Shouldn't we just try to outrun them?"

"That won't work," Dave said definitively. "It's too wide open out here. Someone is going to bust an axle or blow a tire or overturn. We've got no chance out in the open. The cave is the only piece of real estate within fifty miles that's remotely defensible given how outnumbered we are."

"But won't we be trapped in there?"

"Yep," he said. "So, you'd better hope they get tired before we run out of ammo."

Chapter Twenty-One

Carrianne turned around and focused on what was coming ahead.

What was behind them was just too frightening.

They were closing in fast on the mound that contained the cave. Dave had already pointed the Bronco in that direction, and the other Broncos had adjusted course as well.

Dave clicked on the walkie-talkie and announced, "Okay, everyone. Once we stop, we've got about a minute to get into that cave before they'll be on us. Don't waste it."

He clicked off then continued. "Josh and Keith, you guys grab the ammo box. I'm getting one of the statues. Carrianne, can you and Ray grab the other?"

"Why are we even bothering with them?"

"Because those statues might be our only bargaining chip. I have no idea why those bandits are after us, but I've got to think they'll value gold statues more than they value anything else we have to offer."

Carrianne glanced at Ray, who just nodded. There was no sense in arguing further.

As soon as they had skidded to a halt, Ray opened the door. With a yelp, Digger bolted out of the car like someone had shocked her with a cattle prod.

"Digger!" Carrianne shouted.

The dog was already sprinting blindly off into the darkness. Carrianne climbed out of the Bronco to give chase, but Ray grabbed her arm.

"Let her go," he said. "She's probably better off without us at this point."

"She doesn't even know where she is. She'll die in the desert without us."

"She'll survive," Ray said.

And we might not, she thought.

"Fine. Let's just get the sculpture."

They each grabbed one end of the piece from the back of the Bronco and scaled down the rocks with it. Carrianne was in the lead, with Ray following behind. All around them, the others were also scurrying downward toward the cave.

She could hear the sound of engines running hot in the distance. The bandits were bearing down on them.

There was more gunfire. Carrianne reflexively ducked. She couldn't tell where the bullets were landing or if the bandits were just firing wildly into the night.

Then she heard a pop and a loud hiss coming from one of the Broncos' tires.

Were the bandits deliberately aiming for the tires, to disable the vehicle and cut off any chance it could be used for escape? Or was it just a lucky shot? There was no telling. Carrianne concentrated on navigating each rock at her feet by the light of the stars overhead.

One of the bandits fired again. The bullets slammed into some of the boulders above them, creating a rain of fine rock shards. Carrianne flinched again, awaiting a rain of shrapnel.

It never came. Though, from above her, Ray cried out.

She stopped.

"I'm fine," he said. "Just slipped a little. Keep going."

She scarcely needed the encouragement.

A few steps later, she felt welcome relief as the walls of the tunnel closed around her, though she kept her legs churning as they continued down the slope.

She had one hand on the statue and the other on the rock wall beside her. It was her best means of navigating the darkness—that, and her own heavy breathing, which was bouncing off the walls and telling her where they were.

As they reached the end of the tunnel, she saw a light. Someone inside the main cavern had a flashlight and was shining it on the floor of the cave. It was almost like a lighthouse, welcoming them to harbor.

"Let's put this thing down," Ray said once they were through the tunnel. "Against the wall over here should work fine." He was breathing heavily, too.

Without a word, Carrianne pivoted to her left. After a few more steps, they set the statue down.

She then turned to face the rest of the group—or what she hoped was the rest of the group. "Do we have everyone?" she asked.

She reached into her pocket, pulled out her phone, and turned on its flashlight. She wished she had grabbed a real flashlight in addition to the satellite phone. Or maybe even instead of the satellite phone. The thing was basically useless down here.

"I think so," Dave said. "We should probably count off, just in case. Keith, start us off."

"One," came Keith's voice in the darkness.

That was soon followed by a two, a three, and so on. Ahmed counted on behalf of several of the Egyptians.

They soon reached twelve. Carrianne said, "Okay. And I'm lucky thirteen. We're all here. Good work, everyone."

She said it with little cheer.

They were a long, long way from being out of trouble.

Outside, more bandits were congregating. There were a lot of people shouting in Arabic, and engine noises, and brakes screeching.

One of the bandits fired down into the mouth of the tunnel. The bullet didn't reach the main cavern, but its ricochet created another spray of rock.

"They're having a little too much fun up there," Dave said. "Go up close to the mouth of the tunnel and lay down some cover fire. Not too close. If you hit one of them, great. If not, fine. I just want them to back off a little and understand that while we may be cornered, we still have plenty of fight in us."

Carrianne couldn't tell who he was talking to, but her flashlight illuminated Joshua as he disappeared back into the tunnel with his SAW already raised.

A few moments later, the gun roared to life. Its report was deep and resonant. She could feel the reverberations in her chest and wondered if it frightened the bandits as much as it did her.

Everything went silent for a moment. Then, Joshua released another burst.

"Okay, that's good," Dave called up the tunnel. "They get the point. There's no need to waste ammo. Can you tell if it worked?"

"No casualties," Joshua answered. "Though I think one or two of them may have fresh stains in their underwear."

"Good. Can you hang there for a little while? If anyone tries to come down the tunnel, waste 'em."

"Roger that."

"You want me to go up and help?" Keith asked.

"No. That was the whole point of the cave," Dave said. "With an opening that narrow, it only takes one man to hold the position. It would be suicide for any of them to try and come down."

"Just like it would be suicide for us to try to go out," Jerry said.

"Yeah, that's about the size of it," Dave said. "It's a good ol'-fashioned standoff."

What breaks it? Carrianne wondered. She didn't say anything, though. She was just glad to still be alive.

One of the bandits shot into the tunnel again. Compared to the low growl of the SAW, it sounded like a popcorn maker.

Though she had no doubt it would still sting.

"You want me to shoot back?" Joshua asked.

"Nah," Dave said. "We can let them have the last word."

"That's if they're done."

"We'll find out soon enough. But I think that'll be it for a little while."

Carrianne was starting to think Dave had a sixth sense for combat because things at the top of the cave went quiet.

She turned off her flashlight, mindful of the need to preserve the battery. Others did the same, until they were down to just one.

Carrianne's breathing was finally returning to normal.

Then, from outside, there was an odd squelching noise. It sounded like microphone feedback.

It was followed by a voice in accented but clearly enunciated English, speaking through a megaphone. "Attention in the cave. Attention in the cave. We have you trapped. We just want the statues. We will permit you to bring the statues to the surface. Bring them to the surface, and we'll take the statues and go."

Dave swore.

"How the hell do they know about the statues?" Jerry whispered, echoing the thought that was just starting to form in Carrianne's head.

"Because," —Dave hissed—"we have a rat."

Carrianne was almost too shocked by the implications of the accusation as Dave continued.

"Those statues were wrapped in tarps when we brought them out of the cave, and they were wrapped in tarps when we hauled them into camp. There's no way, *no way*, anyone could have guessed what we were carrying. It's why they weren't just satisfied taking our equipment. They knew there was a much, much bigger score to be had. And the only way they could have known that is if one of our people was communicating with them.

"So, really, there's only one question," he finished. "Which one of you hajis sold us out?"

Dave had switched on his flashlight and was shining its beam on the face of one Egyptian after the other.

"Dave, you don't … you don't know that for sure," Carrianne said.

"I sure as hell do. I did three tours in the Middle East and if I learned nothing else during that time, it's that you can't trust a goddamned haji. If they think they can make a nickel off screwing you over, they'll do it every time."

Carrianne didn't want to believe it. But she also knew it was entirely possible Dave was right.

"Would you hold this, please?" he said to Keith, handing him the flashlight. "Keep our rats in the light. I need my hands."

Keith accepted the light and began swinging its beam from the cooks, Ihsan and Bassel, to the laborers, Tariq and Hani, then to Mirza and Ahmed.

All six men looked terrified.

"Alright, take your stuff, put it at your feet, then line up against the wall where I can see you," Dave commanded. "You better keep your hands where I can see them. And spread out a little."

Then he brought up the barrel of his SAW so it was at chest height. "You're not moving fast enough. *Now*, goddammit. And you better shut the hell up about it. I know enough Arabic to understand what you're saying, so keep your damn mouths shut."

As if to prove it, he started speaking in Arabic. Whatever he was saying spurred the remaining stragglers to action. They were all now lined up against the wall of the cave with their hands held over their heads.

Those who had managed to grab some personal belongings during their escape from camp dropped their bags at their feet.

"Okay, Keith, give me the flashlight."

He complied.

"Excellent. Now, search them. Search their bodies. Search their stuff. Let's see what's going on here."

Dave turned to the Egyptians and said, "If any of you move, I'm going to shoot first and ask questions later."

He repeated himself in Arabic then stood still as Keith began patting down Bassel.

Carrianne was still hoping that Dave was completely off base. She had spent weeks in the desert with these men, developing a bond that felt like something more than just professional courtesy.

She had smiled at them over breakfast, labored through the heat of day with them, laughed along during their frantic card games in the tent, washed dishes with them at night. She had lived in community with them.

They had been nothing but kind and gracious and hospitable.

They weren't just colleagues. They were friends.

Weren't they?

She just couldn't believe one of them would have betrayed the rest of the group so completely.

Keith had moved on to Mirza, running his hands over the man's round belly.

Mirza was grumbling something in Arabic, prompting Dave to shift the SAW barrel up toward his head and snarl a warning.

Whatever was said, Mirza stopped talking. But it did nothing to wipe the glare off his face.

Keith moved onto Ahmed next. He was dressed in Western clothing—skinny jeans and a polo shirt—that couldn't have concealed much.

Then, Keith moved down to the bag at Ahmed's feet. It was a largeish messenger-style pouch with a sling for over-the-shoulder carrying. Keith lifted the flap and began a diligent search, which soon yielded a black plastic object that he brought out and studied for a moment.

Only when the flashlight beam struck it did Carrianne realize what it was.

A walkie-talkie. It was not dissimilar to the kind she had been using to communicate with her team in the desert, though it was slightly different from the one that had been issued to Ahmed by Blue Diamond.

Keith walked over and handed the device to Dave.

Without a word—and without taking his gun sights off Ahmed—Dave walked closer to the mouth of the tunnel. As soon as he clicked on the button, he cut into the middle of what sounded like two men talking in Arabic.

Carrianne felt her insides go cold. A two-way radio like that had a relatively short range. A mile or two.

The only people it could have picked up were the bandits.

Ahmed had been using it to communicate with them. He had probably been doing it since the start of the trip. That's how the bandits always knew where they were and where they were going.

Carrianne thought back a few hours. Ahmed had complained of a stomachache and gone back to camp, where he must have radioed his friends just on the other side of the hill about the statues.

That's why their numbers had increased so suddenly. Ahmed had put out the word that there was a major, major bounty to be claimed. In the chaos of fleeing camp, he had somehow found time to radio that they had taken the statues back with them into the cave, which is why the bandits knew they needed to give chase.

It all made sense.

Ahmed was the rat.

Ahmed, who knew the ways of the desert.

Ahmed, who had family living nearby. And friends. Lots and lots of friends, who came for the promise of profit.

Ahmed, who had been making a hundred bucks a week as a taxi driver and who recognized that, even if they had to split the proceeds a hundred ways, selling those statues would have added up to a life-changing fortune.

Carrianne stared at him hard. "Ahmed," she said acidly. "How could you?"

"Princess, surely you don't—"

"Shut it, Ahmed," Carrianne snapped. "I'm not your princess."

She turned to Dave. "Okay, what now?"

"Oh, it's pretty simple, really," Dave said. "I'm going to kill him."

Chapter Twenty-Two

D ave regripped the SAW and grimly announced, "Stand back, everyone."

Ahmed sank to his knees.

"Wait, no, please. I ... I have a wife ... I have a mother. I have—"

"Shut up," Dave roared. "Everyone here has spouses and parents and people who love them. You've put every single one of us in danger. You should have thought of that before you stabbed us all in the back."

Ahmed was crying. He began blubbering something in Arabic. Carrianne thought she recognized a prayer.

The other Egyptians were just looking at him.

It was telling that none of them were even trying to come to his rescue. Were they afraid it would be assumed that they had been conspiring along with Ahmed?

No.

It was that they had been betrayed by him, too.

As she watched Ahmed beg for his life, she felt little sympathy for him. Motivated by nothing more than greed, he had brought this scourge upon them.

He deserved his fate.

"An eye for an eye," Dave said. "That's how justice works around here."

But then, as he raised the barrel of the SAW and brought his finger toward the trigger, Carrianne heard Paw's voice in her head: *There's gonna come a time in your life when you have to decide whether you're the type of person who does the right thing. If you make the decision now, it'll be easier to stick to it later.*

Was she really going to stand by and let this happen? For as satisfying as that might have been, it was still vigilante justice. Even if she wasn't the one pulling the trigger, this was still her expedition.

If she didn't do anything to stop Dave, she would be just as culpable in Ahmed's death as Dave was. And killing Ahmed wasn't right.

She walked over and placed her hand gently on the barrel of his rifle, pushing it down slightly.

"Wait," she said softly. "Don't."

"Why not?"

"I don't know. But we can't just shoot him."

"Yeah, well we can't exactly leave him alive, either," Dave snarled. "We have enough to deal with holding off that mob outside without having to worry about him stabbing us in the back down here."

"Okay, fine. Let him go."

"Are you kidding me? He can tell them about our weaponry, about our numbers, about—"

"He already has," Carrianne said. "He's been telling them everything about us for weeks now. The damage is done."

From one glance at Ahmed, she knew it was true. He looked unmistakably guilty.

"Killing him won't solve anything," she continued. "And it may even make things worse. Let's say the bandits get tired of keeping us down here and decide that stealing the diamond drill and the rest of our stuff is enough of a payoff for them. How are you going to explain this?"

"It was self-defense," Dave said.

"No court would agree. You have to know that."

Dave just swore.

"Fine," he said then turned toward Ahmed.

In one quick, brutal movement, Dave twirled the SAW around and brought the barrel down on Ahmed's head.

He was able to at least partially shield himself from the blow with his arms, but he still yelped in pain.

Keith kicked him once in the gut, eliciting another yell.

Carrianne braced herself for more, but they seemed to have made their point.

"Get out of here," Dave snarled.

Ahmed looked up at Dave, then at Carrianne, then back at Dave.

"Go, rat!" Dave shouted at him. "Hurry, before I change my mind."

Ahmed didn't wait another moment. He gathered his legs underneath him and lunged toward the tunnel.

"Yo, Thing One, there's a rat coming your way," Dave called. "Don't worry. He's not armed. Just let him scurry out of his hole like rats do."

"You got it," Joshua called.

Carrianne heard Ahmed's footfalls growing distant as he scuffled his way up the tunnel in the darkness.

For a moment, there was only silence.

Then, it was broken by an eruption of gunfire.

It wasn't just one person shooting. It was five, ten, fifteen guns going off, all at once. The noise was deafening, and it reverberated down into the cave, where the hard walls only amplified it.

Mixed into the racket was Joshua yelling, though it was impossible to know what he was saying.

The gunfire continued for perhaps fifteen seconds, then stopped as abruptly as it had begun.

"Josh, can I get a report?" Dave asked.

"Uh, yeah, they, uh ... they shot him," Joshua said, sounding shaken. "The moment his head peeked out of the tunnel, they just ... they mowed his ass down."

"Is he dead?"

"Yeah," Joshua reported. "Like, really, really dead."

"Why would they shoot their own man?" Jerry asked.

"Because that's who we're dealing with out there, people who shoot first and ask questions later," Dave said. "They don't care who they kill, even if it's one of their own."

For a moment, no one spoke.

Then Jerry laughed.

"What could possibly be funny?" Carrianne asked.

"Ahmed was the one who *didn't* believe in The Curse of Dust."

The shock of Ahmed's death came at Carrianne in waves—like those that might be found in the ocean.

What is it they say? That one out of every seven is the big one?

That was what this felt like. It was like she was floating along, thinking she was fine, and then suddenly she would get overwhelmed.

Oh my God. Ahmed is dead. They actually shot him.

And if bandits would do that to Ahmed, their friend, the man who had been helping them, they would surely do the same thing to anyone else who tried to come out of the cave.

She and Ahmed had once discussed the nature of humanity. He had said it was unpredictable. And maybe that was true in some cases. But not here. She felt like she knew exactly what these bandits were about.

"Giving them the statues won't work," Carrianne said, breaking a long silence. "Whoever took them up there would just get killed, too. There's no way we can trust them."

"Yeah," Dave said dryly. "You're probably right."

Everyone chewed on this for a moment. By this point, they had all taken seats on the ground. Flashlights were off, to conserve batteries.

The darkness was total.

"Okay, what now?" Jerry asked.

"I don't know. Let's take stock for a moment," Dave suggested. "We know we can't go out there. And as long as our ammo holds out, they can't come in here, either. So, it really comes down to how long we can survive down here."

"A long time, if we had food and water," Javier answered. "Unfortunately, we don't."

"We have *some* water," Keith said. "I brought a full bottle."

"So did I," Jerry volunteered.

A few others had as well. But when they took a full inventory, the grimness of their situation became readily apparent. Between them, they had eighty-six ounces of water.

"There are thirteen of us," Dave said. "Even if we ration it smartly, that won't last long."

This sobering recognition was met with another moment of quiet.

"Blue Diamond should be coming with reinforcements eventually," Carrianne said.

"How soon?" Jerry asked.

"I don't know. A.J. said 24 hours."

"The more pertinent question is: How many?" Dave said. "Is he going to bring enough soldiers to fight that horde outside?"

"I'm not sure. I did manage to send him a text before we went underground. He knows we had to abandon camp and that we're in trouble."

"Did you tell him where we were going?" Jerry said.

"No," Carrianne admitted. "When I sent the text, I didn't know myself."

Dave sighed loudly. "Well, hopefully anyone who shows up and sees that the camp has been ransacked and that there's a bunch of trucks congregating a mile away would figure out what's going on pretty fast."

"Hopefully," Jerry repeated. "Our chance of survival is down to a 'hopefully.'"

"I'm afraid that's the best I got," Dave said.

There was more quiet.

"We can go a long time without food. It really comes down to water," Ray summed up. "Is eighty-six ounces of water going to last us until Blue Diamond shows up with reinforcements?"

"That's about the size of it, yeah," Dave said.

Then, a thought occurred to Carrianne. "Not necessarily. There *is* water down here somewhere. Our readings from earlier today were highly suggestive of that."

Even as the words fell out of her mouth, she realized how precarious they sounded. The scientific language of certainty and uncertainty—*highly suggestive*—was fine if you were talking about mineral plays.

It was a lot less satisfying when you were talking about the possibility of death by dehydration.

"Yeah, but we don't know where it is or whether we can get at it," Jerry said. "If it's just locked up inside the rocks, that doesn't really help us. We don't have drilling equipment anymore."

"It might be seeping out somewhere, though," Carrianne said. "Water never just stays put."

"True," Jerry said.

"What are the chances that there's water down here somewhere?" Dave asked.

"That there's actually water? Ninety-five percent, at least," Carrianne said. "That it's recoverable? I don't know. Jerry, what would you say? Fifty percent?"

"We'd just be guessing," he replied.

"But not zero," Dave said.

"Not zero," Carrianne confirmed.

"Okay, then that goes along with something else I've been

thinking about. Cave systems often have more than one place where they meet with the surface, don't they?"

"It's certainly possible."

"That means there's a not-zero-percent chance there's another way out of here, and there's also a not-zero-percent chance that Kimberly and the others found it, and that's where they are right now. That goes along with a not-zero-percent chance of finding water. If we combine all those not-zeros, we definitely get some chance of improving our situation.

"But we have to go searching for it."

"Which would mean splitting up," Carrianne said.

"Exactly," Dave said. "That cave entrance is the only place where we can reasonably hold off the bandits. So, some of us need to stay here and do that. And then some of us need to explore the rest of the cave. We already know there's a tunnel down farther. That must lead somewhere. Maybe there's a way out, or maybe there's water along the way. It feels like it's worth sending a group to find out."

Carrianne realized she was already nodding. "Yeah. I'm with you. What do you say Jerry, Ray, and I head deeper to see what we can find, and the rest of you stay here and fight the good fight?"

"Okay, but you should have a soldier with you," Dave said. "We only need one gun to hold off the entrance and maybe one more as backup. That leaves another gun to go with you."

"Fine by me," Carrianne said. "Anyone have any objections to this plan?"

"How long are you thinking this expedition will be?" Jerry asked.

"I don't know. A few hours, at least."

"And then we'll come back here?"

"I would think so, yeah. Why?"

"Just thinking about provisions," Jerry said. "For starters, how do we divide the water?"

"If there are four of us, we're a little less than a third of the group," Carrianne said. "We'll take a little less than a third of the water."

"That sounds fair," Javier said.

"Keith, why don't you go up and relieve Thing One?" Dave said. "I'd like to send him along with our explorers. Correct me if I'm wrong, but you've seen more combat. If things get really hairy here—"

"Got it," he said.

A light switched on, and Carrianne heard the sound of Keith's boots scuffing the ground as he walked up the tunnel.

In short order, Joshua returned. They decided it made sense that the exploratory party should have more flashlights—they were the ones who needed to see, after all.

It wasn't long until they set out. Carrianne and Ray were in the lead. Ray had a flashlight in his hand and a knapsack on his back that held their precious water, extra flashlights, and batteries.

Jerry and Joshua were just behind them.

They crossed the length of the main cavern more quickly than they had earlier in the day, now that they weren't focused on exploring every inch of real estate along the way. After a bit of groping in the dark, they found the entrance to the tunnel that led deeper underground.

As they began their descent, Carrianne felt incredibly alert. They still had no idea what obstacle, difficulty, or misfortune had prevented Kimberly and the others from returning.

It was entirely possible that, as great as the danger was facing the group at the mouth of cave, there was equal peril awaiting them somewhere farther down.

With this in mind, Carrianne began taking shorter strides. Truth was, they had no idea what might be looming in the darkness.

Now and then, when she felt a little unsteady—like she was about to lose her balance—she reached out and held Ray's arm for a few seconds.

He didn't object.

As their pace slowed to a cautious shuffle, she once again found herself studying the walls of the tunnel. She had never been in a lava tube, but she thought they tended to feature smooth surfaces. After all, lava was once liquid.

These walls were not smooth. They were craggy and uneven, like they had been hacked at by something—whether it was the forces of erosion, or ...

Or human beings?

This was the thought that had slowly been working its way up into Carrianne's mind. They had clearly found evidence of human habitation—the tools, the scraps of clothing, the statues.

Was it possible that humans had also *created* this cave? Had those craggy walls been chiseled away by hand tools, with the loose rock carried away somewhere else?

It would have been an enormous undertaking, yes, but if the pyramids suggested nothing else, it's that the ancient Egyptians weren't allergic to hard work.

All it took was time. And their civilization had several thousand years of that.

They continued deeper. After several hundred feet—she wasn't exactly counting steps—the tunnel began twisting to the right. Then it straightened out again.

Another few hundred feet passed. No one was speaking. The loudest sound was Jerry's breathing. His labored inhales and exhales reminded Carrianne of how Paw used to sound.

The tunnel took another gradual right turn. It was like they were slowly corkscrewing their way down to the center of the Earth.

Then, as they entered another straightaway, Carrianne thought she saw a foreign shape just beyond the reach of Ray's flashlight beam. A lump, lying along the wall. But there was something about its shape that was itching some unreachable part of Carrianne's brain.

It was too round to fit in with the rest of the cave.

Was it an animal?

"Wait a second," Carrianne said, bringing them to a halt. "Shine your light over there."

Ray's flashlight beam traced a slow path toward the object in question, then settled on it.

For a slow, sickening second, the truth dawned on Carrianne.

It wasn't an animal.

It was a person.

She recognized his buzz-cut head and jutting ears.

Joseph.

He wasn't moving. And there were wounds all over his body.

Deep wounds.

Mortal wounds.

Someone, or something, had slaughtered him and left him for dead.

Chapter Twenty-Three

Carrianne turned to Joshua—to shield him, to protect him, to prepare him.

She wasn't quite sure what she hoped to accomplish. But whatever she was going to do, it was too late. He had already seen it.

The sound coming from him began as a whimper, turned into a low moan, then quickly built into a wail.

He rushed over to his brother and knelt before the lifeless shape. He said Joseph's name repeatedly, as if that would somehow pump life back into the body.

Or maybe he wasn't saying the name. Maybe it was just random syllables, the output of a person who had momentarily lost their connection to real words. In the echo chamber that was the tunnel, it was hard to tell.

Carrianne reached out toward Ray, clamped her hand on his forearm, and squeezed hard enough that she could feel his pulse. Ray had grabbed her wrist with his other hand.

All the while, his flashlight beam remained on what used to be Joseph. No part of him had been spared. It was like he had been turned inside out. The body had been so badly butchered and the gashes were so extensive it was difficult to guess what had caused them.

His clothing had been shredded. There was a dark stain underneath him that was the color of rusted iron.

The sickly smell of blood permeated the air. Carrianne swore she could even taste it.

She risked a glance at his face then immediately regretted doing so. It was just too gruesome.

Who or what had done this?

Had he been set upon by some large, vicious animal—or animals —that lived down here? A pack of dogs?

Or was it the cave itself?

Not natural.

Done by humans.

Were there more bandits hiding down here somewhere? Or Bedouins who had taken up residence? Or evildoers of some other origin?

It had to be, didn't it? She couldn't think of any creature capable of creating this much carnage.

She finally tore her gaze away and buried her face in Ray's chest.

His T-shirt was quickly and strangely wet. Then, she realized it was because she was crying.

Ray wrapped his arms around her, and they stayed in that awkward embrace as Joshua continued his moaning.

Jerry had gone closer to him and had even bent down, but he still wasn't quite making contact. There was something about Joshua that was too volatile to touch—an energy that was about to explode somewhere.

Suddenly, he was on his feet, screaming into the darkness. It was mostly obscenities, but now and then, there were actual sentences.

"Who did this?" he demanded. "Who did this?"

He brought his gun up to chest level and buried the stock against his shoulder.

"You want a fight?" he yelled. "I'll give you a fight. Come on. Come and get it."

He pressed down the trigger, sending a stream of bullets down the tunnel.

In that small enclosure, the sound was so thunderous it seemed to momentarily disable all Carrianne's other senses. It was like she could no longer see, or smell, or taste, or touch. There was only noise, noise, and more noise—so loud it blocked out everything else.

Ray had released his hold of Carrianne. Jerry had rocked back at first but was now making a recovery.

They approached Joshua in tandem. Jerry may not have been in very good shape, but he was still plenty strong. He locked Joshua in a bear hug from behind. Ray went for Joshua's hands, prying them off the gun.

As the racket from the SAW finally died away, she heard Jerry cooing, "Okay, okay. You're okay. Just take it easy."

Joshua was bawling. Ray had moved in front of him to block his view of his brother.

"Just breathe with me, buddy," Jerry was saying. "Come on, take some deep breaths. Nice and easy."

At first, Joshua was gasping more than he was breathing. Jerry kept talking in a soothing voice. Very slowly, Joshua stopped struggling and allowed himself to return to some semblance of sanity.

Carrianne felt herself doing the same.

She repeatedly reminded herself that she was the leader of this expedition. As much as it was tempting to allow this shock to overwhelm her, she needed to get a grip.

The truth was, they were in more trouble than ever.

She used the hem of her T-shirt to blot the tears off her face and gave herself a quick peptalk. *Come on*, Carrianne. *Get it together.*

Jerry and Ray had worked Joshua around so that he was no longer facing Joseph.

Carrianne walked over and positioned herself in front of him. "Okay, look at me," she said. "This is awful, absolutely awful. But there's nothing more we can do for Joseph. We need to focus on the living. I need you. Ray and Jerry need you. The people up at the top of the cave need you. Kimberly, Ciarra, and Jamil might need you more than anything. We have to move forward like they're still out there and we can still help them. We also have to find water or find a way out of here. It's a lot. We're in a bad fix here. You know what I'm saying?"

Joshua, who had at least been tracking her words, nodded slightly. His face was tear-stained, but he had stopped crying for the moment.

"So, I know you want to freak out, but freaking out is not going to solve anything. We've got to keep our heads. I can't have you running off and screaming and wasting ammo shooting at nothing. Whoever or whatever did this is still down here somewhere, which means we've got to keep our wits about us."

He nodded again and exhaled loudly.

"Why don't you drink a little water, okay?" she asked, handing him the bottle from Ray's knapsack.

They all watched him take a too-long pull. She knew they were all thinking the same thing.

How many ounces was that?

"Okay, good," she said. "Now just take a little walk around. Get your head right."

He complied.

Jerry slid up behind her.

"What do we do about the body?" he asked in a quiet grumble. "Do we ... should we take it back up to the others, or ..."

The question tailed off without end.

It was Joshua who stopped walking and provided a firm answer.

"Leave it," he said. "Just leave it. There's nothing more we can do for him right now, anyway. We can come back for him later. Whoever did this is going to pay. That's where my focus is now."

"Okay," Carrianne said. "But no more freakouts?"

"No more freakouts."

"Good," she said. "Now there's basically only two ways we can go here. If we go back, we're safer—we know what's there—but we haven't solved anything. If we go forward, we're probably in greater danger, but maybe we'll find ourselves in a better situation on the other side of it."

"Then we go forward, right?" Ray said.

"Don't see where we really have a choice," Jerry said. "Let's just keep it slow and steady and try not to get ambushed."

"Yeah, good plan," Ray said sarcastically.

"I'll take the lead," Joshua said. "If anything out there even breathes in my direction, I'm going to waste it."

"Again, good plan," Ray said.

Though this time, he wasn't being sarcastic.

Carrianne glanced down at Joseph's mangled corpse, took a deep breath, and managed to start putting one foot ahead of the other again.

The tunnel took another twist as it continued to work its way deeper. They kept following it, their progress slower than it had been before.

Then, they rounded a corner and came across something Carrianne did not expect.

A total and complete dead end.

Carrianne removed a flashlight from Ray's knapsack so she could have a better look.

There was a wall of loose stones blocking the path.

"What the hell?" Joshua said. He kicked a rock with his steel-toed boot, like that would do any good.

How was it possible that the tunnel just ended? If there was no way out—other than the way they had just come—had Joseph's attackers waited patiently until the Blue Diamond expedition team had packed up for the day and then snuck out of the front of the cave? With Kimberly, Ciarra, and Jamil still with them?

Carrianne got up close to one of the boulders and crouched down, shining her flashlight all over it.

Then, she figured it out.

"This is fresh," she announced. "There's a layer of dust on everything else in this cave, but there's no dust on these rocks. That means they must have been moved here recently."

Ray said, "You mean since Joseph ..."

"Exactly," Carrianne said. "Whoever did that to Joseph didn't want to be followed. And they hoped that by putting these rocks here, they would seal off that possibility."

"They've done a good job of it," Jerry said.

"No, this is just a setback," Carrianne said, reaching up toward the top of the wall and tugging on one of the rocks. "Let's get to work."

"You want to take apart this wall by hand?"

"Yeah," she said, like it should have been obvious.

"That could take hours. Days," Jerry said. "We have no idea how thick this wall is. And the whole time we'd be removing those rocks, we'd be sweating out water that we can't afford to lose."

"I'm not leaving three team members behind."

"I'm not saying you should. I'm just saying don't do it the old-fashioned way."

"What are you talking about?"

"There's dynamite in the ammo box."

She just stared at him for a moment.

"Are you crazy?" she asked. "That could cause the whole tunnel to cave in. We'd never get them out."

"Nah," Jerry said. "Explosive energy is just like any other form of energy. It travels the path of least resistance. It would blow out loose rock first."

"You don't know that."

"Sure I do."

"You're absolutely sure?" Carrianne asked.

"Of course."

"Just like you were absolutely sure about the P17 filter."

Jerry looked down at his boots.

"There's also the element of surprise to think about," Joshua interjected. "A huge blast like that would let the enemy know we're coming. At least if we remove the rocks quietly, whoever is on the other side of this wall might think they're still safe."

"Then it's settled," Carrianne said. "Let's get to it."

She returned to the rock she had been attempting to pull out before. Ray and Joshua began moving toward the wall as well.

"This is madness," Jerry protested. "One or two sticks of—"

"Jerry!" Carrianne said sharply. "The decision is made. Are you helping or not?"

Jerry continued his protest, but he did so while yanking at rocks.

The work was exhausting. And grinding. As Jerry had predicted, they were all soon sweating. Carianne had removed her hoodie, which helped some, but she was still leaking precious water.

Their task was also made more difficult by the low visibility. They propped flashlights up on rocks and shined them toward the wall, but it always seemed like the rock Carrianne was digging at was in a dark spot. Or someone would be walking in front of the beam just when she needed to see the most.

They made slow progress, removing the rocks and setting them along the tunnel wall, leaving enough space for them to continue working. As the number of rocks they removed grew, they kept having to walk farther back in the tunnel to stack them.

It wasn't long before she noticed that Jerry's energy was flagging. He just couldn't keep up the same pace as his younger, healthier colleagues.

"I know you're doing the best you can," she said to him quietly at one point. "Don't overdo it."

"I'm fine," he insisted, though Carrianne could tell he wasn't.

Otherwise, they labored in silence. Whenever Carrianne mashed a finger or felt her muscles straining, she resisted the urge to mention it.

Complaining wouldn't help get the rocks out of the way.

As Jerry predicted, they had all soon worked up a vigorous sweat. The cave was no more than sixty degrees, but it didn't matter. Work was work.

Still, no one drank water.

Carrianne did her best to ignore her thirst—and the grit building up in the back of her throat from all the dust they had been kicking up.

An hour later, Ray had just worked loose another rock when he said, "I think we're through. Here, bring me that light."

Joshua passed him a flashlight.

"Yeah," Ray said. "I can definitely see through to the other side. There's more tunnel. I think if we can get just a few more rocks out, we'll be able to make it through."

Knowing that they were nearing the end helped boost everyone's energy level. It still took another twenty minutes before they had created an opening large enough.

"Okay, should we ... just go?" Ray asked.

"Let's catch our breath for a moment," Carrianne said. "And maybe take a drink? What do you say?"

The moment she suggested it, everyone's eyes turned to Ray's knapsack. They were all parched. Jerry, especially, looked like he was about to pass out.

"Just a little," Carrianne said, reminding them.

They passed around the bottle, each taking a judicious drink. When Jerry consumed more than everyone else, no one said anything.

"Before we move on ..." Carrianne said, then paused to formulate a warning that expressed the right degree of caution without sounding paranoid. "Whoever made that wall and whoever killed Joseph obviously doesn't want company and isn't friendly. They also could be very close by. We have to assume they're around every corner."

"They might also set a trap of some sort," Joshua pointed out.

"That's possible, yes."

"You think we should turn off our flashlights?" Ray asked.

"No, because we have no idea what happens to the tunnel. It could suddenly drop down a hole, or—"

"Sure. Right."

"But let's keep the lights pointed down, and let's stay very quiet."

This suggestion was met with agreement.

Carrianne was the first through the opening they had created. She then shined a light for Ray, Joshua, and finally Jerry, who had the tightest squeeze.

On the other side, the tunnel appeared identical to what it had been before. The same rough-hewn walls. The same gentle slope down.

They turned another corner, warily inching their way along, keeping all their senses tuned to the yawning blackness in front of them. The tunnel seemed to be broadening just a little, which made Carrianne wonder what other changes might be coming.

When the beam of Carrianne's flashlight first caught what appeared to be a hole in the side of the wall, she thought maybe it was just the shadows playing tricks on her.

But no. There was definitely a burrow of some sort on the left side. More than one, in fact.

She shifted the light to her right hand so she could get a better angle on what appeared to be a long rectangular opening.

Then she had to resist the urge to scream.

It contained a body.

Chapter Twenty-Four

A s she drew closer, she realized it was not a fresh body.

It was very, very old.

Everything except the head and hands were wrapped in tattered beige cloth. The skin was as black as coal, though the features remained remarkably well-preserved, right down to the folds of the ears and the delicate opening of the nostrils.

Even to Carrianne's untrained eye, it appeared to be the result of classical Egyptian embalming techniques.

"Oh my God," Ray said. "It's ..."

"A mummy," Joshua finished. "An honest-to-goodness mummy. I'll be damned."

The face seemed masculine, so Carrianne decided this was a man. She found herself staring at his cheeks, his eyelids, his lips.

This was someone who had lived in a very different culture many thousands of years ago, and yet being able to study him so intimately made him feel somehow familiar. Like she could have known him.

She could easily imagine his cares and concerns were not so different from hers. He had his work and his family. He had hopes and dreams and aspirations. He had probably loved and been loved.

And when he died, the people around him wanted to ensure that he remained safe and happy for all eternity.

"Check out these little bowls and cups," Ray said, shining his flashlight on a set of small objects down at the mummy's feet.

"I read something about that," Jerry said. "A lot of tombs have them. The ancient Egyptians believed that the dead required nourishment in the afterlife, but they also thought the soul was very small, so it only needed a little bit of food and water. Hence the undersized dishware."

"Uh, guys?" Joshua said. "There are more of them."

Carrianne shifted her flashlight up and realized there was another body just above this one, lying in its own hole that had been chiseled into the wall.

And another body below. The way the bodies were stacked on top of each other, each in its own cubby, almost reminded her of bunks on a ship.

Then, Joshua said, "A lot more."

Carrianne shined her flashlight further down the tunnel where Joshua was already investigating. It was lined with similar crypts on both sides, as far as the light stretched.

These were catacombs—a vast underground repository for the dead.

Was that why the cave had originally been constructed? Was this, in fact, a giant tomb? With the golden ladies and the curse at the entrance?

But, again, why would the curse be warning people not to leave?

Unless Ciarra's hieroglyphics app had translated it wrong? That was certainly possible.

Whatever the case, this was a significant archaeological find. This wasn't just a few mummies. Depending on how far the tunnel stretched, it might be hundreds or even thousands of them.

"Look at all of them," Ray said, walking a few more steps, as awestruck as Carrianne was. "It just keeps going."

"Dude, there's a cat in this one," Joshua called out. "A cat mummy!"

"Egyptians were big into cats," Jerry said.

They let their flashlight beams dance among the dead for a few more minutes as they inspected one corpse after the next.

"Okay, this is creepy as hell, but it's also pretty cool," Joshua said from a bit farther down. "I mean, geez Jerry, some of these guys are older than you."

Jerry chuckled.

Carrianne was glad Joshua was cracking jokes. He was probably still just in shock, but it was better than having him catatonic or in a rage.

"Okay, let's keep our wits about us," Carrianne reminded them. "We don't know where Joseph's killers have gone. They could still be very close by. Don't get distracted, or we might end up joining these people in the afterlife."

It was a reminder to herself as much as anything. It was difficult not to get swept away by the grisly spectacle of it all.

But as they got back underway, she still couldn't stop her mind from churning over the oddities of what they were seeing.

For starters, why would the ancient Egyptians have taken their bodies all the way out here? This place was at least seventy miles from the Nile and probably just as far from any oasis that might have been able to sustain civilization. There were few places in Egypt more out of the way.

It seemed like a very long way to go to bury people, especially in an age long before motorized transport. The journey would have taken several days by camel and required quite a bit of planning to survive in such a harsh desert climate.

Were the Egyptians simply *that* determined to ensure that their dead would remain undisturbed?

Yet they clearly *hadn't* remained undisturbed, despite those efforts. There were modern people down here, somewhere.

Which brought Carrianne to another inexplicable oddity: Why

would those people, whoever they were, have left the catacombs untouched? An authentic Egyptian mummy was worth a lot of money. She was sure there were collectors who would pay tens of thousands of dollars for one—maybe even hundreds of thousands.

Then there were the objects alongside the bodies. Those were valuable, too.

It just seemed difficult to believe the crypts hadn't been plundered, either recently or long ago. Was it possible whoever was down here had only just discovered this bounty when Blue Diamond had opened up the cave?

No. That couldn't be. Whoever attacked Jospeh—and kidnapped Kimberly, Ciarra, and Jamil—had already been down here.

Which meant there *had* to be another way in and out, didn't there? Yet she had seen no evidence of it so far. The tunnel had only continued to go farther down. They had to be hundreds of feet below the surface by now.

Unless it bottomed out at some point, and then started going back up? Did it perhaps come back above the surface a mile or more away?

For the time being, she continued on, shuffling slowly past mummy after mummy, trying to keep herself alert for any danger that may lie ahead.

As they continued, the tunnel grew taller and was soon high enough for four bodies, then five. The dead lined both sides, such that every three or four steps they took yielded another ten bodies.

They had taken hundreds of steps. Which meant thousands of bodies. Carrianne's sense of wonder only increased. This was going to be the work of a lifetime for many Egyptologists just to even attempt to study and catalogue all of this.

She began to notice a change in the air. There was a new odor. Gone was the dry, dustiness that had filled her nose ever since they entered the cave. It had been replaced by something that almost smelled agricultural—like plants growing, and maybe fertilizer? But how was that even possible?

Then Joshua, who had remained in the lead with his gun raised, stopped abruptly.

"Guys, you hear that?" he asked.

Carrianne stopped and tried to still everything, even the sound of her own heartbeat.

And, yes, she heard it—whooshing and burbling and trickling.

She must have grabbed ahold of Ray and squeezed again, because she suddenly felt him squeezing back.

"That's..."—Joshua stopped for a moment to interpret what he was hearing—"That's water, right?"

They followed the noise, which only continued to grow louder.

The closer they got, the more it became obvious: it was, in fact, water.

A lot of it. A stream or a river. Someone from Greasy Creek had no trouble recognizing the sound of liquid tumbling over rocks.

The tunnel kept growing wider and taller. Eventually, there were no more bodies lining the walls. Carrianne was so focused on where the water was coming from, she didn't even note where the catacombs ended—just that they had.

Strictly from judging the quality of the sound, she had the sense that the tunnel would soon be opening into a much larger space.

But before long, that wasn't the thing that was making her most curious.

It was that there seemed to be a faint glow up ahead.

"Hey guys, hold still and turn off your flashlights for a sec," Carrianne said, having to raise her voice to be heard over the rushing of the water, which was now quite close. "I want to see something."

Everyone complied. As her eyes adjusted, her astonishment only increased.

There was a faint blue glow emanating from somewhere in front of them.

"Dude," Joshua asked. "Whiskey tango foxtrot?"

They walked in speechless silence with the lights still off for another few feet until the river came into view.

It was perhaps the most beautiful thing Carrianne had ever seen: a long, wide line of glowing blue water, flowing at a gentle downhill pace for hundreds of feet—maybe thousands, maybe more—until it faded into the unseeable distance.

"Bioluminescence," Jerry said definitively. "I saw it on a vacation in Puerto Rico one time. It's caused by little critters in the water that glow. There's chemistry involved. I used to understand it, but I couldn't explain it anymore. It looks ... well, just like this."

"It's incredible," Carrianne said.

They all stopped and gawked. The river seemed to emerge from a hole in the rocks to the right of them. This was effectively its headwaters, at least as far as this visible underground portion of the river was concerned.

From there, it rolled along at a fairly lazy pace, but there was enough of a current that it never looked the same from one second to the next. The blueness roiled and twisted, sometimes appearing in darker bands or long ribbons that lasted for mere seconds until they reconfigured into some other shape.

The show was spectacular. It was the kind of thing she felt like she could spend the rest of her life staring at and never get bored.

"But this smells like fresh water," Ray said. "At least in Florida, you only get bioluminescence in salt water."

"Like I said, I can't explain it," Jerry said. "But it's happening. So, it must be possible."

"You think it's safe to drink?" Joshua asked.

It was a question of some importance. The potability of this water could mean the difference between life and death, depending on how long they were trapped down here.

"Let's find out," Jerry said.

He walked down the rock embankment toward the edge of the water with one of the bottles in hand. Even in the dim light,

Carrianne could see that the rock close to the water appeared slick with moisture.

"Careful, Jerry," Carrianne said. "Don't go falling in. I don't think anyone here is a trained lifeguard."

"I'll be fine," he said.

Then, he reached out and stuck his fingers in the river.

"It's chilly," he said. "It feels like a stream that's come out of a mountain."

He brought his fingers to his mouth. "Definitely fresh," he said.

Then, he dipped the bottle into the water and filled it. "Okay," he announced. "Here goes nothing."

He took a sip, paused to taste it, then took another sip. He stopped with a great deal of deliberation, as if he was trying to judge whether he was about to keel over dead from some exotic toxin.

But nothing happened.

"It seems fine to me," he announced. "It tastes a bit chalky. But that's probably to be expected since it's been flowing through so much rock. It's probably picking up some calcium, some magnesium, maybe some other minerals. It's not bad, though."

He raised the bottle to his lips and emptied it in one long swig. The others watched him jealously.

"I'm sure it's a damn sight better than dying of thirst," Joshua said. "Here. Gimme the other bottle."

He retrieved their other container. Then, he went down to the water, submerged it for a moment, and lifted it to his lips for a drink.

"Yeah, it's great. Here. Drinks on me."

He handed Carrianne a full bottle. She had never felt so thirsty. She took the container and tilted it back without pause.

The water was immensely satisfying. She passed it to Ray, and he guzzled the rest.

"What do you think?" Ray said. "Should we fill these up and take them back to the others? I'm sure they'd appreciate it. Plus, it feels like they need to know about ... you know ... about Joseph."

Carrianne cast a quick glance at Joshua to see if the mention of his brother's name triggered a reaction. But the soldier seemed to have walled himself off from emotion, at least for the time being.

"I say we press on for a bit," Jerry said. "It's taken us, what, two hours to get down this far? I'm sure we can cut that time down going back. But it'll still take a while. It makes sense to me to explore a little further while we're down here."

"And we still don't know where the others are," Carrianne pointed out. "They may be running out of time."

"Or they may already be dead," Joshua pointed out.

There was no refuting him.

"Still, I think we ought to explore a little more," Jerry pressed. "You never know what we might—"

As if to reinforce the point he was about to make, Ray interrupted. "Wait, what's that?"

He was squinting into the gloom beyond them. Carrianne tried to follow his eyeline, but she wasn't seeing anything.

"What's what?" she asked.

"Hang on. Sorry, I feel like I need to turn on a flashlight. Close your eyes and turn away if you're worried about it wrecking your night vision."

Carrianne did just that. She heard Ray clicking a button, then the sound of his footsteps moving farther down the tunnel.

"Yeah, guys, check this out. You might as well turn your lights on."

Carrianne opened her eyes and walked toward Ray. He was shining his light at an object that was suspended over the river by ropes. It was a large metal disc, not terribly unlike the ones being held by the golden ladies.

Except it was much, much larger.

It was hanging at a forty-five-degree angle and tilted toward the shoreline, where there was another huge metal disc.

There was another one just beyond it.

And another.

There was a long row of them, stretching down the river.

"Turn your lights off for a second, I want to see something," Jerry said.

They all did as asked.

"I thought so," Jerry said.

Sure enough, as soon as the flashlight beams faded out, Carrianne could see the discs were made of highly reflective metal—silver, perhaps?—such that they were glowing blue. They were so bright it was almost like they were the original source of the light.

"Amazing," Carrianne said.

Ray had walked ahead. It was still fairly dim, but between the river and the reflectors, there was enough luminance that he didn't have to worry about falling into a hole or tripping on something.

It was almost like a child's nightlight, glowing bright enough to banish any would-be monsters back under the bed.

"Guys, there's ... like ... soil underneath here," Ray said. "It's ... it's really rich and dark. It looks like something you'd buy in a bag at a nursery. And it has weird stuff growing in it."

Carrianne walked quickly over to Ray, who was pointing to a clump of something sprouting out along the side of the river.

In the gloom, she could just make out a stand of vegetation. As she got closer, she saw it had stalks as thick as her pinky and fine needles that looked like they belonged on a pine tree, except they were too long. The ends of the stalks almost looked like feather dusters and towered eight or ten feet in the air.

The plant was such a pale, pale yellow that it basically passed for white.

"I'll be damned," said Jerry, who was a few steps ahead of Carrianne. "I might be wrong, but I think this is papyrus. I saw something that looked just like this growing along the Nile when we were in Aswan. I pointed it out to Bassel, and he said it was papyrus."

Joshua came up just behind them. He still had his gun at his chest, with his finger just outside the trigger guard, but he was staring with the same kind of wonder as everyone else, not paying attention to his surroundings.

"That's wild," he said.

Ray, who had already moved away from the water, about twenty feet inland, announced, "There's more stuff growing over here. It looks like it's the greens for some kind of a root vegetable. Like a turnip, maybe? Except it's not green, of course. It's white."

"Don't all plants need sunlight?" Carrianne asked in disbelief.

"Well, yeah, I think so," Ray said.

"Then how are these surviving? There's no sun."

"Maybe the bioluminescence from the river is bright enough to make stuff grow?" Ray hypothesized.

"It must be," Carrianne said. "This stuff—whatever it is—seems to be doing okay."

"Yeah, obviously these plants have ... I don't know, adapted to low light somehow."

"Evolution can make all sorts of crazy things happen, I guess. Aren't there plants that grow in caves that don't need light?"

"I think those are lichens. Plants—"

Then Jerry interrupted their conversation in an urgent voice that, while soft, was as deadly serious as Carrianne had ever heard.

"Joshua, drop your gun," he said.

"What?" Joshua said, turning toward him.

"Drop your weapon!" Jerry said in a fierce whisper. "Drop it now, damnit!"

"Are you out of your mind?" Joshua said. "I'm not—Oh God!"

He immediately laid his gun down at his feet.

Carrianne's attention was on Jerry, who was acting so strangely.

"Everyone, put your hands up," Jerry said. "Nice and slow. No sudden moves."

Carrianne complied, though she couldn't figure out what had him so spooked.

Then it became very, very apparent.

From out of the darkness, there were at least a hundred people emerging. They were armed with spears and hatchets.

And they were like no people Carrianne had ever seen.

Chapter Twenty-Five

T heir eyes were huge. Not only were they large in proportion to their faces, but their eyeballs themselves were also oversized—almost like they were about to outgrow their sockets.

They were also black. Which was impossible, wasn't it? Human beings didn't have black eyes. Very dark brown, yes. But not black.

Then, Carrianne realized it wasn't the color of these people's eyes that was so different. It was the anatomical structure. The center portion of their eyes consisted almost entirely of pupils, with only the thinnest sliver of irises. It was as though their eyes were permanently dilated to the widest possible point. Set so close against the whites of their eyes, it only made the overall effect that much more striking. It almost reminded Carrianne of Japanese anime characters, with their dramatic, extra-large eyes.

Then there was their skin. It was so pale it was practically translucent. Carrianne could easily see their veins running blue beneath their arms and shoulders.

Their hair was also very light-colored. It was so blond it almost appeared white.

The total effect—enormous, black, pupil-dominated eyes set into bodies that were almost entirely absent of pigmentation—was both fascinating and shocking to look at.

It was also easy to guess how it had come to be.

These weren't people who had just found this cave in the last few days, weeks, or even years. These were people who had been living here their entire lives—as had their ancestors, and their ancestors' ancestors, going back further than Carrianne could even guess. Just like the plants growing alongside the river, their bodies had evolved to exist in incredibly low light conditions.

How long did it take for changes like this to occur in human beings? Fifty generations? A hundred? More?

It reminded Carrianne of something she had once read about Europeans and their skin color, which had originally been black—just like people from Africa, because that's where Europeans had originally come from.

Then, a genetic mutation for fair skin worked its way through the population. It happened between 6,000 and 8,000 years ago. Researchers theorize it was because lighter-colored skin more easily absorbed Vitamin D in places where there was less sunlight.

The change was believed to have taken between a thousand and 2,000 years. But she had seen the math: a trait that improved survival rates by even one percent didn't actually take *that* long to win out. Given enough generations, it was inevitable.

Had that happened here? If so, these people had a history in this cave that went back a long way.

That's why there were all those corpses in the catacombs. They weren't bodies that had been brought here from a great distance. They were native to this place. They had lived and died in this very cave. And then they had been embalmed in a way that had mummified them.

That also explained why none of the tombs had been looted. The people who created them were still here to keep watch. And no one else had been down here.

The cave really *had* remained sealed all this time.

None of which seemed to have made the people now approaching especially friendly to outsiders. As they drew closer, they had not lowered their weapons, which were made of metal whose edges had been honed to deadly sharpness.

Carrianne could already guess these were blades like the ones that had inflicted the fatal wounds she had seen on Joseph.

But wait, no. It wasn't a guess.

She could actually see the dried bloodstains on some of them.

They hadn't bothered to clean them.

And she wasn't the only one thinking this, because Jerry was continuing a soft, insistent monologue. "Okay, everyone stay nice and still. Keep your hands out where they can see them. No sudden moves. Joshua, whatever you do, don't go toward your gun. If whatever these things are view us as a threat, we're done for."

The people were continuing to inch nearer. Their steps were small. Their weapons remained raised.

Carrianne kept studying them. Their clothes consisted of robes. Some were shorter and cinched at the waist with belts. Others flowed down to the ankles.

They were white except for the collars, which consisted of colorful beads. The patterns reminded her of the woven hats on the table she had fallen into at Sharia as-Souq.

But nothing about these people reminded Carrianne of modern Egyptians. They were dressed like ancient Egyptians. The kind Carrianne had only ever seen illustrated in history books.

There were now ten of them that had broken from the rest of their group and were advancing on Carrianne, Ray, Jerry, and Joshua. They had formed a semi-circle that was growing ever tighter.

Finally, one of them started talking.

It was a man. His voice sounded stern, perhaps like he was giving orders. The language was like nothing Carrianne had ever heard before. It was difficult to say what it even sounded like.

Hebrew, maybe? Or maybe she only thought that because she knew they were somewhat near where Hebrew had originated.

What was clear was that the man wasn't very happy. He was pointing at their hands and was continuing to say the same words, over and over, like somehow repetition would make the meaning clearer.

His gestures and sounds kept getting more aggressive. And even though he was getting closer, he did so with increasing tentativeness.

Then, he shielded his eyes, which were already closed into a squint. And that's when Carrianne finally understood.

"Our flashlights," she said. "I think they want us to shut off our flashlights."

And didn't it make sense? For people whose pupils were practically the size of quarters—who may never have been exposed to sunlight in their entire lives—the beams from flashlights were probably intensely painful. Like searing lasers.

She wasn't holding a flashlight, but Ray and Jerry were. Ray immediately clicked his off. Jerry, who had been warning against sudden moves, did so more slowly.

This seemed to satisfy the man, though not completely. He began pantomiming an underhand throwing motion, which he punctuated with encouraging nods of the head.

"I think ... I think he wants us to toss the flashlights toward him," Carrianne said. "Be careful. They obviously see the flashlights as dangerous, so the last thing we want to do is use them as missiles. Be nice and gentle about it."

Ray went first.

Jerry followed.

As soon as the second flashlight had landed, several of the people moved decisively. They turned their spears upside down and used the blunt parts of the weapons to smash the devices.

There were soon small pieces of plastic and metal clattering about. A battery rolled away from one of them, and that quickly earned a bashing, too.

Carrianne just watched and absorbed the lesson: these people *really* didn't like bright lights.

Once the destruction was complete, the leader started speaking orders to his compatriots.

Two of them stepped forward and began acting out a strange kind of play. One of them had a white rope made of woven fibers—perhaps the papyrus that was growing alongside the river. He was holding up the rope.

The other held out his hands with his wrists together.

Then, the first one took the rope and wrapped it around the other's wrists, fastening the rope in a quick knot.

The man giving the orders was talking the whole time. He kept saying what sounded to Carrianne like "beeta." She didn't know what "beeta" meant exactly, but she could guess.

We're going to tie you up like this.

Carrianne wasn't very fond of the idea. But what choice did they have? They were vastly outnumbered. They were surrounded. Their only means of escape was the river, but jumping into it seemed like a very bad idea.

They had no idea how deep it was. Just that it looked deep. They would also be guessing where it led, or whether there were rapids or waterfalls, or whether it would flow into some underground cavern from which there would be no escape.

For that matter, it might just flow straight into the heart of these people's home, which would just result in their capture, anyway.

Then there was the temperature. If Jerry was right, and it was like a mountain stream, they wouldn't be able to survive long in it before hypothermia set in.

Yes, they were down to one option.

The river wasn't it. And neither was resistance.

"Guys, I think they want to tie us up," Carrianne said. "And I think we have to let them."

Without further hesitation, Carrianne stuck out her hands toward the leader.

"Okay," she said. "Go ahead. Tie me up. It's okay. I understand this will make you feel better."

"Like hell," Joshua said. "We can't just let ourselves get taken hostage."

She ignored him. She was making eye contact with the leader the whole time, which was strangely reassuring. For as unusual as his eyes were compared to what she was used to, they were still human.

So was the understanding that seemed to lurk just beneath them. This was not some maniacal creature with no connection to empathy or compassion.

As she looked at him, something passed between them— something that bridged the gap of all the differences they had.

At the root of it, he was a leader trying to protect his people. Just like Carrianne was. Establishing this allowed her to accept being constrained without feeling overly anxious about it. She felt like she could trust this man.

"Beeta," she said, hoping she was correctly pronouncing ... whatever the word was.

"Beeta," the leader repeated.

One of the leader's men approached her tentatively with a length of rope. She kept nodding and encouraging him—even if he couldn't understand her anymore than she could him.

Eventually, he slid the rope over her wrists and secured them in place with a knot. The rope was thick and strong.

She looked up and saw Ray, Joshua, and Jerry also being bound. Another man grabbed Joshua's gun from the ground. The way he handled the weapon—like he wasn't quite sure which part he was supposed to avoid—told Carrianne he had never seen anything quite like it.

With their ties secured, they were soon marched away.

Where they were going was entirely unclear. So was the path

itself. The surface dwellers did not have eyes adapted to maneuvering in the dim glow of the bioluminescent reflectors. They kept tripping on obstacles that seemed to pop up randomly out of the darkness.

At one point Jerry stumbled so badly, that he would have crashed headfirst had he not been held up by the man who had control of his rope.

They were led past more and more plants until Carrianne realized these were actually fields. All of them were bathed in blue light coming from reflectors that hung from a rock ceiling maybe fifteen or twenty feet up, which made this feel like a massive indoor growing operation.

For as spectacular and strange as the sight was, there were also aspects of it that felt very familiar. These people had planted their crops along a river that they then used for irrigation, much as Egyptians had been doing since the dawn of the Agricultural Revolution 10,000 years ago.

This must have been how they fed themselves. Carrianne recognized what appeared to be beans. And carrots. Possibly potatoes. The leaves were all pale yellow or white as opposed to green. They appeared to be thriving all the same.

How many people were being fed by these fields? Hundreds? Thousands?

Whatever the case, they weren't limited by growing seasons this far underground. There were no changes in sunlight or droughts to worry about, and the temperature remained constant no matter what was happening on the surface.

They probably kept cultivating all year round, harvesting crops as soon as they were mature.

Their dirt was also something to behold. Ray had described it as "rich," and that definitely was the right description. Carrianne was far from being a soil expert, but she guessed anything this dark needed a fair amount of organic material.

Where had that come from? It's not like they could just go collect leaves or grass clippings. Did they have some kind of recycling program? Or was it manure or other waste?

Whatever they were doing, it required a concerted effort, along with a sophisticated understanding that healthy soil was vital for healthy plants.

It had to be a lot of work, though whoever performed it wasn't around at the moment. The fields were empty.

The only people Carrianne saw were the soldiers—these were soldiers, right?—who were continuing to lead her, Ray, Jerry, and Joshua away.

They were concentrating so much on avoiding tripping, they didn't speak. They just kept walking (and stumbling) for some healthy portion of a mile. Nothing about the scenery changed. The river remained on their right side the entire time, continuing to flow with that soft woosh over its rocky bed.

Then, to her left, Carrianne saw for the first time what appeared to be a house.

They had now left the fields—and their glowing reflectors—so the lighting was worse than ever. From what she could make out, the dwelling was rectangular and small, probably not more than a few hundred square feet.

It had a door but no windows, which would be pointless in a place where there wasn't exactly much to see. It appeared to be made of a combination of quarried stone and off-white-colored mudbrick— the kind of materials that would be readily available down here.

Strangely, there was no roof. Then she realized its inhabitants probably never needed one. It's not like they had to worry about being bothered by sun, rain, or wind when they were underground. There were walls for privacy, and that was it.

They were soon passing many structures. While they varied somewhat in shape and size, they were constructed of the same materials. There was no sign of anything made of wood; there were no trees down here. It was all masonry.

This was clearly the residential section of ... whatever it was you would call this. A village? A commune? A civilization? Carrianne couldn't even find the words. And, in any event, it was so dark she was mostly focused on the not-so-easy task of putting one foot in front of the other without falling over.

She was relying on sound as much as anything to tell her what might be coming.

Which was why she was aware that they were about to approach something very different from everything else they had seen so far. Because she suddenly started hearing something above the gentle sounds of the flowing river.

Human voices.

A lot of them.

And they were coming from straight ahead.

Chapter Twenty-Six

There was a faint glow in the distance.

Now that they were farther away from the river, the light was no longer blue. It was warm and yellow, maybe even orange.

It wasn't strong enough to cast a shadow. Its intensity was something less than moonlight.

More like the starlight Carrianne had seen in the desert.

It seemed to be emanating from sconces chiseled into the walls high above them.

"What do you think is making that light?" Carrianne asked.

"I could be wrong, but I think they're burning sodium," Jerry said as he huffed and puffed behind her. "I did an experiment as an undergraduate about a half million years ago where we had to burn sodium. That's pretty much the color it makes right up there."

Carrianne cast her eyes fleetingly upward then returned them to where she was placing her feet. The overhead lighting may have been plenty enough for the people who lived down here, but she felt like she was mostly still in the dark.

"I guess that makes sense," Carrianne said. "It's not like there's a lack of sodium underground."

"Or anywhere else. My guess is they're mining it from somewhere around here."

Any further discussion was halted because they were drawing nearer to whatever gathering of humanity was just ahead. The voices were only growing louder, and they echoed off the rock in a way that reminded Carrianne of a crowded ballroom with a marble floor.

The path they had been traveling had finally widened into something more like a road. There were structures on both sides—houses, she assumed.

Farther back from the road, there appeared to be dwellings that had been chiseled straight into the rock. They reminded Carrianne of photos she had seen of native cliff dwellings in the American West.

Some of them had feeble light coming from them. Others were dark.

She had lost track of time but didn't dare check on her phone. She worried her captors would see it as another light-emitting object in need of destruction.

But it was now probably ten o'clock? Eleven? Sometime in the late evening.

Did that mean the people who lived in the dark houses had gone to sleep? Or were daily rhythms governed by sunrise and sunset completely meaningless down here?

There was no time to ponder it. They were now entering an area that appeared to be some kind of village square.

Or marketplace. It kind of reminded her a little bit of Sharia as-Souq, in the way that it was lined with booths and stalls. Each of them had their own awning or other distinctive decoration that separated them from their neighbor.

And, like Sharia as-Souq, it was alive with activity. There were people everywhere—perhaps even more people than would ordinarily be there to conduct the business of commerce. Carrianne guessed there were several hundred people congregated.

Then, she sensed why.

It was because she and her team were expected. Word had

obviously spread that people from the surface had been detained. And the people living down here wanted to have a look at the strangers.

The leader who had directed the group's capture was just ahead. As he entered the middle of the village square, he said something in a loud, authoritative voice.

As soon as he spoke, the crowd quieted, which confirmed to Carrianne that they had been awaiting their arrival.

The villagers were now just gawking, probably fascinated by the visitors' tiny eyes and pigmented skin.

There were women—the first she had seen—as well as men. It was difficult to guess anyone's ages. Absent the damaging rays of the sun, their skin was far less wrinkled, and it had no moles, sunspots, or any other signs of the things that ravaged people through the years up on the surface.

There were definitely young people, though. Babies and toddlers. Children and teenagers.

Carrianne tried to let herself be reassured by their presence. It was another reminder that, for as different as they may have been, these were still just people trying to live their lives.

In peace, right? This was ultimately peaceful, wasn't it?

That remained an open question. Being tied up and paraded through town for all the populace to see definitely made her feel less like a human and more like an object. A bug under glass. An oddity. A circus freak.

She stared back at the people who were staring at her. Now and then, she would see someone turn and whisper something. She tried not to be unnerved by it and remained calm.

Which was maybe easier said than done.

"I wish I still had my gun," Joshua said quietly from behind her.

"You'd be dead if you did," Jerry said.

"Maybe it's better to go down swinging," Joshua replied. "I feel like we're being led to our execution or something."

"These people might not mean us any harm," Ray said.

"Yeah, tell that to my brother," Joshua said.

"If they wanted to kill us, they would have done it already—right when they first saw us," Carrianne said. "There's no need to walk us a mile away."

"Unless they wanted to do it in front of an audience," Joshua said. "Don't you think that's what happened to the others?"

"There are children here. I don't think they'd kill us in front of babies."

"You don't know that," Jerry said. "Hangings used to be big community events back in the day. People brought their kids and everything."

"My point exactly," Joshua said. "We never should have let them tie us up. We've lost all control of the situation."

They stopped talking as they turned to the left. In the meager glow of the sodium lights, Carrianne saw what appeared to be a set of steps that had been carved out of the rock in perfect, even measure. Each riser and each tread were precisely the same.

They led to a construction that was—by far—the largest and most impressive they had seen so far.

Built into the rock, it was fronted by a broad portico with scalloped columns that towered several stories high. Just inside the columns were several large, imposing statues that also appeared to have been sculpted out of the surrounding rock.

These were gods. Egyptian gods. She recognized Isis and Osiris; Anubis, with his jackal-like head; and another god she couldn't identify, except to say that he looked like a pharaoh, complete with the stick of a beard extending down from his chin.

Which must have meant this was a temple.

They were soon being marched up the steps. As they did so, the citizenry seemed to be following behind them, though they stopped at the foot of the steps.

Like they were expecting some kind of show.

Was Joshua right? Was there about to be a ritual sacrifice?

There was no telling. But Carrianne felt spurts of panic coursing through her body as they reached the top of the steps.

She was waiting for the order to halt, turn around, and face a crowd that was expecting blood.

Instead, they were marched straight through an opening between Osiris and Anubis, out of sight of the townspeople and into the heart of the temple.

There was a flicker of sodium fire coming from near the ceiling of a large, open space. It felt like this was the area where they would hold whatever ceremonies or observances that happened here.

It wasn't especially bright—nothing down here was—but there was better visibility than anywhere else they had been, if only because now there were surrounding walls for the light to bounce off of.

Carrianne focused on those walls for the first time. They weren't especially easy to make out, but she recognized hieroglyphics. Which ended any doubt she may have had.

In their dress, in their religious practice, and now even in their writings, these people were exactly like ancient Egyptians.

Yet somehow here they were, thriving in the present day.

Any opportunity Carrianne had to marvel at this was short lived, because they were still on the move, being tugged through this main chamber and through one of the smaller doors that led to a long hallway.

Then, it was down some steps, which weren't lit. The leader had grabbed what appeared to be some kind of torch. Carrianne couldn't see it well enough to understand how it worked, though it wasn't a live flame—just a burning ember of some sort.

It cast just the smallest hint of a glow, which seemed to be plenty for him.

She leaned her shoulder against the wall to help her keep her balance as her feet felt their way from one tread to the next. Her captors seemed to have no problem navigating in near total darkness.

They went what felt like two stories down, then three. Wherever they were being led, it was definitely beneath the main sanctuary.

Was this going to be an underground holding cell?

A dungeon?

How far *did* this go down? They were hundreds of feet underground already, but that didn't mean they couldn't go much deeper. Paw had taken her into coal mines that tunneled more than a mile into the Earth.

Finally, they were moving horizontally again, down a hallway of some sort. She could see a light at the end of it. They were moving toward it and ... what else, exactly?

There was no telling.

But as they reached what appeared to be their destination, she was greeted by two things.

One was a section of metal bars, anchored firmly into the surrounding stone. This she had been somewhat expecting. This *was* a prison, after all.

The other was something she wasn't expecting.

Someone was saying her name.

"Carrianne!"

She recognized the voice instantly. "Ciarra!" she called back.

Then, it was Kimberly excitedly saying, "Hey, guys!"

Carrianne felt enormous relief just knowing they were alive. She could also make out Jamil, scrambling to his feet to greet the newcomers.

They were soon being led through a swinging barred door into a holding area that was maybe forty feet wide and thirty feet deep—about the size of the downstairs of a typical suburban house.

Carrianne looked upward as her hands were untied. The ceiling was an uneven arch that climbed to perhaps twelve or fourteen feet. Unlike the smooth, beautiful, exacting surfaces in the main body of the temple—which appeared to have been carved by the most skilled artisans—this was jagged, having been chiseled roughly from the rock and left as is, without any thought to its appearance.

A single glowing piece of sodium just outside the bars lit the entire space. The leader closed the cell door and set a lock into place. He and the other soldiers departed without further comment.

No one stayed behind to guard them. There probably wasn't a need. They were securely locked in a hole in the ground, behind bars that looked like they were made of iron, underneath a temple, several miles from anything or anyone that might have saved them.

"It's nice to see you," Ciarra said. "It's also not nice to see you, if you know what I mean."

"Yeah, totally," Carrianne said.

"What happened to you guys?"

Carrianne shared their story then said, "What about you?"

"It sounds pretty similar, except when the Kemet found us ..." Ciarra paused, seeing the bewildered look on Carrianne's face. "They call themselves Kemet, by the way. Just like—"

"Ancient Egyptians, yeah. I've sort of been piecing that together."

"Right, so when the Kemet found us, we were in the tunnel and Joseph ... He ... I don't know how to say this."

She was looking toward Joshua.

Carrianne spared her the difficulty of explaining, quietly saying, "We found his body. They left it in the tunnel."

Ciarra sighed. "It was awful. Just awful. We heard something coming—it was the Kemet, of course. But we didn't know that at the time. We couldn't see them. We thought maybe it was bandits or nomads or ... we didn't know, obviously. Joseph kept shouting at them in English to stop. And I was translating into Arabic. They just kept coming, so he fired off some warning shots, just to scare off whoever it was. He wasn't aiming at anyone. He was shooting at the floor. I don't think he hit anyone. But ... the next thing we knew, there were spears coming from everywhere. They knocked him over, and then there were eight or ten people just ..."

She stopped speaking for a moment. The memory of it was clearly overwhelming and painful.

After taking a moment to compose herself, she continued. "Anyhow, Jamil, Kimberly, and I just raised our hands. We didn't try to resist. The Kemet are actually pretty peaceful if you don't try to shoot them. They've been very kind to us so far. And their culture is ... well, it's remarkable. I don't mean to sound too much like an ESG liaison, but I think we have a lot to learn from them. Did you see their town?"

"Yeah. We were led through it."

"It's incredible, isn't it? You should hear the story behind it."

"The story?" Carrianne said. "You mean you've been talking to them?"

"Yeah. All the priests speak Arabic."

"How do they know Arabic?"

"Because we're not the first people from the surface to come down to this cave," Ciarra said.

She read the confusion on Carrianne's face and said, "I should probably start at the beginning."

Chapter Twenty-Seven

C iarra began with a question. "You're familiar with King Menes, yes?"

"He's the guy who united the Upper and Lower Kingdoms of Egypt," Carrianne said.

"Right. Egyptologists like to debate whether he was a real person or not. They think he might have also gone by the name 'Narmer,' and they go through all this stuff about how he might be part legend, like King Arthur. Or how he might be a combination of several different people, like William Shakespeare. Or how a woman he was with, Neithhotep, might have been his queen, or she might have been his daughter, and blah, blah, blah. They're basing it all on stuff they've read on walls, or broken bits of tablets here and there, and it's all pretty sketchy because it was 5,000 years ago, and who really knows, right?"

"Right."

"The people down here know, that's who. The Kemet. Or at least they sound like they know. They talk about this stuff like it's totally real, because Menes—let's just call him Menes, to keep it simple— isn't just some historical figure. He's someone their grandparents'

grandparents' grandparents—etcetera, etcetera, etcetera—actually knew. They have all this stuff documented in writing, too. But there's also a very strong oral tradition. They've been telling each other this story for a long, long time."

"Which means their version might be wrong, too," Carrianne pointed out. "Like a game of telephone, where one person repeats a story to the next person, who repeats it to the next person, and so on and so forth until it becomes unrecognizable."

"Oh, for sure. But the point is, this is what the people down here believe. And they believe it with total conviction, with no doubt whatsoever. To them, Menes *is* one guy who unquestionably united Upper and Lower Egypt. It wasn't easy because the Upper and Lower Kingdoms had been fighting each other for hundreds of years. Menes was from the Upper Kingdom—Memphis, which is near where Cairo is today. He came down to the area around Aswan and kicked ass, not just with his military, but also administratively. He put systems in place, systems that were meant to last. And, obviously, they did last. It sounds like he was a very strong leader. Mind you, as far as these people are concerned, Menes wasn't just a guy. He was a living god.

"Anyhow, once he did all that hard work of uniting the kingdoms, he was pretty keen to keep it all going. He was concerned about his legacy, like any good monarch is. So, when his wife, Neithhotep, got pregnant, he was pretty excited. Then, she had not one baby but two. Twins. Both boys."

"I bet it was a shock," Carrianne said. "They didn't exactly have ultrasounds back then."

"Nope. And for Menes, this was a real problem. He worried that having two boys with equal claim to be his successor and two kingdoms that had only recently been united would lead to civil war. One twin would take the Upper Kingdom, and the other twin would take the Lower Kingdom, and the two kingdoms would just go back to fighting each other all the time, just like they always had. And he didn't want that. He wanted peace. He thought about just killing one and letting the other have it all, because that's how they tended to solve problems back then. But he couldn't. It would have broken Neithhotep's heart."

Jerry interjected. "So, he may have been a crappy dad, but at least he was a good husband."

Ciarra went on. "Anyway, Menes had this dilemma, and how did he solve it? How did he prevent his two sons from ever competing with each other? What he came up with was what you might call the ultimate two-state solution. He decided one son would rule the above-ground world. What he called this son translates as 'The Day Pharaoh.'

"But, at the same time, he immediately dedicated an enormous number of resources to creating a glorious new kingdom for the other son—*below* ground. He formed an army of workers and engineers, using all that good Egyptian know-how—the kind of stuff that eventually created the pyramids. They spent twenty years chiseling out a new home, and they brought down everything that would be needed to thrive. As the story goes, Menes himself created a river for these people—because he was a god, and gods can do that sort of thing. He also gifted them with crops that they could use to feed themselves and the keen eyesight to see in the dark. He gave them everything they needed. And you can guess what he called the son who got to rule it all."

"The Night Pharaoh," Carrianne said.

"Exactly. Part of Menes' plan was to make sure that the two kingdoms would never interact, so there was no mention of The Night Pharaoh or the creation of his realm in any official records. The location of the cave was a big secret, and the people who came down here never came back. So, after a few generations, the kingdom ruled by The Day Pharaohs forgot The Night Pharaohs even existed. Or maybe they just assumed they had died off. Who knows? They stopped calling themselves The Day Pharaoh because, as far as they were concerned, there was only one line of Pharaohs. But The Night Pharaohs have been down here all along, ruling in an unbroken chain, with one passing on their divine leadership to the next for the last 5,000 years."

"So, these people that have captured us—who call themselves the Kemet, just like ancient Egyptians did—are still following the orders of a pharaoh ... again, just like ancient Egyptians."

"Yes."

"Incredible," Ray said.

"I don't know," Joshua said. "If you ask me, The Night Pharaoh got the short end of the stick."

"From your surface-dwelling perspective, maybe," Ciarra said. "But guess which one is still here? There's been no one to conquer The Night Pharaohs, no armies coming in from Mesopotamia or Rome or anywhere else. Unlike the Kemet up there, the Kemet down here have been able to exist in peace, almost entirely undisturbed."

"But not totally undisturbed," Carrianne pointed out. "Because we're here."

"Yeah, and there have been others through the years. Just because we forgot about them that doesn't mean they've had the luxury of forgetting about us. They've maintained some knowledge of the above-ground world this whole time. They know that there's a lot more of us than there are of them. They know we have technology that they don't have and that if we ever became aware of their existence, it would probably be a real problem for them. Remaining separate has become a necessary part of survival for them.

"Remember that hieroglyphic curse we found up at the entrance to the cave, the one that said if anyone left, they'd face certain death? That's a big rule down here. You *don't* go up to the surface, period. It's become baked into these people's belief system. And, when you think about it, the curse is sort of true for them. With their eyes and skin, if any of them wandered up to the desert at two o'clock in the afternoon, they'd be in a world of hurt. They've taken great pains to keep the two worlds apart. Their priests and their pharaoh constantly reinforce the message that the above-ground world is nothing but bad news and they're much better off down here. But that gets me back to where we started. You were asking how they know Arabic."

Ciarra directed the comment at Carrianne, who said, "Yeah, what's the deal with that?"

"People from the surface have been accidentally stumbling on this place for a long time. Some of that contact has definitely been beneficial. Because it means, for example, that they've been bringing their diseases down with them—allowing the Kemet to develop natural immunities, just like the people above them.

"Anyway, the main point is, for the last 1,500 years or so, none of the people from our world have spoken Egyptian, because that language died out. They've spoken Arabic. The priests taught themselves Arabic so they could communicate with the outsiders, and they've passed knowledge of Arabic down through the generations. They've even gotten themselves a copy of the Quran so they can study it. It's part of the priesthood's role to stay sharp with the language—just in case."

"And you've learned all of this ... how?" Carrianne asked.

"The lead priest, Akh, explained it to me. From what Akh said, they haven't had outsiders down here in a long time. None of the priests currently alive have ever interacted with anyone from the surface. There used to be a lot more ways in and out of here. But about 100 years ago or so—when the outside world was starting to get a lot more mobile and a lot more curious—the Kemet closed up all the tunnels."

Kimberly cut in. "We think the origin of The Curse of Dust is from before they sealed the entrances. The curse used to be a real thing. People came out this way and tripped on one of the tunnels that led down here. And then they never came back. It really was like the desert swallowed them up."

Carrianne felt like she was missing something that was now slowly creeping on her in the worst way. "So, wait, if the desert swallowed them up, that means the Kemet ... never let them go?"

Even in the low light, she could see Carrianne and Kimberly exchanging grim looks.

Ciarra then said, "Yeah, that's ... I don't even know how to tell you this. As Akh has explained to me, once you come across the Kemet, you have to stay. It's for their protection. They'll treat us as guests, and they'll feed us and take care of us. They truly mean us no harm. We just can't leave."

"So, we're also their prisoners."

"That's right."

"For how long?"

"For forever," Ciarra said. "And Akh has made it very clear to me that the penalty for even trying to escape is death."

Their discussion continued, though none of it changed the fundamental desperation of their circumstances.

They were locked deep underground in a dark hole.

They were not permitted to leave.

And the Kemet saw it as so necessary to their very survival that nothing about this would change.

Ciarra, Kimberly, and Jamil had remained in reasonably good spirits about this because they were under the impression that they would eventually be okay—that Dave, Keith, Joshua, and everyone else would soon come for them.

That's when it became Carrianne's turn to deliver bad news: Dave and Keith had their hands full with the bandits. They were not coming to rescue anyone.

Not soon.

Maybe not ever.

That was the worst-case scenario that now seemed horribly possible.

If the bandits were able to overwhelm Dave and Keith and kill the others with them, there would be no one left who was even aware that seven people were still trapped much deeper in the cave.

They certainly wouldn't be aware that there was an entire civilization capable of doing the trapping.

Carrianne told herself that, surely, the reinforcements from Blue Diamond would chase away the bandits and then try to figure out where the rest of the team had gone.

Except what if A.J. assumed that the rest of the expedition had been killed and that their bodies were simply missing, never to be recovered?

What if the Kemet were right now figuring out how these four newest outsiders had gotten in and were sealing up the tunnel again? Would A.J.'s people reach the dead end and give up?

Was it really possible no one was going to come after them?

She decided not to voice her fears. Morale down here was bad enough already.

The conversation in the holding cell eventually wound down. They were all exhausted.

Carrianne pulled out her phone and looked at the time. It was 2 a.m.

Definitely bedtime.

She powered down her phone to save her battery. Then, she let Ciarra give her a tour of their accommodations, such as they were. This consisted of a toilet that had been chiseled into a burrow in the corner, a cistern filled with water, some portable sleeping pads, and a pile of blankets.

The blankets were made of a rough, scratchy fabric. The pads, which seemed to have been stuffed with some kind of straw, were not much softer.

But it was still better than lying on bare rock.

Carrianne fell asleep fast—and hard.

. . .

She wasn't sure how much time had passed when she started to come out of her slumber. A noise coming from outside the cell stirred her awake.

Her eyes opened. The light—that dim glow from the sodium—hadn't changed. But something in her brain told her it was morning.

Several of the Kemet were at the cell door. They were carrying baskets. Before her eyes could decide what was going on, her nose told her that there was food nearby. It smelled like something that had been freshly baked.

She rose and walked over to the bars, where a Kemet man smiled at her, spoke words she did not understand, and held out a piece of flatbread.

He was dressed differently from the soldiers, making her wonder if he was a priest.

If he was, he would know Arabic.

"*Shukran,*" she said. It was the word for "thank you" in Arabic.

"*Afwan,*" she heard back. You're welcome.

She accepted the bread, aware she was famished. It was warm and, as she discovered when she bit into it, delicious.

Ray appeared at her side with a weary smile. He also accepted some bread, chewing it ravenously.

"We should wake everyone else up," she said. "I don't want anyone to miss breakfast."

"Good thought," he said.

Carrianne began rousting people. Jamil came to quickly and readily clued into what was happening.

She reached Ciarra and Kimberly next. Joshua also appeared, having been awakened by Ray.

Then, from along the wall, Ray called out. "Hey, we have a problem over here."

"What's the matter?" Carrianne asked, following the sound of his voice over to where he was kneeling next to Jerry on one of the sleeping pads.

"He's not waking up," Ray said.

Chapter Twenty-Eight

Carrianne rushed over to them.

Ray had one hand on Jerry, who was on his side, facing the wall. His bushy white hair stood out against the dark surroundings.

It was difficult to see whether his eyes were open or closed, and Carrianne didn't dare shine her phone light on him to check. Not when the Kemet priest was on the other side of the bars, peering in on them.

She got down on her knees next to Ray. Jerry's body was warm. She checked for a pulse and found it easily.

It was strong and regular. And he was breathing. If anything, he was breathing too much. The breaths were fast and deep, like he couldn't get enough air no matter how hard he tried.

His exhales had a strange, fruity smelling odor.

"Jerry, buddy, can you hear me?" Ray asked.

There was no answer.

"Jerry, you gotta wake up and talk to us. What's the matter?"

He finally managed to say, "Don't ... feel ..."

That was as far as he got. He couldn't even finish the thought.

"Jerry, come on, talk to us. What's happening?"

But Carrianne could already guess—Jerry was in diabetic ketoacidosis. "He needs his insulin," she said. "His blood sugar is too high."

"Jerry is diabetic?" Ray asked.

"He was hiding it from everyone at Blue Diamond because they wouldn't let him go out into the desert if they knew. He's been sneaking insulin ever since he came out here. I caught him injecting it one time. He said it was something he had been managing for years, and he would be fine."

She left it at that. Jerry continued forcing unnaturally deep breaths in and out. The others had come around behind Carrianne and Ray.

"He doesn't look fine," Ray said.

"He's also been storing his insulin at room temperature," Carrianne said. "He swore that was no problem, too, but I'm sure it's not helping."

She shook him gently, then not-so-gently. "Jerry, Jerry you gotta wake up. We're trying to help you. Where's your insulin?"

No answer.

"Jerry, we have to get you some insulin or ... or bad things could happen."

She turned to Joshua. "Did Jerry bring a bag down?"

"I don't think so. We put the water and the extra flashlights in Ray's bag."

"It's over by the pad I was sleeping on," Ray said.

From behind Carrianne, there was movement as someone went to retrieve it.

Then, she heard Kimberly ask, "Okay. What am I looking for?"

"A hypodermic needle and a clear glass vial."

"There's nothing like that in here."

Joshua swore.

Kimberly brought the bag over. They all took turns searching through it. There was no insulin.

"His breath smells really weird," Kimberly said.

"Yeah. Kind of fruity, right?" Carrianne said.

"To me it smells more like acetone."

"Ass-a-tone?" Joshua snickered.

"No, acetone," Kimberly said, then spelled it out. "Also known as nail polish remover."

"That can't be good," Joshua said.

"I'm sure it's related to the diabetes somehow," Kimberly replied. "I took organic chemistry as an undergraduate, when I thought I might be a doctor. Acetone is considered a ketone. Some ketones in your body are good and natural. But if you have too many, it essentially makes your blood poison. I forget whether it's the liver going crazy or the kidneys going crazy or a combination of both. But it's definitely, *definitely* not good. He needs help."

Maybe it was because Jerry was breathing so fiercely—and futilely—but Carrianne suddenly felt like she couldn't get enough air into her lungs, either.

Or enough ideas in her head. What do you do for a diabetic who doesn't have insulin?

"Come on, let's get him up," she told Ray.

"Are you sure? Won't that hurt him?"

"I don't think so. If the problem is that his blood sugar is too high, getting him up and moving around a little will help burn off some of the sugar."

Ray shrugged but said, "Okay. How are we going to do this?"

"Grab his shoulders," she said. "I'll get his legs. Let's see if we can at least get him sitting up against the wall."

They went to work. Jerry had to weigh at least 230 pounds, if not 250; and, at the moment, it was all dead weight. They yanked and tugged until they finally got him into an upright position, facing the middle of the room.

His eyes were open but glassy. They weren't tracking anything. Beneath his white mustache, his mouth hung open. He was obviously disoriented.

"Jerry, hi," Carrianne said with her face close to his. "Where's your insulin? Did you bring any insulin with you?"

His response was to slump over and vomit.

"Oh man," Ray said. "This is bad."

"Yeah, and I'm worried it's only going to get worse."

They attempted to get him back up, but he wouldn't stay.

Next, they held him up and tried to pour some water into his mouth. Those efforts weren't very successful, either.

Eventually, they decided to let him lie down again. They huddled in the middle of the cell.

The Kemet priest who had brought them breakfast was still there and was looking on with concern, but Carrianne ignored him. It's not like they had to worry about him eavesdropping.

"Okay, does anyone have any expertise with diabetes?" Carrianne asked.

No one spoke.

"Yeah, me neither," she admitted. "But I'm pretty sure if we don't get Jerry insulin, he's only going to get sicker."

"He's in a certain amount of organ failure already if his breath smells like that," Kimberly said. "Should we be ... I mean, do you think he could die?"

"I don't know. But yes. We have to be thinking in those terms. He's not in shape to travel, obviously, so we need to get someone out of here who can go back to the top of the cave, find his insulin, and bring it back down here. I'm pretty sure he stashed it somewhere up there."

"What makes you think that?" Ray asked.

"Because before we left, he asked how long I thought we'd be gone for. In hindsight, he was thinking about whether he needed to pack his insulin."

"I don't understand," Kimberly said. "I realize we're talking about a stubborn old mule, but why wouldn't he pack it just in case?"

"Because he worried he'd be bringing attention to it. If Blue Diamond knew about his diabetes, they'd take him off the expedition.

And it sounds like he really needs the money. When I told him it would be just a few hours, he did the math and decided he was okay to leave his insulin behind."

"Yeah, I guess that makes sense," Kimberly said. "So how do we get back up there?"

Carrianne turned to Ciarra. "You think the priests would let us send someone back to the mouth of the cave with a solemn promise the person would come back? Explain to them it's a life-or-death situation. If the person didn't come back, our friend could die."

"I can try," Ciarra said.

She went over to the cell bars and began a conversation with the priest. She was pointing to Jerry. But, of course, the priest had already seen that one of the outsiders was in distress.

He quickly departed.

"What's the deal?" Carrianne asked.

"He's going to talk to Akh," Ciarra reported.

"Did he sound sympathetic, at least?"

"It's hard to say. I guess we'll find out soon enough."

They lapsed into silence as they waited for a reply. Jerry was lying down on his pad. He moaned occasionally, but no words came out of him.

After a while, Carrianne heard footsteps coming their way. The man who emerged was taller than the other priest. And older. She could tell from the way the flesh under his chin and on his neck had gone loose. Even though there wasn't sunlight to age people down here, there was still gravity.

He had a smooth, shaved dome of a head that looked like a lightbulb.

"That's Akh," Ciarra said softly.

"He's the boss, right?" Carrianne asked.

"Yeah."

Ciarra stepped forward. She and Akh began an exchange in flowing Arabic.

But it didn't take fluency to know the conversation wasn't going well. Ciarra's body language quickly made that quite clear.

"It's a no-go," she said. "His worry is that whoever goes back to the surface will come back with reinforcements, and that would put all the Kemet in danger. He didn't use these exact words, but he knows they're outgunned down here."

Carrianne sighed. Akh was glaring at her from the other side of the bars, as if daring her to contradict him.

"Tell him Jerry will die if he doesn't get medicine," she said.

"I already did."

"Do it again."

Ciarra did as told. Akh's reply was short. Then he turned and walked away.

"What did he say?" Carrianne asked.

"He said, 'Sometimes people die.'"

Carrianne waited until the sound of Akh's footsteps had faded away then went to Ray's bag.

She removed the flashlights, kept the water bottles, then put the bag on her shoulders.

She went to the cell door and reached around to the other side.

"What are you doing?" Ciarra asked.

"Finding my own way out," she said.

She put a hand to the back of her head, pulled out a bobby pin, and stuck it inside the lock.

"And how are you going to do that?" Ciarra asked.

"My dad was a locksmith," she said as she worked the bobby pin around. "I wouldn't say he taught me everything, but he taught me enough. This is a really straightforward pin-tumbler lock. And it's only got three pins. This shouldn't be hard."

"So, you're, what, picking the lock?"

"Yep."

She was out of practice, but this really was a rudimentary lock. And it had plenty of room inside, which made it easier to work with. The Kemet had obviously become decent metal workers over the last 5,000 years underground, but they still didn't have access to the kind of tool-and-die expertise that went into making your typical Master Lock, the small marvel of engineering that it was.

Back when she was a girl who spent hours doing this for fun, this would have been no challenge whatsoever. Now, it just took a little bit of patience to get everything lined up right. Luckily, there was a certain amount of muscle memory with picking locks that never entirely went away.

"Do you think the priests will notice you're gone?" Ciarra asked.

"Maybe they will, maybe they won't. They're priests, not corrections officers. And they obviously haven't had prisoners in a long time, so they don't seem to know how to do it. I mean, they didn't even search us when we came in. Did they search you?"

"No."

Carrianne took a moment to toss her cap to Kimberly.

"If you hear them coming back, put this on. Keep moving around the cell and alternate between wearing it and not wearing it. To the Kemet, we probably look similar enough. Let's just hope the hat is enough to confuse them."

Ray stepped forward and bravely announced, "I'm going with you."

"No, you're not. Having two of us leave would make it that much more obvious that people are missing, not to mention that two people slinking out of here would be easier to spot than one. Besides, they've made it clear that the penalty for escape is death. It doesn't make sense for more than one of us to take that risk."

"Then it should be me," Ray said.

"Nonsense. Jerry is my problem, not yours."

"I'll be faster getting back up the tunnel. I have longer legs. And if I get caught, I'll have a better chance of outrunning the soldiers."

With the pins set properly, she stuck in three bobby pins that, together, were strong enough to turn the lock. She opened the door then immediately shut it behind herself.

"If you want to get out, you'll just have to pick the lock," she said, removing the bobby pins and sticking them in her pocket. "Now, if you'll excuse me."

She pulled her hoodie up over her head then disappeared up the tunnel before anyone could object.

Her attire favored concealment: the black hoodie, midnight blue jeans and brown boots—plus Ray's black backpack. The dark ensemble would camouflage her well in the dim underground.

Still, it would not overcome her chief disadvantage: the Kemet could see her a lot more easily than she could see them.

Once she got away from the cell, the tunnel was pitch black. She was tempted to pull out her phone and use its flashlight, but she talked herself out of it. Not only would it wreck her night vision, but it would also make her a beacon if anyone happened to be nearby.

She would simply have to go by feel rather than sight. She groped along with her hand on the wall, trying to move as silently as possible so her ears would be able to tell her if anyone was coming.

Her main fear, beyond being discovered, was getting lost. She wasn't totally sure if there was just one tunnel—the one they had walked down on their way to the dungeon—or if there were other offshoots. If she unwittingly took a wrong turn, she worried she would wind up going in circles underground.

There were several switchbacks. She remembered that much. She also knew that the tunnel they had taken kept sloping down. Therefore, as long as she was going uphill, she was hopefully heading in the right direction.

She moved as quickly as she dared, mindful of the passing of time. A priest had just come to serve them breakfast. How long until another came with lunch? Three hours? Four?

Having Kimberly wear her hat might or might not delay their captors noticing someone was missing. But eventually the priests would surely notice there were only six people in the cell rather than seven.

She just had to push herself to move as fast as she could while staying undetected. It felt like the highest stakes game of hide and seek she had ever played.

The first switchback came soon enough. She found it easily enough in the dark. The wall she was tracing her hand along took a hairpin turn to the left.

A little way farther up, it switched back the other way. She stumbled a few times. The footing wasn't the problem; it was that the blackness was so total it was easy to get disoriented.

She kept pushing through more turns. At no point did she feel confronted with a decision. There was only one way to go. She was fairly certain she was making good progress toward the ground level of the temple and was almost daring to feel optimistic.

Then, she heard a faint shuffling sound.

She stopped, wondering if perhaps it was just her own footsteps echoing back at her.

But, even when she stood completely still, the noise only grew louder.

There was no doubt. Someone was coming.

Chapter Twenty-Nine

Carrianne's first instinct was to flatten herself along the wall of the tunnel and hope she stayed invisible as the person slid past her.

But no. That wouldn't work.

Just because she couldn't see a thing didn't mean the Kemet coming toward her was similarly afflicted. It would probably be someone—a priest, a soldier, it didn't really matter—with one of those torches she had seen earlier.

The light coming from those things wasn't much. But it was still something. Especially to someone with eyeballs perfectly tuned to the task of seeing in almost no light.

Carrianne would be as obvious as a fly swimming in milk.

Realizing this, her next thought was to retreat down the tunnel.

But what would that ultimately accomplish for her? She would just be hoping the person, what, stopped coming? Or turned off somewhere?

Both of those scenarios seemed unlikely. She was already pretty sure that this passageway went straight to the dungeon—and nowhere else. She would just be backtracking only to wind up where she had started. Except she wouldn't have time to pick the lock, so she would have to explain why she was on the wrong side of the bars.

The person was coming closer. And she could already make out a very slight brightening.

That cinched it. There would be no hiding in the dark. With each passing second, her circumstance was only becoming more dire, yet she couldn't seem to get herself unstuck. She only had two options—forward or reverse—both of which were untenable in their own ways.

She was moments away from being found out. As soon as the person rounded one more corner, she would be in plain view.

Then, a thought came to her.

It was, possibly, a terrible idea.

But it suddenly struck her as the only viable option.

She would take her biggest weakness—the Kemet's superior night vision—and turn it to her advantage.

She was thinking about the way those Kemet soldiers had attacked the flashlights Ray and Jerry had been holding.

These were people who really, *really* didn't like light—people who, collectively, hadn't been exposed to much of it over the last 5,000 years.

Turning downhill, away from the person approaching, she reached her hand into her pocket, brought out her cellphone, and powered it on. Then, she tapped one button on it and immediately held it against her chest.

She turned back uphill and started running through the tunnel as quickly and silently as she could. She nearly collided with a wall as she encountered the next switchback and just barely managed to make the turn.

From there, it was nothing but a short straightaway between her and the Kemet coming her way. She could now see he was a man, probably a priest, and quite possibly the same priest who had served her breakfast.

It didn't really matter.

Whoever it was, she was about to give him the shock of his life.

She ran straight toward him. She could see his head tilting a little. It was a universal sign of human curiosity, and she could almost see the half-thoughts forming in his mind.

What is ...

Who is ...

Why is ...

This wasn't something that was supposed to happen in a temple where this man had probably spent decades without ever once being accosted or threatened.

Which, she hoped, would make how she planned to launch this attack all that much more effective.

She closed in fast—ten feet, then five feet. He had recoiled a little but still wasn't doing anything to ward her off or protect himself.

So, he was totally exposed when, at the last possible second, she brought her phone away from her chest and held it to his face.

With the flashlight on.

The beam from the phone went directly into his very sensitive eyes.

She held it there for less than a full second—she barely even broke stride—but the result was exactly as she had hoped.

The man immediately dropped his torch and howled in pain. Out of the corner of her eye, Carrianne could see his hands going to his eyes, but she didn't stop to watch him writhe.

She was once again using the flashlight to illuminate her way, which made her trip back up the tunnel much easier and quicker. She was soon charging up the stairs and back into the main sanctuary, which was as empty as it had been earlier.

The cries of pain echoing from the tunnel grew fainter as she put more distance between herself and the suffering Kemet.

She dashed through the main chamber, out the only exit she knew of, past the statues of the gods and out onto the portico.

It was empty. There were no people anywhere. At least none that she could see.

That faint glow from the burning sodium was smoldering from somewhere high on the wall behind her. It didn't provide much light, but it was at least something. Carrianne turned off her phone's flashlight and stuck the device back in her pocket.

At this point, all it would do was alert the Kemet to her location.

She ran down the steps and was immediately confronted with a decision. If she went the way she had come, she would be heading straight into the town square, which felt like a terrible idea. Even if it wasn't as crowded as it had been when she and the other prisoners were paraded through, there would still be people.

There were two other pathways that looked to be possibilities. One angled off to the left, into what may or may not have been another residential area. The other was a hard right that traced along the wall of the cave.

The one to the left felt like it would be taking her further underground—and away from the tunnel that led up to the mouth of the cave—so she turned right.

As she put distance between herself and the temple, she had the sense she was running parallel to the main street but behind the shops and stalls. The wall of the cave remained on her right. This felt like the Kemet equivalent of a back alley.

She wasn't sure what she'd do if she encountered more people. At least so far, it was just her.

But it probably wasn't going to stay that way for long. There were, what, five hundred people living here underground? A thousand? The housing she had seen already would hold a few hundred people, but she was convinced she hadn't seen everything. The fields she had passed certainly seemed capable of sustaining a robust population, and they would also need a fair number of people to till and harvest them.

From behind her, she heard shouting in that not-Hebrew language of the Kemet, coming from the temple.

The alarm was being sounded. Whether it was priests or soldiers, there were now people on the alert that one of the prisoners had escaped.

People who would surely be coming after her.

Did they have some way of communicating with others in more distant parts of the village? Of sounding a wider alert?

Was she going to round a corner and run into a band of soldiers waiting to pounce on her? What would they do with her when they caught her?

She didn't want to think about that. She just kept sprinting.

Her best hope was that these were people who weren't used to dealing with the unexpected. If what the priests had told Ciarra was true, none of them would have dealt with an intruder in their lifetimes.

She just had to find a way to stay a step ahead of them. They didn't know which way she was headed.

Of course, neither did she.

The horrifying thought occurred to her that if the alley she was traveling suddenly dead-ended, she was probably done for. But it continued twisting and winding along the backside of the shops.

Then, in the distance, she saw it opening up a little. There was an intersection that offered her two choices—straight or left.

If she went straight, the path continued. It was impossible to say how long. She didn't like how it seemed to be turning further to the right, which would only jam her up more against the cave wall.

It just felt like that way would eventually end.

Going on nothing but a hunch, she veered left.

The path widened into something more like a street. She was now going toward the middle of the cave; toward the residential area she had passed through the previous night. And, eventually, toward the river.

As had been the case before, there didn't seem to be anyone out. It was like going through a neighborhood in the middle of the day, when no one was home.

Then, just ahead, there was a woman—a youngish woman,

perhaps twenty or twenty-five, carrying a child on her hip. She was a head shorter than Carrianne. She had those huge eyes and ghostly pale skin and wore a white robe with an ornamented collar.

But there was still something very ordinary about her. Like you could stick her in suburban America, put a Starbucks cup in her hand, and she would blend in.

She seemed to watch with fascination—and no real sense of danger or alarm—as this stranger sprinted past.

For a moment, Carrianne thought nothing would come of this interaction—that the Kemet were so unaccustomed to outsiders after such a long isolation they didn't even know how to react to one.

Then, the woman screamed.

Carrianne didn't dare stop.

Whatever hope she had of remaining undetected had probably been a fantasy, anyway.

She reached into her pocket for her phone and turned on the flashlight. It would certainly help her be able to run faster without stumbling. Maybe it would also make anyone else she encountered too scared to come closer.

That, and it was the only weapon she had.

She was approaching the street she and the others had been on earlier. She knew that going left would have taken her immediately back to the village square.

That was a nonstarter. She prepared to veer to the right, knowing that was the way that would eventually lead out of the cave.

But then she took a glance in that direction.

There was a soldier just up the path.

She could only sort of make him out, though she was fairly certain she was seeing his back. He seemed to be unaware she was racing past.

Still, it effectively eliminated the possibility of going out the cave the way she had come in it.

She crossed the street, still running at close to full speed. Her lungs were already starting to burn, and she could feel her legs growing thick with lactic acid buildup.

But there was no time for pain. She just had to push through.

As her feet continued pounding across the stone surface beneath her, she felt like she was getting closer to the river. Its blue glow was somewhere ahead of her.

Whether reaching the water would ultimately be beneficial to her escape—or a complete disaster—was just one more thing she didn't know.

The path ahead forked. There was no immediate way of telling which way to go. But it felt like left went further downhill, while right was slightly uphill.

And uphill was ultimately where she needed to go.

She turned right.

Mudbrick houses, whose off-white walls reflected her flashlight beam back at her, continued to line both sides of the road.

There was still almost no one out. Maybe everyone else was off working somewhere? Or asleep? Or just ... elsewhere?

The only exception was an elderly man, who was sitting on a chair in front of one of the houses. He was mostly bald, with a few straggly strands of white hair sticking out from the sides of his head.

As Carrianne dashed by, he barely moved. Mostly, he just stared at her with his mouth agape.

The street sloped suddenly downward, and the row of houses abruptly ended. She was once again running through fields overhung with large silver reflectors. The path she was on had plants of varying sizes on all sides.

They were mostly a blur. It's not like she was going to stop to identify them.

There were irrigation ditches partially filled with water on either side of her. Carrianne had the brief thought about whether she could hide in one of them, if only to give herself a chance to catch her breath and regroup.

Then, she saw something better. Looming ahead of her was a stand of that papyrus-like plant she had seen before. Its tallest stalks were at least eight feet, maybe even higher. The vegetation beneath was a thick mesh of white needles.

Without a second thought, she slowed just enough to part a few of the stalks and climb inside. The growth in the middle was so thick that it was difficult to find a place to stand. But that made it plenty thick enough to conceal her.

She let the plants close behind her, and she shut off her flashlight. Then, she stood, trying to stay quiet and listen as she gasped for air.

At first, she worried that someone had seen her disappear into the plants—or, for that matter, that the thunderous beating of her own heart would give her away. But there seemed to be no one aware of her presence. There was no screaming, no shouts behind her, no soldiers bearing down on her.

She was safe for the moment.

But she was far from out of trouble.

Chapter Thirty

C arrianne allowed her breathing to return to normal and her eyes to readjust to the permanent dusk of the river's blue glow.

Then, she risked a look outside her papyrus hiding place at her surroundings.

That's when she saw the dock. It was maybe fifty yards upstream —really not that far at all compared to how far she had just run.

The dock was home to several boats, small vessels with upturned bows and a platform for a person to stand in back and row. They looked like a cross between a canoe and a gondola, except they had two oars—rather than one—that were fixed to the sides of the boat by tall oarlocks.

Carrianne had never seen anything quite like them. But that was less interesting to her than the more pressing question: Could she figure out how to pilot one?

She considered this for a moment and decided that yes, she could. It just didn't look all that complicated.

What's more, the river struck her as a much better way to travel back up to the mouth of the tunnel than a street that was probably swarming with soldiers by now. The Kemet wouldn't be expecting her to take to the water.

She crouched low and emerged from her hiding spot. As she scanned ahead, she saw that this stretch of papyrus extended to a point just short of the dock. She could walk along the bank of the river using the plants to shield her from view. They were tall enough that she didn't even have to stoop.

When she reached the dock, she didn't hesitate. She climbed onto the nearest boat, untied it, and pushed off into the river.

The boat's setup was simple, and it somehow felt intuitive to her. She was able to easily figure out where to stand and how to push the oars to send her lurching forward.

As she began making her way up the river, she glanced up at the silver reflectors, hanging from the ceiling above her. Each one appeared to have been perfectly angled toward a reflector on land. It was a remarkable feat of engineering, though she really didn't have time to appreciate it or take it all in.

Her focus was on getting away.

She steered herself toward the left side of the river. There were no fields, structures, or other signs of civilization on that side. It was just a sheer stone wall that the river was slowly eroding.

It took work to battle against the current. But if she kept up a good stroke pace and pushed as hard as she could, she was able to make decent progress.

After perhaps a half-hour of steady effort, she reached the headwaters of the river, where it emerged from that hole in the rock.

She paddled until the ceiling was too low for her to go any farther, then steered over to the shoreline. She recognized exactly where she was. This was near the tunnel entrance. She could see the spot where Jerry had filled his water bottle and declared the liquid potable.

The riverbank didn't have any people on it, as had been the case the first time she had come across it. The area at the top of the bank was wide open. Unlike other areas alongside the river, it was not planted with crops. It seemed to serve no real purpose whatsoever.

There was nowhere to tie up the boat, so she just guided it over to a shallow spot and stepped off. As soon as she had disembarked, the empty craft began drifting back down the river.

She knelt and quickly filled the two water bottles from Ray's bag, knowing there were six very thirsty people at the entrance to the cave that would appreciate the gesture.

Without another backwards glance, she walked through the open area then entered the tunnel. As the blue light of the river faded, she turned on her flashlight. She was soon jogging alongside the long line of crypts that had so fascinated all of them on their way down.

She now understood this was where generations of Kemet had been laid to rest. More than likely, in keeping with Egyptian tradition, the Kemet hadn't mummified everyone. It was an honor reserved for the highest status people—the leaders, the wealthy, maybe the high priests.

It was thousands of years' worth of lives that had been led inside this cave.

She was still thinking about that when she reached the rock wall that she, Ray, Jerry, and Joshua had partially dismantled on their way down.

It didn't appear to have been touched. It had the same narrow opening they had created at the top.

Carrianne was a bit surprised to find the Kemet hadn't done anything. Did they not realize the hole was there? Had they not gotten around to fixing it yet? Or were they trying to come up with a more permanent solution for sealing the passageway?

There was no time to ponder their lack of action. She was just grateful for it as she kept moving, clambering through the crevice at the top, then continuing to follow the tunnel as it snaked toward the surface.

She worried about how long the flashlight on her phone would last. She knew that LED bulbs sipped energy and barely drained the battery. But it still wouldn't shine forever.

Finally, she reached the main cave. The first thing to greet her was the sound of gunfire. It was coming from one of the SAWs. That throaty growl was unmistakable. She was cheered by the racket. It meant Dave and Keith were still fighting the good fight.

She hastened her pace, swiftly covering the several hundred yards that remained.

But as she approached, she immediately got the sense that something was terribly wrong. Dave was standing at the opening that led to the tunnel, though he was no longer firing.

Bassel, Hani, Ihsan, and Tariq were huddled against the wall, looking miserable. Mirza was now holding one of the SAWs. Javier was pacing.

And Keith was nowhere to be seen.

Carrianne's first thought was that he must have been farther up the tunnel.

But no. Keith wouldn't be in the tunnel without his gun. And Dave wouldn't be pumping rounds into the tunnel from where he was standing if Keith was somewhere in there. The risk of him being hurt by friendly fire would be too great.

Then, she got closer and saw Keith.

He was lying on the ground, very still.

Too still.

With dread rising in her, she walked up and shined the light on him, confirming her worst fear.

Blood oozed from his ears. His face was badly burned on one side and covered in soot. His torso looked like something had crushed it.

An unlit cigar peeked out of his breast pocket.

His eyes were open and unblinking.

She turned away immediately, unable to look at him for another moment, and held out a hand against the rock wall to steady herself.

The world was suddenly spinning a little too fast.

She knelt down and bowed her head, staring at the dusty floor of the cave. Her insides felt like someone had locked them in a vise and was now squeezing.

"Oh, Keith," she blurted, and she realized there were tears on her face.

This was too much.

Too much carnage.

Too much dying.

First Ahmed. Then Joseph. And now Keith.

The sting of Ahmed's death had been mixed with hurt and bewilderment over his betrayal. It was hard to know what to think.

With Keith, there was no such mix of emotions.

It was just devastating.

She kept expecting Dave to see her and come over to her—to explain, to comfort, to commiserate, whatever. But he was rooted in his spot at the entrance to the tunnel. Now and then, he squeezed off more rounds, filling the cavern with the SAW's thunderous report for a few moments until everything lapsed back into silence.

Finally, she rose to her feet and staggered over to him.

His face was a grim picture of concentration. He was a man who had been pushed to the very edge.

"What happened to Keith?" she asked quietly.

"We didn't realize they had grenades," Dave said, his voice hoarse from yelling. "They threw one down the hole and Keith ... He just didn't have time to react and ..."

His voice faded away.

"I'm sorry," she said. "I'm so, so sorry."

"We're still hanging on," Dave said. "The grenades forced us back from the mouth of the tunnel. The bandits are down in the tunnel now, and they're getting closer. But at least so far, we've been able to hold them off. I've got to be honest. I'm pretty tired after being at this all night, but hopefully so are they. They—"

Triggered by nothing she could discern, Dave suddenly tackled her, throwing his body over hers while yelling, "Get down!"

Carrianne felt the air getting knocked out of her as Dave's full weight landed on her. She was about to protest—with a yell? a grunt?

It never even got a chance to form.

From just up the tunnel, a grenade detonated. There was a flash of light, and the noise of the explosion left her feeling concussed and a little deaf.

Dave quickly picked himself up off her, shouldered the SAW, and fired a few rounds up the tunnel.

"We're still here you cocksuckers!" he yelled. "You're gonna have to do better than that!"

Carrianne propped herself up, took a moment to collect herself, then got back to her feet and returned to Dave. He was just staring up the tunnel, waiting for the next assault.

"We were able to retrieve Keith's gun, and it still works," he said, then nodded toward Mirza. "I've taught some of the other guys how to use it, and they're taking turns relieving me. Tariq had a turn, and he was okay. Javier is a little quick on the trigger. Mirza's not bad. Hang on."

He lifted the barrel of the SAW but did not squeeze off a round.

"Sorry. I thought one of those bastards was trying to sneak down. Anyhow, what's going on down there? You guys find any water yet? I don't mean to complain, but this is hard work. We're getting pretty thirsty."

"Yeah, actually. Here," she said, unshouldering Ray's backpack.

She handed him one of the bottles. Without a word, he opened the top and chugged. She gave the other bottle to the four men huddled against the wall. They muttered their thanks.

Having emptied the bottle, Dave handed it back to her.

"I'll take a refill whenever you have a chance," he said.

"Yeah, I'm not sure how soon that's going to happen."

"Why?"

As briefly as she could, she told him about the Kemet—including about how she had escaped but now planned to go back down.

Dave showed little reaction as he listened to the report. He seemed to be running everything through a risk calculator in his head.

None of the numbers coming back were very promising.

"So, what you're telling me is we're stuck between a rock and a hard place," he said. "Or, more accurately, stuck between people who want to give us the death penalty and people who want to give us life in prison."

"Yeah, that's about the size of it."

"But you're going to go back down to prison because ... because Jerry needs his medicine?"

"Yeah."

He scoffed. "You're a better person than me."

Then, from farther up the tunnel, another grenade exploded.

"Not that being up here is any great shakes," he said.

"A.J. is coming with reinforcements. He said something about the ETS emergency response team, which could have boots on the ground in twenty-four hours."

"Yeah, those guys are the best," Dave said. "I just hope they get here soon. Our ammo is holding out so far, but if those a-holes up there get lucky with a grenade, this will get un-fun in a hurry."

"Just a few more hours," she said. "I talked to him around six last night. So—"

"Right. And then you're thinking once we get the situation up here under control, we can worry about you guys down there?"

"Yeah, I guess that's our best hope at the moment. Unless we can convince the Kemet to let us go."

"You think that'll happen?"

"I don't know. They can't really think it's tenable to keep us forever, but—"

"But this is a civilization that's been chugging along on its own for 5,000 years, so who the hell knows?"

"Yeah, basically."

"Well, good luck. I don't blame you if you want to stay up here, but if you want to go, Jerry's stuff is right over there," Dave said, jerking his head toward the wall.

"Thanks."

She went over to Jerry's bag and quickly found a box of insulin vials and some needles. Not knowing how much he would need—or how long he would need it—she took all of it and tucked it into Ray's bag.

"Good luck to you, too," she said. Then, for what little good it would do him, she added, "I'm sorry about everything."

His only response was to fire a few more rounds up the tunnel.

She set back out across the cave then down into the tunnel. With her phone light still going strong, she soon reached the dismantled rock wall. She shimmied over the top and kept going, past the crypts, which were now starting to feel like a familiar part of the landscape.

As she neared the end of the tunnel, she thought she heard something coming toward her.

There was a soft clink of metal hitting metal.

Kemet soldiers?

A patrol, perhaps?

She switched off her flashlight and stuffed her phone back into her pocket. She didn't want them to see her as a threat.

Then, she stood very still and spread her arms out wide, with her palms showing and her fingers splayed. She knew they would see her before she could see them, and she wanted it to be very clear she didn't have a weapon and didn't plan to resist.

She wished she could let them know she was there in a way that was somehow disarming. But how could she accomplish that without a shared language?

Then, a thought popped into her head.

Just a single word.

Sing.

She should sing. Did the ancient Egyptians sing? They must have. Every human culture she knew of sang and made music.

The first song that came to mind was a popular one in her native culture: "Country Roads" by John Denver.

"Almost heaven," she began tentatively. "West Virginia."

She waited. Nothing happened.

"Blue Ridge Mountains," she continued. "Shenandoah River."

She thought maybe she heard a shuffling and a scraping of feet on gritty rock. She kept going.

"Life is old—"

Before she could finish, she stopped because in the small hint of light that was now leaking from down the tunnel, she could just barely make out several soldiers, with their spears at the ready, stepping forward.

"Beeta," she said, echoing the syllables she had heard the leader use before when he tied her up.

Then, she slowly brought her wrists together. "Beeta," she said again.

From somewhere in the darkness, she heard the familiar voice of the leader reply, "Beeta."

He emerged, holding one of those faintly lit torches.

She thrust out her arms and soon felt the rasp of papyrus rope tightening around her wrists.

The leader looked at her in an odd way.

He seemed almost fearful.

Why should *he* be afraid of *her*?

Shouldn't it be the other way around?

His soldiers also seemed to be treating her with greater deference. She couldn't begin to guess why. She just let them lead her back down the tunnel.

They didn't slow down as they went through the fields and toward the village. She suspected they were taking her straight back down to the dungeon.

As they entered the residential section, there were still very few people out.

Where is everyone? she wanted to ask, though she knew she wouldn't get an answer.

She just allowed herself to be a spectacle: the prisoner, once again being forcibly marched through their village.

The marketplace had more people bustling about—it was now late morning, right? Time for business?—and they, too, stopped to stare. But the soldiers kept up their brisk pace.

Then it was up the steps of the temple and back down into its bowels. When they reached the cell again, there was a priest standing outside the bars. He seemed to have been waiting there, as though he expected the newly returned prisoner to be arriving at any moment.

"Carrianne!" Ray called when he saw her. "You're okay, thank God."

The priest was clutching an iron key that was shaped like an oversized toothbrush. Carrianne felt like she recognized how the teeth fit the pins she had picked earlier.

As the leader untied her wrists, the priest stuck the key into the lock, turned it, and opened the cell door for her.

She slid through quickly so he could shut it behind her. She worried the priest was going to search Ray's bag—or punish her in some way—but he seemed to be apprehensive of her, too, just like the soldiers had been. It's like he wanted to keep her well beyond arm's length.

Odd.

But she didn't give it further thought. She accepted a quick hug from Ray then went over to Jerry, who was still lying on a pad against the wall. The odor around him was a mix of vomit and that fruity, acetone breath he kept expelling.

Now that Kimberly had helped her identify the odor, it really did smell a bit like nail polish remover.

"How's he doing?" she asked.

"Bad," Kimberly said. "I wouldn't say he's in a coma, but I wouldn't say he's been lucid, either. He's just sort of moaning a lot."

"Well, hopefully this will perk him up," she said.

She removed one of the syringes, filled it up, and rolled Jerry onto his back. Fighting her squeamishness, she lifted his shirt and stuck the needle into his stomach, just like she had seen him do to himself.

For the first fifteen minutes or so, nothing happened. She worried that maybe she had administered the insulin incorrectly, or that it was simply too late to reverse whatever damage had been done.

While she waited, she told the others the terrible news about Keith and about how Dave and the others were now in the fight of their lives at the mouth of cave.

Everyone was quiet for a while after that, which made it easy to notice that Jerry seemed to be struggling less.

Then, roughly half an hour after she had administered the insulin, Jerry sat up on his own.

"Hey, everyone," he said. "Sorry I was a little out of it. Did I miss anything?"

Carrianne was about to answer, but she could hear people coming back down the tunnel. All seven prisoners expectantly turned their eyes toward the bars.

It was the same priest as before. He was joined by Akh, the head priest.

As Akh began speaking, the other priest was already opening the cell door.

"What's happening?" Carrianne asked.

Ciarra finished listening then said, "The pharaoh wants to see you."

Chapter Thirty-One

There was no opportunity to ask questions. Akh and the other priest were already walking back up the tunnel. It was clear they expected Carrianne and Ciarra to follow them.

To a certain extent, whatever Carrianne wanted to know—Why? What's happening? What does he want from me?—didn't really matter.

The pharaoh's requests were not to be denied.

Akh was setting a rapid pace. The other priest had a torch with him, but that wasn't really enough light to prevent Carrianne and Ciarra from stumbling now and then.

They passed quickly into the large space of the temple's main sanctuary, then through a portal that had escaped Carrianne's notice earlier. There was nothing to mark it as being any different from any of the other openings.

The hallway it led to was nondescript as well—just a square passageway chiseled out of the rock.

Then, they passed a pair of spear-wielding soldiers and were ushered into a chamber that, even though she could barely see it in the dim light, almost made Carrianne's jaw drop.

It was a massive room, with huge columns towering up to the ceiling. Its opulence was astonishing. The floor was populated by statues in both gold and silver, with precious gems set in them.

Rich tapestries covered parts of the walls. In other spots, the walls were exposed, but they contained colorfully painted reliefs and hieroglyphics that went as high as Carrianne could see—and, surely, much higher.

Important stories were being told in these pictures and pictographs, though Carrianne and Ciarra were being hurried along so quickly they didn't have time to stop and study them long enough to understand what was being conveyed.

There were riches everywhere she looked.

Soon, they were climbing a large set of steps, though it was difficult to see where they led because the top of it was so high.

But when they got there, Carrianne finally understood.

This was the pharaoh's throne room.

And there, at the center of everyone's attention, was the pharaoh.

He appeared to be fifty. Or sixty. Or forty. It was hard to tell with his unlined, bright white skin. He certainly had a regal bearing about him.

Unlike the other Kemet she had seen—all of whom were slender —the pharaoh had a pronounced ice cream scoop belly. Whether this was a sign of status or the result of being fed the best food the Kemet had to offer (or just more of it), she didn't know.

He had a double chin, chunky arms, and sausage-like fingers to match.

He was sitting on a throne that had been intricately crafted in gold, complete with sculpted gold lion heads at the base of the seat.

His robe was a version of the same off-white garment that all the Kemet wore, though his had even more colorful ornamentation at the collar and cuffs. His headdress looked like something straight out of King Tut's tomb, with alternating blue and gold horizontal stripes and a serpent coming out of the forehead.

There were other people around, some of whom appeared to be

priests. Others were perhaps advisors of a different sort. Military. Economic. It was hard to say. They were all men, and they were all focused on the pharaoh, toward whom they were suitably deferential.

The pharaoh was a god, after all.

Akh and the other priest bowed as they approached, so Carrianne and Ciarra did the same.

The pharaoh clearly had an agenda because he did not wait for anyone else before he began talking. He spoke in Arabic, which made sense—as pharaoh, he was the highest of the high priests.

Ciarra watched him carefully and immediately began translating. "He says that you must be a powerful sorceress," she said.

"Huh?" Carrianne asked.

Ciarra listened a little more then said, "He seems to be under the impression that you escaped the cell through the use of magic and then conjured light to temporarily blind one of his priests."

This must have been why the soldiers and the priest had been so afraid of her. They believed she could mess them up with magic.

"Uh, okay, sure," she said. "At what point do I tell him he's cracked?"

"Not yet. Let's just see where this goes. You have to remember, to the ancient Egyptians, magic was very real. It was the explanation for a lot of things they couldn't understand."

Ciarra uttered a short sentence to the pharaoh, who resumed his monologue.

"He says he fears he has been cursed. He says he feels ill, and none of them can seem to do anything for him. He is tired of being sick all the time. He wants you to use your magic powers to cure him."

"Oh lord," Carrianne said. "This is seriously messed up. Tell him I don't have any magical powers."

Ciarra did as asked.

The pharaoh's face immediately creased with anger. His tone became sharper.

"He says you're lying. He says if you don't use your powers to help him, he will punish all the surface dwellers, starting with me. He says he will start by putting me to death, right here and now."

"Are you serious?" Carrianne asked.

"I don't want to find out. So, honestly, I don't care that you're not Merlin. Just humor him. Do something that looks like magic. Lay hands on him, whatever. Maybe if he believes you're that powerful, there will be a placebo effect or something."

Carrianne swallowed hard. "Yeah, sure. Then let's make this good, I guess. Tell him ... tell him I need to examine him."

Ciarra spoke. The pharaoh sat up a little straighter and seemed to be welcoming Carrianne to approach.

Carrianne bowed again and walked toward the throne. The various advisors and priests nearby were clearly on high alert, and she noticed one soldier gripping a hatchet.

As she drew closer, she saw there was a gold side table next to him, covered in a large pile of what appeared to be fruit. She recognized what looked like an albino strawberry. And what was maybe white grapes. And maybe figs?

She pointed to the bounty and said, "He must really like fruit."

Ciarra translated, then listened as Akh began talking.

"Akh says that comes from the pharaoh's garden. Only the pharaoh is allowed to eat from the garden. It's one of his special privileges as a god."

"Almost sounds like the forbidden fruit from the Garden of Eden."

"Yeah, except these guys have been underground since before the writing of the Old Testament, so they wouldn't know about that."

"Good point," Carrianne said. "I guess we know why he's so fat. He sits around eating fruit all day and probably never does any actual work. Don't translate that."

"Definitely not."

Carrianne was now next to the pharaoh, who was looking at her expectantly, with the same stern face. She didn't have the first clue where to begin. Did she ask him to undress? Did she take his pulse? Try to listen to his heart?

Then, she caught a strange but familiar odor coming from him.

He smelled fruity, but not like mango.

More like acetone.

Nail polish remover.

His breath wasn't nearly as powerfully tinged as Jerry's had been, but it was still noticeable. And, in an instant, it helped Carrianne understand. The pharaoh who gorged himself on fruit and never exercised was, unsurprisingly, becoming a diabetic.

"I have really good news for him, for you, and for everyone," she said. "I think I'm going to be able to do some magic after all."

"Really?" Ciarra said. "You serious?"

"Yeah, but tell him there's a price. Tell him if I cure him, he has to let me and my friends go, otherwise there will be no end to the curse. Tell him it's only right that we return to our world and leave them to theirs. Tell him if we are allowed to go, we will keep the secret of what exists down here, and that I will cast a powerful spell that will keep outsiders away."

Ciarra translated.

Then, there was silence as the pharaoh listened to and then considered this offer. He entered into a brief discussion with his advisors, though they had switched languages, so Ciarra didn't know what was being said.

Then, the pharaoh looked at Ciarra and spoke definitively.

"He says he agrees to your terms. But if you don't cure him, he will put us all to death."

Carrianne had Ciarra explain that they needed to return to the dungeon, so she could work some magic.

Akh led them back down to the cell. Carrianne went

immediately to Jerry, who was still sitting up and looked like he had continued to improve while she was gone.

"How much insulin do you need to get you through the next day or so?" she asked.

"Not too much," he said. "The vial I've already started has enough doses left in it for sure. Why do you ask?"

"Because I need the rest of your stash," she said. "I think I can use it to get us out of here."

"Then, by all means, have at it," he said.

She took the box with the remaining vials, along with most of Jerry's needles. She then had Akh escort her back to the throne room.

Once she was back in audience with the pharaoh, she held up one of the vials.

"This is a very powerful potion," she said, and Ciarra began translating. "It will make you feel much better. But I have to inject it into your stomach."

She held up the needle and pantomimed bringing its sharp edge toward her stomach.

This made several of the advisors visibly nervous, but the pharaoh nodded and seemed to be girding himself for it.

"Tell Akh to take note of what I'm doing," Carrianne said. "It sounds like this is about to become his job."

Ciarra conveyed the words. Akh drew closer and watched as Carrianne filled the syringe.

She looked at the pharaoh while pointing to her own belly. "I need to inject it here."

There was some awkwardness as the pharaoh lifted his robe and exposed his large, round stomach. She stuck the needle in and depressed the plunger.

The pharaoh grunted a little but was otherwise stoic.

"The Kemet pray, right?" she asked.

"Of course," Ciarra said.

"Good. Tell them we're going to pray now. All of us must pray for the next half-hour. Tell them this is very important and that the magic won't work otherwise. We're going to pray, and then the gods will be pleased, and the magic will take hold."

"Are you serious?"

"Yes."

"You had better be right."

"This guy has type 2 diabetes and has probably felt like crap for years," Carrianne said. "The insulin is going to make him feel like a new man, trust me."

"If you say so."

Ciarra spoke, and the room quieted.

Akh began what sounded like a prayer. It was long and somber. When he was done, another priest took over.

The pharaoh remained quiet. His eyes were closed.

They continued their prayers, with each priest taking a turn.

Suddenly, amid one of the prayers, the pharaoh said something that brought everyone to attention.

Everything in the room briefly stopped, including Carrianne's breathing.

He spoke a few words, which were met with a palpable outburst of joy.

"He says he feels much better!" Ciarra gushed. "He says you are a great sorceress."

"Okay, good," Carrianne said. "Now, this is very important. Tell him the potion will make him feel better for a while, and that he should take the potion whenever he feels bad. But in the long run, the real cure will be up to him. Explain to him the fruit from the pharaoh's garden is poisoning him. That is why he is suffering from this curse while none of his people are. Tell him he needs to stick to eating vegetables and then try to explain exercise to him. He needs to move his body—march like his soldiers march, work the fields like his people do, however you want to explain it. If he eats like his people and works like his people, he will feel much better, and soon he won't need the potion anymore."

Ciarra communicated the full message.

When she was through, the pharaoh was smiling.

"He says he is very grateful, and now he will fulfill his promise and let you and your fellow surface dwellers go free."

Carrianne smiled back and was about to thank him when a young-looking man burst into the throne room and ran up the steps.

Through ragged breathing, he spoke with great urgency.

All around Carrianne and Ciarra, there were shouts of dismay. The advisors began having a frantic conversation.

One of the men, who looked like he was part of the military, sprinted out of the room.

"What's happening?" Carrianne asked.

"I don't know. Hang on."

Ciarra conferred with Akh, whose face had gone ashen.

"Oh no," Ciarra said when he was done.

"What's the deal?" Carrianne asked.

"It's the bandits. They must have gotten past Dave and the others, because they're now at the wall. They're taking it apart, stone by stone. It sounds like they're going to break through any minute now."

Chapter Thirty-Two

Carrianne felt herself rock backwards as she absorbed the news. Her thoughts immediately went to the men who had likely just lost their lives defending the top of the cave. Something must have gone dreadfully wrong for them. Had a grenade rolled too far? Had they run out of ammo? Had they let their guard slip—or made some other mistake—and paid the price?

There was no way of knowing. All she could do was mourn them. It was simply terrible—that all those people were ultimately worth less to these bandits than two gold statues.

But she quickly realized that, as awful as it was and as much as she might want to surrender to those emotions, there was something even worse about to happen.

The bandits were coming. They had no idea that by continuing down the tunnel, they were essentially kicking a hornet's nest. The Kemet would come swarming at them with the ferocity of people protecting their home.

A battle was inevitable.

The Kemet had spears and hatchets, superior numbers and better vision.

But the bandits had guns.

It would be a bloodbath for both sides.

And it would only get worse if the bandits managed to win. If they succeeded in breaking through, they wouldn't show restraint.

She was thinking of the young woman with the baby on her hip and the old man sitting in front of his house. These were people who just wanted to live in peace, without bothering anyone.

Yet the bandits wouldn't hesitate to slaughter them—not once they saw the riches waiting for them. Forget the mummies, the artifacts, the artwork, or anything of cultural significance. The silver reflectors alone would be worth a fortune. They easily weighed a hundred pounds each. Melted down, they could be sold for, what, twenty thousand dollars? Forty thousand? More?

And that was just one reflector. There were *thousands* of them covering the river and fields, which put their total value in the many, many millions. A hundred million? More?

Suffice it to say: a lot. Enough to give the bandits all the motivation they needed to press forward.

Could the Kemet really defeat these modern-day scavengers with what was essentially Bronze Age weaponry?

There was no way of knowing. But she knew, as long as she could still stand, she had to do everything she could to help them.

She turned to the pharaoh and looked him in the eye. "Please let me and my friends join you in this fight. I know some of what I do may seem like magic to you, but it's really just advanced technology. And the people coming down the tunnel have advanced technology, too."

She let Ciarra catch up with the translation before continuing.

"My friends and I have tried to be good people. We are peaceful. We respect your culture, your civilization. We don't want to see you get hurt.

"The people coming down the tunnel are not good people. If they're able to break through your defenses, they will kill all of your people and take your treasure. We call them bandits. All they do is steal things, break things, and hurt people. In fact, the only reason we're here now is because we were trying to escape them. They would have killed us." She bowed her head. "They succeeded at killing some of our group."

Ciarra kept talking as Carrianne waited. When Ciarra had finished, Carrianne resumed.

"Let us help you fight this terrible enemy. Together" —she meshed her hands together— "we will defeat them."

Maybe it was her imagination, but the pharaoh seemed to understand. He was nodding even before Ciarra had finished translating.

"He said you are a very wise and powerful leader, and he is honored to join forces and fight with you."

Carrianne smiled at him. Then, she made one final request: to have Joshua's gun returned to her.

It was its own form of magic.

Joshua had already squeezed off twenty or thirty bullets when he was in his mad rage, but the SAW's belt contained two hundred rounds. So, it could still be a powerful tool on their side.

One of the priests was soon presenting it to Carrianne. She accepted it and carried it with her as Akh and the other priest escorted her and Ciarra back down to the dungeon.

When they arrived, they explained to the rest of their group all that had transpired.

Their news was met with a combination of anguish, relief, and fear.

A lot of fear.

They quickly collected their things. Jerry brushed off all offers of assistance, insisting he was feeling much better. They soon departed and worked their way back up the tunnel for what Carrianne hoped would be the last time.

When they exited the temple, what they found was quite different than anything they had seen before.

There were hundreds of people massing there under the dim

glow of the sodium lights. There was a lot of noise—voices, loud and soft, giving commands and having conversations—but it was surprisingly orderly, given the circumstances.

This was an emergency, though not an entirely unexpected one. She had the sense these people had trained for this.

She could see most of the people had weapons. They were ready to defend themselves.

Akh uttered something to Ciarra, who then conveyed the message to the others.

"He says he will join us as we go to the headwaters of the river. He says the soldiers are already there. That is where the battle will take place, and it's where our help will be needed most."

"Okay, let's head out, then," Carrianne said.

They had just reached the bottom of the steps when the pharaoh appeared at the top of them. The Kemet quieted in an instant. All eyes had turned toward their leader.

As he began talking, the silence among the rest of the group was total. He was speaking in the Kemet's native language, but some things didn't need translation. His brief oration was met with a roar of approval from the people.

"I'm feeling inspired, and I don't even know why," Ray shouted over the noise.

"For sure," Jerry replied. "Now let's go help save the day."

They followed Akh and his bald head through the residential section of the village, which was now empty. After they passed the fields, they reached the headwaters of the river.

The area now felt familiar to Carrianne. The ever-changing blue ribbon of river continued its gentle flow to their left.

Akh led them to a spot just short of the wide-open area. It was a small rock berm, maybe five feet high, at the edge of the fields. The mouth of the tunnel was barely visible in the distance to their right.

As Akh spoke, he made a show of crouching behind the berm, making himself small.

"He wants us to hide here," Ciarra said, in case it wasn't already obvious. "He says we have to make sure we're out of sight."

Carrianne looked around, expecting to see platoons of Kemet soldiers at the ready.

There were none.

"Just ... by ourselves?" she asked.

"Yes. He says this is where we are supposed to be. He's stressed to me that we absolutely cannot move from here."

"Okay, when should I start shooting bandits?" Joshua asked.

Ciarra relayed the question, then reported back, "Not yet. For right now, he just wants us to stay here."

Akh was still motioning for people to get low. One by one, the seven members of their group followed the instructions, finding places behind the rock.

The priest said something to Ciarra then stood quickly and disappeared from their view.

"He reiterated that we *have* to stay here," she said.

"Yeah, I kind of got that already," Jerry said.

He seemed to Carrianne to be in good spirits. After how sick he had been feeling, anything—even the stress of an imminent clash with bandits—was an improvement.

Joshua, on the other hand, was clearly jumpy. Carrianne couldn't decide whether he was itching for a fight, whether he didn't like being told what to do, or whether he was just apprehensive.

Maybe it was all three.

When Akh returned, he began talking in earnest with Ciarra, who translated in short bursts.

"He says their scouts have been keeping watch on the bandits ... They have removed the rest of the wall and are coming this way ... This is a good place for us to sit tight ... We should be patient and not ... not leap at ... hang on, he's going for some kind of metaphor, and I don't get it."

She asked a question of Akh, which resulted in a short dialogue between the two before she resumed.

"Yeah, basically, he's asking us to chill. Joshua shouldn't use his weapon until the time is right."

"And what time is that?" Joshua asked.

Ciarra posed the question to Akh, who answered quickly.

"He says you'll know—that it will be very clear. But whatever you do, don't shoot too soon."

"In other words, don't fire until you see the whites of their eyes?" Jerry asked.

"I'm pretty sure the Bunker Hill reference would be lost on them, but yeah," Ciarra said. "That's the general idea."

Joshua grumbled something inaudible as the group settled in to wait. For how long remained unclear.

Fifteen minutes passed. Then twenty. Nothing happened.

Then, it was an hour.

Still nothing. It only made Carrianne that much more unsettled that they were so completely on their own.

Were they the sacrificial lambs? Set off on their own to be easy pickings for the bandits? Did the pharaoh and his advisors believe that Carrianne would be able to use her "magic" to protect them?

Where *were* the rest of the Kemet? The hundred or so soldiers she had seen? The thousand or so citizens who seemed to be massing for a defense?

Every so often, Akh came with more updates. The bandits were slowly working their way in this direction. He kept urging patience.

In between Akh's visits, there remained muted conversation behind the berm. Carrianne kept shushing them, feeling like an anxious stage manager reminding the cast to stay quiet while they were waiting behind the curtains offstage.

More time passed. Another hour? More? Carrianne wasn't sure. She didn't want to tax the battery on her phone by constantly powering it on to check.

Nothing was happening. And yet something soon would. It was a strange combination of boredom and terror.

Joshua kept making noises of exasperation that she gradually learned to tune out.

Then, at last, the first group of bandits arrived at the mouth of the tunnel.

Carrianne stiffened when she heard them. She risked a quick glance over the berm.

There were only four of them. They had flashlights and were waving them around as they walked slowly into the open space. None of them had weapons at the ready. One had a long rifle hanging loosely from a strap across his chest.

Their movements were loose, easy. They did not seem to be particularly wary of anything. They were acting like they had already defeated all resistance.

She couldn't understand their Arabic, but she didn't really need to. They were having the same reaction she, Ray, Jerry, and Joshua had when they had first come to this spot. They were marveling at the river, the cave, all of it.

One of the bandits called loudly up the tunnel.

"He just told his buddies they have to come see this, that they won't believe it," Ciarra whispered.

"This is stupid," Joshua hissed. "Why are we letting them just waltz in here? The tunnel is a great choke point. It's a lot easier to defend than this huge cave. We should be jamming them in the tunnel."

Carrianne watched as the knuckle on his index finger went white from pressing against the trigger guard too hard.

"Just hold your fire," she said. "This is the Kemet's home turf. We have to trust that they know how to defend it."

"Yeah, against the Macedonians and the Hittites. This is a little different."

More bandits kept showing up. They, in turn, called for others to join them. Ten became twenty, then thirty, then forty. They were all jabbering loudly, quite unaware anyone was watching them.

"I could take out half of them right now," Joshua said. "They wouldn't even have time to grab their weapons. I can *take* them."

Carrianne reached out and put her hand on the barrel of the SAW to prevent him from doing anything rash.

The number of bandits had finally stopped increasing. They were starting to fan out and explore. There was still no reaction from the Kemet, and no indication there would be one.

Carrianne's dread was only rising. She was starting to think the Kemet had abandoned them. They would be left to fight this battle on their own.

It would be Joshua against roughly fifty men—impossible odds, even if he had the element of surprise.

She was just settling into this horrible reality when, to her right, there came a heart-stopping yell.

In one shocking moment, two things happened.

From above the bandits, a deadly hail of iron spears rained down.

And, from below, a dense matrix of sharpened spikes shot up with lethal force from hidden holes in the ground.

Carrianne could now just barely make out that the spears had come from several platoons of Kemet who had been hiding on a rock ledge that overhung the tunnel opening.

There were more coming now. And more. The spears were laying waste to the bandits who hadn't already been impaled by the spikes.

Suddenly, it all made sense to Carrianne. Why did the Kemet have this wide-open area at the mouth of the tunnel with seemingly nothing in it?

Because it was grounds for the perfect trap.

The bandits who were merely wounded—not killed instantly—began howling in pain and fear.

Adding to the chaos, Joshua had sprung into action. This, clearly, was the signal he had been waiting for. He poked his head above the berm, rested the SAW's tripod legs on top of it, and began laying down a deadly layer of fire at roughly chest height.

Carrianne watched as the SAW's rounds ripped through the bandits' bodies with horrific effect.

The few who were still capable of responding groped for their weapons and began firing back, but they didn't even know what they were aiming at. They couldn't see any of their attackers. They were just firing randomly into the darkness.

Then, coming from her right, there was another primal roar, even louder than the one that had signaled the springing of the trap.

A company of Kemet soldiers emerged from seemingly nowhere and were charging at the bandits head on, heedless of the danger.

"Stop shooting!" Carrianne yelled at Joshua. "Hold your fire!"

Joshua had already eased his finger off the trigger.

Carrianne was glad she couldn't see too much of what was happening. What little she could make out was as grotesque as it was brutal.

The Kemet soldiers had set upon the bandits with savage power, using their hatchets to butcher the injured and uninjured alike. There were more cries of agony ... and the sickening sound of metal burying itself in muscle, fat, and bone.

A few of the remaining bandits were trying to raise their hands in surrender.

They were given no quarter.

Other bandits were attempting to retreat. But they didn't get very far. They were still being mowed down from above with lethal efficiency by the spear-throwing Kemet, who combined excellent aim with a seemingly endless supply of projectiles.

Between the air and surface attacks, any bandit who had dared come through the mouth of the tunnel was eviscerated.

The main thrust of Kemet soldiers was now pouring up the tunnel, going after any bandits that might have remained there. If there were any left—and Carrianne couldn't tell from her spot behind the berm—they didn't stand a chance.

They had no idea what was coming, and the Kemet soldiers were disciplined, fearless, and ferocious.

Carrianne had been expecting a battle. Instead, it had been a massacre as one-sided as any in history. The Kemet had been preparing for this for the better part of 5,000 years. And they rose to the occasion.

Carrianne anxiously listened for sounds of continued fighting coming from the tunnel. She heard nothing.

There was no one left to fight.

It wasn't long before Akh was approaching them and speaking with low urgency.

"They're going to seal the tunnel now," Ciarra reported. "And he says this time they're going to seal it permanently. I don't know what that means, exactly, but it's pretty clear it's time for us to make our departure."

Chapter Thirty-Three

T heir trip topside was mercifully uneventful.

Joshua led the way, keeping himself and his SAW poised to respond to danger at any moment. But that proved to be unnecessary. There were no living bandits anywhere in the cave.

The Kemet were in the midst of dragging the bloodied bodies deeper underground, where they would presumably never be seen again.

The Curse of Dust had struck again.

As they emerged from the cave, they squinted and shielded their eyes against the brightness that now somehow felt almost foreign.

Whatever bandits had been at the surface were now long gone, too—either dead or chased away.

The only signs they had even been there were a few bodies, already covered in black bags, and several burned out husks of pickup trucks.

It wasn't difficult to guess the agent of this destruction. Two hulking Black Hawk helicopters with ETS logos were at rest not far from the entrance to the cave. Milling around them were roughly two dozen mercenaries in full combat gear.

Each chopper had several half-full pods of missiles hanging off their underside, along with their forward-fixed 50-caliber machine guns.

Carrianne could imagine the scene as those helicopters—with all that firepower—had shown up and laid waste to the bandits who were still outside the cave. Those not smart enough or fast enough to run away had paid the ultimate price.

Here and there were blackened pockmarks in the desert, further hints of the broader devastation. Only two of the Broncos were still there, and their tires were popped. The other two Broncos were gone, perhaps stolen by the bandits.

At the camp, in the distance, she could still see the tall boom of the diamond drill, which told her the bandits had not yet gotten around to removing all of the equipment before the attack had come. Other things at the camp—the smaller items that could be carried more easily—had surely been looted.

Whatever had happened, Blue Diamond was once again firmly in control of the area. It had spared no expense in bringing in ETS's most elite emergency response team.

And there, in the middle of it, like a kid who just couldn't get enough of the toys he had assembled, was A.J. Sebastian. He had on aviator glasses. His square jaw, with its dimpled chin, seemed to be jutting out just a little further than usual.

Despite all the death and destruction, this was somehow a triumphant moment for him.

Carrianne didn't share his jubilation. Neither did anyone else who had emerged from the cave. They were in a quiet daze, all lost in various stages of their own grief—and relief.

There was something surreal about it. In just a few hours, they had gone from fearing for their own lives, to watching the Kemet rout the bandits, to escaping from a place where they thought they might be locked up for the rest of time.

And now, they were squinting into a desert sun that was still hanging low in the sky—the last remnants of a day that felt like it had lasted a year. The air was delightfully warm compared to the uniform sixty-degree chill of the subterranean realm they had just been trapped in.

Everything else just seemed wrong.

Carrianne had taken sixteen people out into the desert. She was returning with only six of them.

Dave, Keith, and Joseph had died in the line of duty, defending the people they had been hired to protect.

Ahmed had died of his own treachery.

The rest—Javier and Mirza; the cooks, Bassel and Ihsan; and the laborers, Tariq and Hani—had been collateral damage.

It was devastating.

Even though she had not even begun to sort out the emotions, she already knew she would never totally outlive the guilt of surviving while the others hadn't.

But she would find a way to carry on all the same. Meemaw still needed her. And it would hardly honor the sacrifice all those people had made if she just tucked her tail and ran away from life.

She certainly knew what Paw would have to say about it: *You're only a failure if you quit, and no one can make you quit but you.*

She sighed and looked over at A.J. Sebastian, who was still walking around like ... Well, another Paw-ism was immediately coming to mind: *Like the only rooster in a henhouse.*

A.J. was barking orders at the ETS soldiers, who were being compensated well to humor him. She supposed, on some level, she was like that, too.

It made her even more depressed.

But then, as she studied him a little closer, she realized exactly what he was doing—he was coordinating the loading of the gold statues onto one of the helicopters.

Indignation welled up in her. There was no more confusion in her mind about what needed to be done with those statues.

She now understood to whom those statues *really* belonged. And it wasn't Blue Diamond Resources.

Even if she couldn't ensure they were returned to the Kemet, their rightful owners, she could at least try to see to it that they were put in the care of the Kemet's distant cousins.

Carrianne summoned her resolve and approached A.J. "What's your plan for those?" she asked.

"Oh, don't worry about them. I'll take care of it."

"You're turning them over to the authorities, right?"

"Yeah, sure," he said, unconvincingly.

"A.J., don't B.S. me. I don't care what kind of moral gymnastics you do to try and justify it. Those statues aren't ours. You need to alert the Ministry of Tourism and Antiquities immediately. Technically, we weren't even supposed to touch them once we found them."

He looked at her through his aviator glasses. "You're kidding, right?"

"Not even a little bit."

"Did you hit your head down there or something?"

"No. Don't you dare steal those statues."

"I'm not stealing anything," he said. "We paid a lot of money for this expedition. My dad and his stupid SWAGs are very expensive, in case you didn't know. We've been bleeding money for months now. He doesn't care. He'd rather go bankrupt than admit he's wrong about the Western Desert—or anything else, for that matter. This is the only thing we have to show for all our efforts. With luck, we'll even turn a little profit. Finders keepers."

"No. That's not how it works. You know better. I'm not going to look the other way on this, A.J. If you don't go through proper channels, I'm going to have no choice but to report you."

He laughed. "Well, that's very brave and self-righteous of you, but you can't. You can't say a word."

"Why not?"

"You signed a nondisclosure agreement, remember? That thing is beyond ironclad. You go to the authorities, and it'll cost you five million bucks. You really have that much in your bank account?"

"NDAs don't cover illegal activities, and what you're doing by taking those statues is unquestionably illegal. I don't know if Egypt has whistleblower laws, but it doesn't matter. America certainly does, and the agreement I signed said it was governed under the laws of the State of Colorado."

A.J. stopped and looked at her in disbelief. "You really want to make an issue out of this?"

"Try me."

"Why are you bothering?"

"Sometimes you don't need a reason to do the right thing."

He scoffed. "Look, even if the authorities do something—and I doubt they will—I'll either bribe them or bury them in lawyer's fees until they can't breathe. You'll be destroying your career for nothing. Because you better believe I'll have my dad put out the word in the industry that we made a huge mistake in hiring you. You were not only inexperienced, but you were also completely inept. You only filed this frivolous complaint against us because you're a disgruntled ex-employee and you wanted to distract from the fact that you failed massively in your first and only expedition. You'll be radioactive. No one will want to come within a thousand miles of offering you a job. You might as well go back to Greasy Creek and herd pigs, or whatever it is people do there, because you're finished as a geologist."

"At least people in Greasy Creek know the difference between right and wrong," Carrianne shot back.

"Great. Have fun with that. Now, as of this moment, you're fired. As soon as we get back to the warehouse, pack up your stuff and get out. What you do after that is up to you. But I'd think twice about throwing your life away to be the hero of all Egypt. Believe me, the only people who remove more precious antiquities from this country than foreigners are the Egyptians themselves."

Carrianne didn't bother arguing further. He was clearly past the point of moral reasoning.

And, besides, whatever further conversation they would have on the subject was about to be interrupted.

Strangely, there were people on camels that had just emerged from the other side of a rocky outcropping. They were wearing flowing robes and colorful headdresses.

It was the Bedouins. And, quite inexplicably, they appeared to be heading toward Carrianne and A.J.

Carrianne watched with confusion as the camels lurched closer.

There were eleven of them altogether. They had obviously come from the Bedouin encampment she had seen the other day. And now they were on the move.

But why, in the middle of a huge empty desert, did they choose a path that would put them in the middle of a bunch of heavily armed strangers—who happened to be the only people for at least fifty miles in any direction?

"What the hell is this?" A.J. muttered.

There was no obvious answer.

But then, as they got closer, Carrianne felt her mouth hanging open in astonishment. She blinked twice, because she couldn't quite believe it.

The man on the lead camel wasn't a Bedouin.

It was Inspector Mahmoud Yousef of the Egyptian Mineral Resources Authority. His Bedouin-like clothing aside, there was no question in her mind it was him. She recognized his mustache.

He was probably still wearing his pocket protector under his robe.

He was, actually, exactly the kind of person she needed.

Without a second thought, Carrianne walked over to Ciarra, who had been leaning against the strut of one of the helicopters, drinking a bottle of water.

"Hey, would you mind doing some translating for me?"

"Sure," Ciarra said, lifting herself to her feet.

Carrianne led her up to Yousef, who was climbing off his camel near a still-befuddled A.J.

"Inspector Yousef, I have to report a violation of our exploration license," Carrianne said. "A.J. Sebastian is improperly removing antiquities that belong to the Egyptian people. He's in the middle of doing so right now."

She pointed toward the helicopter.

Ciarra began translating, but Yousef interrupted her. "Are you willing to testify to that?" he asked in flawless English.

Carrianne tried not to look surprised.

Yousef knew English?

She answered his question with a very firm, "Yes, absolutely."

"Very good. I intend to see to it he is prosecuted to the fullest extent of the law."

The other riders had also dismounted from their camels and had begun unwrapping the statues. Several of them had pulled digital cameras out from under their robes and were taking photos of the antiquities. The soldiers were exchanging inquiring glances—*What's happening? Should we be trying to stop this?*—but they did not intercede.

Yousef was brandishing a pair of handcuffs. "A.J. Sebastian, you are under arrest for stealing the treasures of Egypt."

A.J. broke into a wild smile. "Oh, Inspector, I think there's been a misunderstanding. I was only having those statues loaded onto the helicopter so I could safely return them to the proper authorities."

"That's not—" Carrianne began to say.

Yousef held up a hand to stop her. "Is that what you intended to do with the Anubis statue you sold in Turkey two weeks ago? What about the scarabs you've been offering for two thousand dollars each on the dark web? Or the gold Ankh necklace you sold for fifty thousand to the collector from St. Petersburg that you met at that hotel in Cairo? Or the marble bust of Julius Caesar that you're trying to get half a million for?"

A.J.'s lips had snapped shut. He looked like he had swallowed a desert cactus.

Yousef turned to Carrianne. "I'm not with the Egyptian Mineral Resources Authority. I'm a special agent for the Ministry of Tourism and Antiquities. We've been conducting a multi-pronged investigation into Blue Diamond's activities in the country for months now. We've been watching you quite closely for the last several weeks, so I'm aware you have not been a part of this conspiracy."

Carianne thought back to when Yousef had last shown up in camp at dusk—seemingly out of nowhere—and then driven off in his Jeep by himself. She thought it strange that he would be striking out into the desert for such a long journey as night was falling.

Obviously, he had been coming from a lot closer than she had realized. That Bedouin encampment wasn't really a Bedouin encampment.

What was it that Ahmed had once said? *The Bedouin are never lacking in surprises.*

Yousef continued. "Your boss has been using Blue Diamond's legitimate exploration activities as a front to smuggle antiquities out of the country. I'm afraid the statues he has on the helicopter are only a small part of a much, much larger operation. He has been purchasing items from thieves throughout the country. He then hides the stolen objects among the core samples that his exploration teams produce, so he has been able to move his treasures freely throughout the country without fear of detection. You may have noticed he was always keen to make sure there was always a fresh flow of core samples?"

Carrianne thought back to A.J.'s response when the diamond rig broke down. *We need those core samples pronto.* He then reiterated it the next day.

"Yes," she said.

"He loaded them onto the plane, along with the smuggled objects," Yousef said. "From the plane, they went to a truck. But on the way to the processing laboratory, the truck often made one extra stop at the yacht he has docked just outside Alexandria. The stolen items were brought aboard and then sailed out of the country on the pretense of weekend pleasure cruises. Isn't that right, Mr. Sebastian?"

Carrianne flashed back to the objects wrapped in blue tarps she had seen when she had inadvertently stumbled on the boat's cargo hold. Was that actually contraband?

Then, she remembered his words from when they first met: *I take her out on longer trips on weekends just because it seems like a shame to keep her in the harbor all the time.*

A.J.'s grim expression had not changed, even as his wrists were secured behind his back with Yousef's handcuffs.

"I believe you have been aboard Mr. Sebastian's yacht?" Yousef asked Carrianne.

"Yes."

"Then you have met another one of our agents. She has been posing as a Russian prostitute named Tatiana. She pretended to be drug-addicted and to not understand English very well. But all the while, she has been cataloguing the extensive nature of Mr. Sebastian's crimes. In addition to what she has seen firsthand, he had many, many sensitive conversations around her that he didn't think she would grasp. As a bonus, we'll also be able to prosecute him for solicitation."

A.J. now appeared ready to pass out.

"It is convenient for us that we are catching him in the act with the reflector statues," Yousef continued. "But even if a sympathetic court accepts his flimsy explanation that he was going to return them to the proper officials, we still have overwhelming evidence of his habitual law-breaking. It has been exhaustively well documented by a dedicated team of agents."

"Did ... did anyone on my team know about any of this?" Carrianne asked.

"I don't believe so," Yousef said. "Simply by continuing to generate core samples, you were unwittingly doing your part. Most of

Mr. Sebastian's criminal actions happened away from other Blue Diamond employees. They appear to be unaware he was using the facility in Aswan as a clearinghouse for the illicit transactions he made in the lower half of the country."

Carrianne thought back to the lumpy objects draped in white cloth she had seen on the pallets back at the warehouse that first day she was in Aswan.

Supplies.

A.J. had said they were supplies.

"So, was all this ... everything we did out in the field, looking for resources ... was it all just a scam?"

"Oh, no. The licenses were quite legitimate. I'm sure if you had found anything, Blue Diamond would have been happy to profit off of it. Gold is gold, Ms. Kaucher. It appears Mr. Sebastian was acting on his own, with a limited number of confederates. We are still reviewing financial documents, but so far, it appears the money trail begins and ends with Mr. Sebastian. We have no evidence that his father or anyone else at Blue Diamond Resources back in America was aware of the illegal activities. As far as they were concerned, this was a perfectly legitimate operation."

Carrianne shook her head, which was swimming.

"So, what happens now?" she asked.

"Your exploration licenses have been suspended as of a few hours ago. Blue Diamond is officially banned from any further exploration in the country. I'm afraid your visas are being revoked as well. You will have to leave the country as soon as possible. We may ask you to return to testify someday. We'll deal with that when the time comes."

"I understand," Carrianne said.

"Now, if you'll excuse me, I have to deliver a criminal into police custody."

Chapter Thirty-Four

E ven though everything Yousef had said made sense, Carrianne was still stunned by what happened next.

Yousef got on a two-way radio and ordered a vehicle to come and pick up A.J., who was soon loaded and taken away.

He didn't say a word the entire time.

But Carrianne doubted his silence—or all the lawyers he was about to hire, or even the bribes he would surely try to offer—would save him this time.

The Ministry of Tourism and Antiquities had dedicated a lot of time and resources to this investigation. It wasn't going to let itself be bullied or influenced by A.J. Sebastian's money.

As soon as A.J. was gone, Carrianne looked around, a little bit stupefied. What was she supposed to do now? What was her team supposed to do?

It would soon be dark. Were they going to try to spend the night at what was left of their camp? How were they supposed to get back to civilization?

Her thoughts were interrupted when she heard someone calling her name.

It was Joshua. He was walking toward her, so she met him halfway.

"What's up?" she asked.

"One of the Black Hawks is taking off in a little while. Most of the soldiers are staying here overnight to keep an eye on the equipment that hasn't been stolen, so there's room for you and the others if you want. It's probably your best ticket out of here. Maybe even your only ticket. I don't think the Broncos are drivable."

"That sounds great," she said. "Thank you. I'll let the others know."

He nodded and was turning to tend to other business when Carrianne stopped him.

"Wait a second," she said. "I think we need to have a quick team meeting about ... about everything. Call it a final debriefing."

He shrugged. "Sure."

"Okay, meet me at the mouth of the cave in five minutes."

As she set about rounding up the others, she was remembering the words of Ben Franklin. Or was it Mark Twain?

Two people can keep a secret if one of them is dead.

What would those guys have said about *seven* people?

That was the question filling her mind as she found the rest of her greatly depleted team—Jerry, Kimberly, Ciarra, Jamil, and Ray—and assembled them in a huddle by themselves near the mouth of the cave.

Before she could even bring them to order, Jerry jumped in.

"For the record, I was going to recommend we return those statues to the proper people," he said. "I wasn't going to let A.J. take them."

"Sure, Jerry, whatever," Ciarra said coldly.

"No, really!" he insisted.

"Okay, everyone, let's just stay focused," Carrianne said before they could continue the argument. "We have something a lot bigger than those two statues to talk about. In the next day or so, if not sooner, we're all going to be heading our separate ways. But wherever we go next, we all share one thing. We're the only people who know about the Kemet."

She paused over this point to let the significance of that truth sink in.

Then, she added, "And we *have* to keep it that way."

Another pause. She looked around the circle and tried to make eye contact with everyone.

"Those people have been living peacefully beneath the sands for 5,000 years," she continued. "They deserve the chance to continue that way. But their way of life, their culture, probably their very survival now depends on us. If the outside world finds out about them, I just don't think ... well, let's just say the rest of humanity's track record with people who are a little bit different from them isn't very good."

"That's for sure," Ciarra said.

"Blue Diamond isn't allowed to do any more exploration in Egypt. And, in case you haven't heard, we're all getting kicked out of the country—everyone other than Jamil, obviously. I doubt anyone is going to take our place trying to find minerals in this empty desert, and I don't think any bandits are going to be coming back this way, either. Pretty soon, this is going to revert to being the empty patch of desert it's always been.

"I'm still going to recommend to Inspector Yousef that he seal up the cave to prevent any wandering curiosity seekers from going down there. And we have to trust that the Kemet will protect things from their end. But the seven of us must agree to stay silent about this. It's really the only way to protect the Kemet long term. There's no blood oath we can take or document we can sign to assure it. We all just have to agree. Can we all do that?"

One by one, they went around the circle. Each person solemnly swore they would keep the secret.

Carrianne had to hope that would be sufficient.

The meeting broke up a short while later. The mercenaries had patched up the tires on one of the Broncos and were offering rides up to the main camp so everyone could gather their things—or what was left of them after the looters had picked them over—before they boarded the helicopter for their ride back to Aswan.

Carrianne was just coming out of her tent with her rucksack when she was met by Ray, who seemed to have been waiting for her there.

"Hey," he said, in his typically shy fashion.

"Hey," she said back.

"I found the drone," he said. "It turns out a random place in the desert is a pretty good place to hide valuable electronics. Thanks for that."

"No problem."

"The ETS guys are making room for it on the chopper. SkyKings is going to be thrilled I'm bringing it back."

"Yeah. Congratulations."

"So, yeah," he said, toeing at some dirt that seemed to have become very interesting to him all of a sudden. "Hopefully they won't try to cancel my contract when I get back. But I guess I'll deal with that when or if it happens. What's… what's next for you? Once you leave the country?"

"Honestly, I don't even know. I gave up my apartment in Colorado, and it sounds like I don't have a job anymore. I'm basically unemployed and homeless. I'll probably go back to Greasy Creek and live with my grandmother while I figure things out."

He risked a glance at her then asked, "Have you ever wanted to go to Florida?"

"I don't know. Why?"

"I've got a little place in Orlando, not far from SkyKings headquarters. It's not much—just a little one-bedroom with a tiny kitchen and a bathroom that only fits one person at a time. But you're … you're welcome to join me there."

She put down her rucksack and studied him. "Ray, are you really asking me to move in with you? Doesn't that seem a little, I don't know, sudden?"

"Well, don't think of it as moving in," he said. "Think of it as ... as ..."

"As what, shacking up?"

He smiled. "I was trying to find a nicer way of putting it than that. But, look, I think we have something worth exploring, you and me. Don't you? I don't think we can do that if you're in Kentucky. And don't use the excuse that we work together, because it's pretty clear that's not a problem anymore."

She laughed. "Yeah, I suppose you're right."

"Is that a yes, then? You'll come to Florida with me?"

"I'll think about it," she said. "We've had a lot come at us in the last day or two. I feel like I at least need a decent night's sleep before I make any big decisions."

"Okay, that's fair. But don't ..."

"Don't what?"

Ray looked back down at the ground for another moment then up at her. His dark brown eyes were as intense as she had ever seen them.

"It's just ... if this winds up being the last time I ever see you, I think it'll be one of the biggest regrets I ever had. Promise me, one way or another, we'll see each other again."

"Okay. I can do that."

She wrapped her arms around his torso, leaning into his chest, allowing herself to enjoy the feeling of her body against his.

Their moment was interrupted by an unexpected sound.

Barking.

Carrianne pulled herself away to see a dog with only half a left ear wagging its tail enthusiastically.

"Digger!" Ray called. "C'mere, girl! C'mere!"

The dog ran toward them. Ray held his arms out wide, but Digger went like a rocket toward Carrianne.

She reached into her pocket and found a dog biscuit. It had snapped in half at some point, but Digger didn't seem to mind as

Carrianne fed the pieces to her. She just happily chomped away while Carrianne petted the back of her head.

"Well, I guess we know who she likes better," Ray said.

"It's bribery, nothing more," Carrianne said.

As soon as Digger was done with the biscuit, she went over to Ray and buried her snout in his leg.

"I think she knows who her human really is," Carrianne said.

"If I were able to bring Digger back to Florida with me ... I mean, you'd *have* to visit us, right?"

"You think you can get her into the States?"

"I'm sure I'll have to quarantine her and do some paperwork and whatnot. But it's not like she has anything to stay here for."

"No, I guess not," Carrianne said then grinned. "She's pretty much like the rest of us in that, huh?"

Ray just laughed.

Before too much longer, they were all strapped into the Black Hawk. As its powerful rotors lifted them into the air, Carrianne took one final glance through the gathering darkness down at the cave opening.

It was still yawning wide open.

And, somewhere in the back of her mind, Carrianne wondered if this really was the last time she'd ever see it.

www.ingramcontent.com/pod-product-compliance
Lightning Source LLC
Chambersburg PA
CBHW050008120726
47903CB00006B/1683